PROTECTING THE MOUNTAIN MAN'S TREASURE

BROTHERS OF SAPPHIRE RANCH
BOOK THREE

MISTY M. BELLER

Misty M. Beller
BOOKS

ISBN-13 Trade Paperback: 978-1-954810-72-3

ISBN-13 Large Print Paperback: 978-1-954810-73-0

ISBN-13 Casebound Hardback: 978-1-954810-74-7

To Pop,
Since you passed, I've realized anew how much you've been part of
nearly every special memory of my life.
Your legacy lives on in so many ways, and I look forward to the day I
see you again.

Seek ye the Lord while he may be found, call ye upon him while he is near:

Let the wicked forsake his way, and the unrighteous man his thoughts: and let him return unto the Lord, and he will have mercy upon him; and to our God, for he will abundantly pardon.

For my thoughts are not your thoughts, neither are your ways my ways, saith the Lord.

For as the heavens are higher than the earth, so are my ways higher than your ways, and my thoughts than your thoughts.

Isaiah 55:6-9 (KJV)

CHAPTER 1

*T*he sun hung low in the sky, casting a golden glow over the bustling streets of New York City as Jude Coulter stepped out of the ornate office building. The marble and opulence felt foreign compared to the rugged mountains of his family ranch in the Montana Territory.

"Have an excellent day, Mr. Coulter." The uniformed man who'd opened the door for him gave a half bow before closing it behind him.

Jude nodded his thanks, though the fellow had already disappeared. He tightened his grip on the carpet bag in his hand and started down the cascade of steps to the street.

Should he have had the money sent to the train station by delivery wagon instead of carrying it in plain sight? It could have traveled in a padded unmarked crate, the same way he'd brought the sapphires from their ranch all the way to this massive city.

It had seemed safer to always keep the payment in his possession, especially since it fit perfectly in this bag.

The hackney carriage he'd ridden in from the train station still waited for him on the street, as he'd instructed. The driver glanced back at him as he climbed in. Did he wonder what was in the bag? Jude had left the satchel with his personal items in storage at the train depot, so he'd not carried anything with him into the office building.

"The station, sir?"

"Yes. Thank you." He should have thought to give the direction, not expected the fellow to read his mind. He was out of his element here, no question.

The driver called to the horse, and the coach lurched forward, weaving into the flow of traffic.

Flow might be a generous word. More like a swirl.

Hordes of people and vehicles moved in every direction, their sounds melding into a discordant chorus. Shouts. Calls from street vendors. Horses snorting and shod hooves clopping against cement and stone. Wagon wheels, the creaking of so many harnesses. Too many sounds to dissect, and the effort tightened his body until his head pounded.

He closed his eyes and brought up a memory of the creek on their ranch, the peaceful murmur as it flowed over rocks. That was where they'd first found the sapphires. Blue and pink stones lying visible among all the brown and gold-flecked pebbles.

The gold wasn't real, of course. Just pretty mica. Which was why the place wasn't overrun with miners like other parts of the Montana Territory. But Dat had realized the significance of the other colored stones.

Jude had loved working with him back then. As the sapphires became their family's main source of income, he'd worked harder and harder to help Dat. Finally, he could help make up for his mistakes—especially that one that nearly caused their family to starve one winter.

When Dat and Mum passed on, both of them so quickly, he'd expected Jericho to take over the running of the mine. As the oldest brother, it was his right. Some might even say his duty. But Jericho'd had his hands full with the rest of the ranch. The horses, the younger boys, and their only sister Lucy. And they'd all been grieving.

The mine had become Jude's solace during that time, as he spent long days by himself at the creek, searching for more sapphires. Digging deeper in the areas that had yielded the most.

The rest of the family started looking to him with questions about the sapphires. He managed it by himself, bringing Jonah or Jericho to help when he needed them. The mine had become his contribution to the family.

His responsibility.

"Here we are." The driver called out just as the rig jolted to a stop.

Jude scanned the busy station. Even more people packed in here than on the street. He gripped his bag and stepped from the cart, then reached into his jacket pocket and pulled out payment for the driver. "Thank you."

The driver's teeth flashed as he nodded. "Any time."

Jude re-secured his grip on the satchel and turned toward the end of the station, where he'd left his other carpetbag in locked storage. He hadn't needed much for this journey, just a change of clothes, his Bible, and a few sundries.

As he approached the storage room, the porter who'd helped him before was speaking to a dark-haired woman. Jude waited a respectful distance away while the man gathered her luggage, but their conversation was easy to hear. She inquired about the western routes available through the Pennsylvania Railroad, and the porter was explaining her options where the track split in Scranton.

Though she didn't say so exactly, Jude guessed she was traveling by herself. That seemed odd for any woman, but especially someone young and pretty like this one. Maybe things were done differently in the city.

She was a little thing. Not bigger than a minute with her dark hair pulled back in a tight knot. Though she was asking questions, she seemed to know exactly what answers she needed. As though the man was simply filling the gaps in her knowledge.

"Thank you, sir. Good day." Her final words held a light accent that hadn't showed in her earlier questions. Not strong, but...different.

When she turned to walk past Jude, she offered a polite smile. Her dark eyes held just a hint of a slant, a look that made her beauty even more striking than he'd first thought.

He dipped his chin in greeting. Should he also say hello?

She passed before he could decide, so he turned to the porter.

"How can I help you, sir?" The man looked like he was forcing pleasantness he didn't feel. Dealing with strangers all day couldn't be easy.

"I have a bag in holding." Jude motioned toward his piece. "That one. Name's Coulter."

The porter pulled the carpet bag out of the fenced area. "May I see your ticket, please?"

Jude pulled the stub from his pocket and held it up for the man to see.

The porter nodded. "Very good." He handed over the bag, then pointed to a large metal sign suspended from the rafters beside the train tracks. "You'll be leaving from platform number three."

After thanking the man, Jude meandered toward the spot. A crowd had already gathered, but he worked his way around the edge until he reached a place to stand and wait on the platform.

It would be a quarter hour before the train arrived, but he'd pass the time here. The sooner he boarded, the sooner he would get to the Montana Territory.

And home.

He'd never realized how important the peace and quiet of the mountain wilderness were to him.

❦

*A*ngela Larkin watched the man from a distance, doing her best to keep a bored look that showed neither the target of her gaze nor the way her heart pounded louder than the incoming train, which squealed to a stop at the station. She would probably have a long journey, unless she could learn what she needed right away, though that was unlikely. If she had to travel all the way to the western territories—even California —she was prepared to do so.

She'd been given a significant responsibility with this assignment, and she would fulfill her part no matter what it required. Not only had she been tasked with a critical role for the country she'd come to love, but Winston was relying on her. All the Treasury agents were relying on her, though most of them probably didn't know it. Even Lawrence and Martin, those two who always worked as a pair and took delight in boasting of their accomplishments for the department.

Winston hadn't given this task to them, even though they'd been agents much longer than she had. They'd probably been passed over for this role because neither of them possessed a hint of tact. Only brawn and the ability to intimidate when they wished.

She took a deep breath and smoothed the folds in her dress. She was more than capable of this assignment. She would prove Winston did well in trusting her with the job.

The arriving passengers cleared off the train, and the porter called for boarding to begin. She followed the surge of people pushing toward the cars. One thing she'd learned early in this city was to travel with the flow when possible. You could weave your way through as you needed to, but you'd reach your goal much faster by working with people than trying to outsmart them. That motto generally proved accurate not only in traffic, but in accomplishing her work too.

As she boarded one of the passenger cars, she did her best to keep her target in view, though keeping plenty of people between them. He settled onto a bench near the rear of the car, and she slid into a seat three rows in front of him. His back was to her, as she'd hoped. He wouldn't see how often she watched him.

When all had been loaded, the train shuddered, then started forward with an unsteady rocking motion. An older man still standing in the aisle stumbled. Her target started to jump up to help him, but he grunted and sank onto his bench before Coulter could act.

As the train picked up speed and the view through the windows changed from city streets to rolling countryside, the rocking of the car eased into a smoother rhythm.

She reached for the book in her bag, but she'd barely opened to her marker when a movement ahead caught her notice.

Coulter rose and stepped into the aisle. He paused for a moment, gripping his seat back and bracing his legs as he found his balance.

She kept her focus on the page, watching him from the edge of her vision. Should she look up and smile? Sometimes it was better for the target to be aware of her, seeing her as just another passenger. Especially if she had a convincing backstory. More often though, she succeeded best when she faded into the background.

So she kept her gaze on the page in her hand as he stepped slowly down the aisle toward her. The outside deck connecting the cars was through the door behind her, and he probably wanted air.

As he passed beside her, the train jerked violently.

Gasps filled the air, and Coulter grabbed onto her seat back to keep from tumbling. A scraping sounded behind her, and she spun to see its source.

"Watch out." Coulter lunged behind her, diving for a box that slid off the upper shelf.

A woman screamed.

Angela lost sight of him as he pulled the box sideways, away from the elderly woman on the bench behind Angela.

A crash sounded, and Angela leaped from her seat to make sure her target hadn't been hurt.

The woman behind her screamed again, the one he'd just saved with his quick actions.

But Coulter lay on the floor, his head slumped against the side of the crate. Eyes closed.

Angela sprang to his side, dropping to her knees.

His chest rose with a breath. A good sign. She dared to touch his shoulder for a gentle shake. "Mr. Coulter."

He didn't blink. No hint of alertness.

The box behind his head tilted him at an awkward angle, pushing his chin into his neck. With one hand under his head, she pulled the crate out and laid him flat on the train floor.

He still didn't open his eyes.

Her mind scrambled for what to do next. She needed help. She was skilled at many things, but her medical knowledge wasn't nearly strong enough for this situation.

She looked up at the worried faces gathered around them. "Is anyone a doctor?"

No matter what, she couldn't let anything happen to Jude

Coulter, not until he led her back to the source of the sapphires he'd just delivered.

A great deal more than her job depended on her succeeding in this mission.

CHAPTER 2

"*A* doctor! Is anyone a doctor?" Angela repeated her plea, her heart racing as she scanned the concerned faces around her.

The request wove through the crowded train car, repeated by voices down the row. But no one answered the call. Could there be no physician at all on this train?

She raised her voice to be heard above the murmuring passengers and noisy rattle of the wheels. "Check the other cars!"

Again, her request was shouted down the row of gawkers.

A new tension pulled in her chest as she turned back to Jude. Hopefully, a doctor could be found, but this man needed help now.

He still lay on the floor, his head rocking loosely with the rhythm of the train. Why hadn't he awakened yet?

She rested her finger on his lip and concentrated to make sure she felt air coming from his nose.

Yes. He was definitely breathing.

Should she try to wake him? Or let him rest? She sent a quick glance down the length of him, searching for limbs at awkward angles or any other sign of distress. Nothing that she could find.

A groan sounded from the man's mouth.

She jerked her focus back to his face. His eyes were still closed, his skin pale now. Maybe she'd heard the sound wrong. It might have been the rumble of the wheels on an uneven stretch of track.

But then Jude's chin shifted sideways, and his eyes clenched tighter as he groaned again.

Relief allowed breath to thread through her aching chest.

Once more, a moan leaked out from his deepest parts. The pained expression deepened, creasing his well-placed features as he cracked open his eyes. He squinted, as though his head ached or the light hurt his eyes.

His gaze didn't seem focused as he looked around, moving only his eyes—not shifting his head at all.

She adjusted her position to catch his notice. "Are you injured?"

He flicked a glance at her, and even that slight motion made him wince. His eyes closed again, then after a second, he cracked them open. "Where am I?" His voice had a raspy quality, not the way he'd sounded when he was talking to the porter at the station. He tried to clear his throat, but it came out as a weak effort since he still didn't move his head. "What happened?"

The murmuring around them increased, but she kept her focus on Jude. "You're on a train, leaving New York City."

Surprise widened his eyes a little, furrowing his brow. "New York? Why?"

Should she answer that for him? Not with so many people listening, certainly. She shifted the direction of the conversation. "You were trying to protect one of the passengers when a box fell from an upper compartment. I think you took quite a knock to your head. Are you injured elsewhere?"

He squinted again, his eyes turning distant. Maybe testing each of his limbs for pain. "Why would I be in the city? Jericho delivers..."

Her pulse leapt. Who was Jericho? Already she was learning important details.

The people had quieted as he spoke but now started talking amongst themselves again. One woman behind her spoke in a high-pitched voice, though she seemed to be trying to affect a quiet tone.

"He doesn't seem to know what he's about. He's taken leave of his senses, I dare say."

Angela crouched over him before she realized what she was doing. Like a mother hen spreading her wings to protect her chick.

Mr. Coulter didn't seem sure of himself, but one could hardly say he'd taken leave of his senses. He knew about New York after all. And this Jericho, whoever he was.

But...he did seem confused about *his* presence here. Had he lost a portion of his memories? She should test him.

She straightened a little to give him space. "You don't remember why you came to New York?"

He turned his troubled squint toward her. "I don't..." Then he closed his eyes, smoothing out the creases on his forehead. "My head hurts so. I can't remember anything."

An idea slipped in, one so daring it couldn't possibly work. Could it?

She would have to lie, something she avoided as much as she could during assignments. She avoided lying at any time, but doing so was always harder when she worked as an agent. The very nature of the role was a lie, really.

But this story wouldn't be a falsehood. More like a disguise. And Jude would benefit, for she'd be better able to care for him as he recovered.

She cleared the rasp from her throat, pushing down her

doubts in the process. "Just rest, dear. I'll find a place where you can be more comfortable."

Jude's eyes popped open, wider than before. He cringed and focused on her. "Do I...? Who are you?"

She let her jaw drop to show her shock, then quickly snapped it shut in a show of working to regain her composure. Then she lowered her voice, infusing both gentleness and hurt into her tone. "What do you mean, Jude? I'm your wife. Angela." She couldn't breathe as she waited for his response. This would determine whether he'd truly lost enough memory for the ruse to work.

Confusion clouded out the surprise in his eyes as he raised a hand to cover his face. "I don't... I don't remember anything." Those last words came out more like a groan than a statement.

She allowed a slow breath of relief as she rested a soothing hand on his arm. "Rest, dear. Don't worry . Once you recover, your memories will come back." She could only hope that would be a long time from now, after he took her to wherever the sapphires were mined.

For now, she needed to see to his comfort. Turning her focus to those gathered around, she searched for the uniform of a porter. There, behind a young couple who clung to each other like newlyweds.

She met the porter's gaze. "My husband has been injured, sir. He needs a place to lie down and rest."

The porter's chin dipped in acknowledgement. "I'm sorry, ma'am. There's no Pullman car on this train. I could spread out blankets in the next car over. The aisle's wider, and he'd have enough room to be comfortable."

She frowned, just enough to show her frustration for the meager accommodations. Like the businessmen's wives would do. "See to it, then. And thank you." She couldn't help tagging on that last bit. He was doing the best he could in the circumstance.

As the man hurried away, she turned back to Mr. Coulter.

Jude. She must call him Jude if she wanted this to work.

Could he even walk to the next car? She should have considered that before sending the porter off on the errand.

"Thank you." He murmured the words with his eyes closed.

She gentled her tone. "With my help, do you think you can walk to the next car?"

"I can walk." His words sounded tight, almost hard. Like Papa's voice when he'd gone to work on the days his ague flared. *Pushing through the pain*, he called it.

She sat quietly to wait, letting her gaze roam Jude's face.

A pleasing sight. Handsome, but not like the dandies in the city, with hair greased and combed perfectly. Jude's appeal was more rugged, his features strong and a little wild. Somewhat like Papa's had been, though this man possessed darker brown hair to Papa's red. And Jude was younger, of course. Closer to her own age.

The porter's return drew her focus away from Jude. "I have a bed ready. Can he...?" His focus darted to Jude.

"I can walk." Jude's growl sounded, though he didn't open his eyes. He was paying attention though.

"Very good."

She shifted to her knees so she could better help. As he strained up to his elbows, she braced one hand at his back to push and gripped his upper arm with the other. The rippling strength beneath both of her palms nearly made her let go. This man was like a draft horse, though he didn't look overly brawny at a glance. Clearly, that was all muscle under his shirt.

As Jude moved to his hands and knees, she shifted to a crouch to help him stand. The porter assisted on Jude's other side. She half-expected him to shake them both away. He seemed the type to hide weakness.

But he allowed them to help him up, then turn him the direction the porter motioned. There was only enough room in the aisle for two, so the porter moved ahead and she stayed at Jude's side, gripping his elbow with both hands.

Both of their belongings were still at their seats in this car, but she'd have to come back for them.

The porter led them through the door at the end and onto the gangway connection between the trains. When the rush of wind blew against them, Jude ducked, squeezing his eyes shut.

She needed to talk to him more like a wife would, keeping up an encouraging monologue. "Let's get you out of the wind, dear."

As she guided him into the next car, blessed silence settled thick in the air. This compartment was more open, with a spacious aisle and larger, more comfortable seats. It must be the first-class car. There were half as many people in here, and those who weren't napping looked at her and Jude with a frown. Clearly, they didn't look like first-class train car material.

The porter led them to the far end, then motioned to blankets he'd laid on the floor to make a bed. The makeshift pallet was tucked between two facing benches, but part of the blankets extended into the walkway.

The porter pointed to the door nearby. "This is the forward-most car, so that door only leads to the engine. You'll get little traffic through here, just the conductor or engineer."

She smiled her gratitude. "Wonderful. Thank you for your help."

"Yes, thanks." Jude managed the clipped words as he braced his hands on the seat and lowered himself to his knees on the blankets.

She tried to reach out and help him, but there was little she could do in the small space, and he managed to turn and lay back without her aid.

As his head rested, he let out a long sigh. "Much better. Thank you."

There was just enough room between the seats for her to

drop to her knees beside him, and she did so. A doting wife would want to be there to help him with any need.

The porter still hovered behind her, so she turned to look up at him. "Could you bring a cool, wet cloth for his head? And maybe tea and crackers, in case his stomach is unwell from the headache. Ginger tea if you have it, with a spoon of honey."

He gave a half bow. "I'll see what I can locate."

As he turned and maneuvered down the aisle, the reality of how impractical her requests were settled. Hot tea on a moving train? As far as she knew, they didn't serve food on board. Passengers were allowed to purchase from vendors at each stop. They certainly wouldn't have hot tea or crackers. A cool wet rag might be impossible too.

"I'm all right." Jude's quiet mumble drew her gaze back to him. "I don't need anything. I'll just rest here. I'll be fine." He kept his eyes closed as he spoke, and his words sounded almost breathy, like he was half-asleep. "What did you say your name was?"

She swallowed. At least he was speaking too softly for nearby passengers to understand. "Angela. Your wife."

He continued in that breathy mumble. "Thanks for helping. I'm sure I'll remember everything after a little sleep."

She rested her hand on his arm. "Sleep, my dear. I'll be here if you need me."

Jude didn't answer, and it looked like his face was relaxing into slumber. Should she move onto one of the seats? That was likely what a society lady would do. Kneeling on the floor would be unseemly. But she hesitated to leave his side. She couldn't stay on her knees for hours, so she eased around to sit with her back against the train car, beside Jude's head.

She should probably return to gather their things before she settled. But as she braced an elbow on the seat to push herself up to her feet without disturbing Jude, the door at the far end of the car opened, allowing in the bluster of the wind along with the porter.

He didn't have towel or mug, but he was carrying her valise and wrap, along with the two bags Jude had been carrying earlier.

She smiled as the man approached. "Thank you. That was exactly what I was about to go in search of." She pointed to the seat beside her. "Place them here, if you please."

He did so, then turned without a word toward the nearby door—the one he'd said led to the engine. Maybe he needed to update the conductor on their injured passenger.

She let herself relax against the wall, thankful for a chance to gather her thoughts and make a plan. She hated lying. Being an undercover agent required telling falsehoods at times to maintain a disguise, but she avoided that tactic whenever possible.

This lie hadn't been necessary for her safety, but it would make her work so much easier.

She pushed the line of thought away. What was done was done. She couldn't change it now. Not until they left the train.

Best examine their surroundings for anything unusual. The rhythmic clatter of the wheels against the tracks provided a constant rumble of background noise. The steady sway of the carriage seemed to lull some of the passengers in this car into a sense of calm, while others shifted restlessly in their seats, unable to find comfort.

She moved her focus back to Jude, so close beside her. His chest rose and fell in deep, even breaths as he slept, his face shadowed by pain. What would happen when he awoke? Would his memories return in full force, exposing her for the imposter she was?

CHAPTER 3

*J*ude pushed through the murky darkness to force his eyes open. His head throbbed as if a blacksmith pounded his skull into a different shape. His stomach roiled too, just on the edge of casting up whatever he'd last eaten.

He managed to squint his eyes enough to see his surroundings. He lay on blankets with a hard floor beneath. A moving floor. Was his bed hanging on ropes?

Then the rhythmic click-clacking broke through his awareness. A train? That would explain the rocking motion. And the domed shape of the ceiling above.

A dull ache pulsed above his right ear, and when he reached up to touch the tender spot, his fingers brushed a swollen lump. The contact sent a fresh bolt of searing pain through his head.

Rustling sounded beside him. He started to turn and look, but the throbbing stopped him .

A woman shifted into his line of sight, her dark eyes filled with concern. She sure was a pretty thing, he could see that even with his dim vision.

"Are you feeling better?" Her voice sounded as appealing as

she was. And gentle, though there was a hint of worry. Did he know her?

She was waiting for an answer, so he struggled to find words. Feeling better than what exactly? He couldn't remember what had happened before he fell asleep.

"I don't know." His voice rasped, so he tried to clear it without increasing the pounding in his head. "What happened?"

"You were struck by a falling crate." Her brow furrowed. "Do you remember any of it?"

He let his eyes close as he strained to find any recollection of that. A box of sapphires? "Where did it happen?"

"On the train. Right after we left New York City."

His eyes opened of their own accord, and not even the throbbing could stop him from staring at her. "New York? Why was I there?"

But he knew, even without her answering. The Coulters only went to New York once a year, and for only one purpose— to deliver the year's shipment of sapphires to Mr. Tiffany. But Jude wasn't the one who made the trip. Only Jericho left the ranch—whether for a supply run to Missoula Mills or a delivery to New York City.

Was something wrong with Jericho? Was that why Jude had been sent?

He pushed back that worry before it clouded the few senses he had left.

Did this woman work for Tiffany? How did he know her? Was she aware of the sapphires?

She still hadn't answered his question. Did she not want to mention the gemstones? He and his family never spoke of them to strangers. It was their closest kept secret. Even when they were all at home on the ranch, they referred to the stones as *strawberries*.

Maybe he should ask a different question. "Who are you?"

Her uncertainty shifted to a look of hurt, then she forced a smile. "I know you hit your head, but I hoped you'd remember. I'm Angela. Your wife."

It took a moment before the meaning of her words penetrated. His...*wife?*

The pulsing in his head increased, more like the thunder of a hundred horses galloping over his skull, pounding him with every hoofbeat. He managed to croak out another question...just to clarify. Because surely he'd heard wrong. "My...wife?"

Her smile turned sad. "You didn't remember the last time you woke either. We met on the train to New York. You swept me off my feet, as they say, and we married in the city. This is our wedding trip, but we're also traveling back to your home."

He took a moment to study her—to really examine her face and strain for any hint of recollection. The effort only made worse the pounding in his head, but he didn't let that stop him.

Still...he could find no memory of her. He couldn't recall anything other than recent memories, certainly nothing about a journey to New York. But surely he would remember falling in love and getting married.

Maybe in a different setting? If she were his wife, they would have... But picturing her lounging on a bed didn't bring any hint of recognition either. It did, however, make his breath come a little faster. He squashed that image before it could take hold. At least the portrait his mind had created included her fully clothed.

She was certainly pretty enough to catch his eye, but he would never have jumped into marriage with only a few weeks —or maybe days?—acquaintance. She couldn't be speaking the truth. But why would she say such a thing?

A new thought slipped in. Had she been in trouble? Had he married her to save her reputation? That sounded more like him, though surely he could have helped her without such drastic measures. Unless he'd been the one to sully her character in the first place? Surely not.

He squinted, trying to bring back such a memory. "How did you say we met?"

"On the train to New York. You were sitting in the seat across from me, and once we started talking, we...well, things progressed from there. You were so charming and dashing, I couldn't help but fall in love nearly from that first conversation." Her voice held a sweet yearning, and she rested her hand on his arm.

She couldn't be talking about *him*, though. He'd never been called charming or dashing. And he certainly wasn't the type to sweep a woman off her feet, as she'd said before.

All this strain was making his head hurt worse, and his vision was starting to blur. He let his eyes close so he could think better. "You said we're going to the Montana Territory?"

"I...think that's the place you said." Her voice was more tentative than before. He'd like to look at her again, to gauge whether she was lying or if he really hadn't told her much about his home and family. The latter was quite possible if they'd only just met.

And it reinforced the theory that he'd married her to help her out of a tight spot. Maybe he'd planned to see her settled near her family, then move on. They could be married in name only, if what she needed was the protection of his name.

With his eyes closed, he tested that line of thought. "You have family somewhere?"

A short pause. "My mother lives in New York City."

He was taking her *away* from her family? That didn't add up. "Your father?"

"He was killed. Four years ago. During the draft riots." A touch of sadness tinged her voice. Real or feigned?

"Aunts? Uncles? Grandparents? Any other kin?" He sounded like an army sergeant barking commands. But he didn't have the strength for softness.

"No. At least, not that I've ever met. My mother has relatives in...another country." Her voice hitched, and it sounded like those last words weren't what she'd started to say. "I've never met them though. At least, not that I remember. I was five when we moved to America."

He forced his eyes to open. What country did she mean? A country where the women were all beautiful perhaps? He'd never heard of such a place, but he wouldn't mind visiting. Her eyes did have a hint of a lift at the outer edges, but he wasn't educated enough to know if that signaled anything specific.

He might as well ask, because it sounded like something he should know. "What country is your mother from?"

Her eyes dipped for a heartbeat, then she lifted her gaze and her chin. "China. My mother is the daughter of an Englishman and a Chinese woman. My father is an Irishman." She spoke the nationalities like they were a shield she was positioning in front of herself, preparing for him to attack with a saber or a spear or something.

He'd not be wielding weapons, at least not about the countries her family hailed from. He let his eyes close again. "My dat's parents were from England. My mum talked about Germany some. I think maybe one or both of her parents came from there. I wish I'd asked more of the details when they were alive. It's nice you know so much about your family's history."

They needed to get back to more pertinent topics though. If he wasn't taking her to family where she could settle, maybe she had friends she planned to live with. It was worth asking.

"Where exactly are we going? I mean, where am I taking you?" He didn't have the strength to be diplomatic anymore.

Her voice came out tentative. "To your home. I'm looking forward to keeping house for you. Being mistress of the place and seeing to your happiness there."

He squeezed his eyes. Being mistress of the bunkhouse he shared with four brothers and a nephew? This entire conversation was as addled as his mind, and he didn't have the strength to sort through the nonsense to find the truth.

He raised a hand to cover his eyes. Maybe blocking out more light would ease the throbbing. "How long 'til we reach St. Louis?" At least he remembered enough to know that was where they'd change from the train to a steamship for the journey up the Missouri River.

"Four more days, I think. We'll need to change trains tomorrow, the porter said."

Four days then. He had to have his wits about him by then. Surely after a good night's sleep, all this would make sense.

"Jude, please try not to worry." Angela's voice sounded so kind. So gentle. "Your memories will return. Rest now."

Despite the confusion clouding his thoughts, her words wrapped around him like a warm blanket. Then something soft and cool—the brush of her fingertips?—stroked across his brow. Her touch soothed in a way he'd never felt, easing the churning inside him.

He let his body relax, let the darkness take over, and welcomed sleep with a final prayer. *Please, Lord, show me what I'm missing.*

CHAPTER 4

*J*ude stared out the train window, his eyes tracing the miles and miles of grassland rolling by. Clusters of trees occasionally broke up the prairie, but barely a hill could be seen. His chest ached for the sight of mountains. The massive rocky peaks rising up in every direction.

How many months till he reached home? Two and a half, most likely. They should reach St. Louis tomorrow morning, then board a steamship where they'd travel nearly two months up the Missouri. From there, he'd have another three weeks on horseback to the ranch. Maybe he could shorten that final ride a little.

The rhythmic clack of the wheels on the track beneath him had finally begun to feel normal, something he barely heard anymore. Maybe that had to do with his head not aching so much these days. In fact, sometimes he didn't even feel the faint throbbing that lingered. The bump above his ear was still just as large though.

He glanced down at the worn leather satchel resting at his feet, filled with money. The pounding in his head changed to a knot of worry twisting in his gut. What was happening with his family? Was Jericho sick or injured? Jude searched the recesses of his mind once more, seeking some clue as to why *he'd* been sent with the sapphires. Why Jericho would have allowed him to leave the ranch instead of taking the burden on himself. Only fog and shadows filled the spaces where his memory should be. He clenched his jaw against the frustration.

The far door of the train car opened, bringing in a gust of wind as Angela stepped inside. She had a hand pressed to her hair, probably to keep the wind from whipping all the strands free of the knot she used to contain it. Her gaze searched him out immediately, and a warm smile lit her face as she started up the aisle toward him.

The sight of her always eased something inside him, and if it weren't for this lingering headache, he might be tempted to return that smile. But all the questions surrounding her made it hard to let himself relax enough to settle in and enjoy her company.

"Good evening." She sank onto the seat beside him, her dark eyes sparkling with genuine warmth as she held up a bundle of cloth she'd balled in her hand. "Mrs. Williams sent two more cookies for you. She said she purchased them at that last stop but she can't possibly eat them after the entire sandwich she also bought for her evening meal.

Now a smile slipped out as he reached for one of the cookies. "I told her she didn't need to do this." The poor woman still felt too much guilt for being, as she put it, *the cause of such a tragic injury, poor dear.* Apparently, he'd been trying to save her from a toppling crate when he'd tripped and the box had hit this own head instead. She came to visit every day and brought some sort of baked good she purchased at a station.

"I don't think it's guilt so much anymore," Angela said. "She just likes to feed you."

He bit into the soft gingersnap, letting the tangy flavor

spread though his mouth before he swallowed. "I do appreciate these sweets." He'd have to walk back to the woman's car and let her know that.

Angela still held out the cloth and the second cookie, so he motioned for her to take it. "That one's yours."

She pinched her mouth as uncertainty darkened her eyes. "I think she intended them both for you."

He shook his head and swallowed the next bite. "That's why she got two. One for each of us." He certainly wouldn't be so rude as to eat them both. Though this final bite was making him want more. Maybe he could find some ginger in St. Louis to take home for the girls to make these.

A new thought jolted...supplies. Jericho always ordered crates full of the things they couldn't easily get from Fort Benton or Missoula Mills. Had Jude left an order with a mercantile in St. Louis on his way east? Was he supposed to pick them up or have them delivered to the steamer once he located a ship to take him upriver?

"What is it?" Angela was watching him, her brow pinched. Those dark eyes were so blasted pretty, and when she stared up at him from this close...

He tore his gaze away, focusing them instead to the empty seat opposite them. "I just realized I might have left an order with a dry goods supplier in St. Louis. I don't know who it would be though." Another scan of his memory produced no clues. "Hopefully, I'll recognize the place when I see it." There were surely half a dozen such places in a city so big. Maybe twice that.

"Do you remember what you might have ordered?" Angela sounded hesitant. She probably didn't want his lack of memories to upset him. She was kind like that. He needed to do a better job of keeping his frustrations to himself.

He searched his mind for what Jericho used to bring home. "Probably bolt goods, a saddle and some other leatherwork, maybe tools. My brother Jericho usually does this trip each year. I can't remember what all he brings."

She tipped her head. "I can't remember what you said. Jericho is...older or younger than you?"

He slid a look at her. Anyone who met Jericho would know instantly he was the oldest. And they didn't even have to look at him to know, just watch how he took charge and guided them all like a mother hen. "He's the oldest, then Jonah. I'm third in line, then Gilead, Miles, and Samson."

Her eyes had rounded as though this was the first time she was hearing how many brothers he had. Surely he'd told her.

Curiosity sparked in her gaze. "Do the others live near you?"

So he hadn't told her about the ranch. Or at least not that there were only a house and bunkhouse. He must have still been protecting the mine. But why would he marry the woman if he didn't trust her enough to tell her his family's closely guarded secret?

She was waiting for his answer still. He stopped himself before nodding, as that motion always increased the throbbing in his head. "You could say that. The women are in the main house, and I'm out in the bunkhouse with my brothers and our nephew, Sean." He couldn't remember the specific details about who stayed where in the cabin, but he had a lower bed in the corner of the bunkhouse. That he knew.

Was it his imagination or did she lose a bit of color? Maybe he was wrong though, for she dipped her chin and then a smile warmed her eyes, though her mouth didn't join the action. "I've always wondered what it would be like to have a big family. It was only me and my brother, and he died when I was six."

A pang tightened his chest. "I'm sorry to hear that. Our older sister died, too, but that was only two years ago. That's why Sean and Lillian, her children, live with us."

Now, Angela's eyes held a sadness that seemed more for him than for her. How could one set of eyes show so much emotion in a single breath? "They're lucky to have you. But I'm sorry about your sister. "How did...?"

She left the question open, and he could only assume she was asking how Lucy died. "Fever. She lived in one of the mining camps. Jericho went to check on her and the children. Arrived just in time to be there for the end."

A burn crept into his eyes, but he steeled himself against it. He'd not cried over Lucy in a while. Why did tears threaten now?

Angela placed a hand on his arm. Not presumptuous. At least it didn't feel that way. She hadn't really touched him so far, the way a wife would a husband. This act felt like solace. Understanding maybe.

When he looked at her face again, her eyes shimmered with the emotion he'd just held back. "I'm sorry, Jude. I can imagine how hard that was. For all of you." She swallowed, allowing a few seconds to pass before she continued. "Chen was killed not long after we arrived in New York. We lived at the edge of Chinatown, and a group of Chinese boys didn't like that he looked so much like our father." She gave a sad smile. "I look like our mother. Most people didn't think Chen and I were full siblings. Anyway, they picked on him every time he left the tenement to go sell the baked goods *A-ma* made. Then one day they cornered him in an alley. Later, they said they only planned to teach him a lesson. That he was sitting up and talking when they left him. Dat found his body when he didn't come home that night."

Horror stole his words as his mind sorted through her words. How could any lads treat another in such a... He couldn't even let himself think the words that tried to come. "They killed him because he didn't look like they thought he should? Did they give any other reason?"

Angela gave a small shake of her head. "That's what Chen had said they teased him about, and it's the reason they gave for hitting him." Her mouth formed a thin line, and her voice came harder. "That's all some people care about, whether another looks the same as them. After all, wasn't a war just fought about that very thing?"

The way he understood it, that wasn't at all the reason the South left the Union. It was more the right for each state to determine their laws. But he didn't aim to discuss politics with her. Especially not when she deserved his care.

He turned his arm and shifted so he could take her hand in his. Hers was so small, nearly half the size of his own. That meant he could close his fingers around hers and protect her. As he did so, he met her gaze. "I'm sorry. Chen didn't deserve that pain, and neither did you and your family. I know it was a while ago, but I'll be praying the Lord gives you peace about the situation."

She studied him, her eyes narrowed a little. Did she not want peace? She seemed hesitant to speak, so he waited, letting the silence settle. Most people didn't like quiet in conversation. It made them restless. Even nervous sometimes. But she didn't seem to mind lack of talking.

At last, she seemed ready to say what was on her mind. "My father was Catholic."

Not what he'd expected her to say. But if she was ready to talk about her faith, he definitely wanted to know where she stood. "He was?" He kept his voice steady, even curious.

Her brows gathered. "He didn't talk about it much. Neither of my parents did. My a-ma's family didn't really have a religion. They followed Confucius's teachings, not a god or anything like that. I don't remember ever hearing my parents argue about religion, we just...never really talked about it. Papa took us to Mass a few times on Easter, but that's the only time I ever heard about God."

A knot tightened in the pit of his stomach.

He'd married an unbeliever? *Lord, help me.* He had to work

harder this time to keep his voice level. "And what do *you* believe?" Combining Catholicism with the moral teachings of an ancient scholar didn't usually add up to a Christian who loved the one true God, but the Father could accomplish anything. He made a donkey speak to Balaam, so he could certainly plant a Christian influence in a young woman's life.

But she shrugged, killing that hope and twisting the knot in his middle even tighter. "I respect all religions. I don't attend services or anything, but I do work hard to live a moral life."

She smiled at him, as though she expected him to be pleased with that answer. It only made his chest ache. *Lord, give me the words. Please.*

He'd never really had to share his faith. His parents hadn't come to truly know God until they moved to the Montana Territory, but even back in Kansas, most people called themselves Christians.

"What do *you* believe?" Her tone sounded curious and innocent, as though they were discussing whether he preferred roast chicken or beefsteak for dinner.

Surely he'd told her before. Maybe his bump on the head had affected *her* memory too. Regardless, this question gave him the chance to share his faith.

He swallowed, sent up another prayer for wisdom, then met her gaze. "I believe in the one true God. Yahweh, who created the heavens and the earth. He loved each of us so much that He sent His only Son to earth as a man to die a miserable death, so that our sins wouldn't separate us from a holy God. He loved each of us so much that He couldn't stand the thought of losing a relationship with us." He willed her to understand the depth of his words. "He couldn't stand the thought of sin separating me from Him. Or separating you from Him. He loves you so much that if you were the only person alive, he still would have sent Jesus to bear the death that sin brings. The holy God, our Father, wants nothing more than to hold us close for eternity."

She was staring at him, and this time her eyes were impossible to read. Maybe she was trying to understand the magnitude of what he'd said. Or maybe she was trying not to let him see her disdain.

Lord, soften her heart. Let Your truth sink into fallow ground.

At last, her mouth shifted into something like a smile, though her eyes didn't join in. "Your faith is important to you. That's admirable." Though she didn't sound like she admired him at all for such strong beliefs. More like she didn't know what to do with them.

He couldn't help asking, "Have we not talked about this before?" If they really were married, he would have done his best to help her understand the life-changing power of God's love. As often as he could.

A shutter seemed to slip over her gaze as she dipped her chin. "You've mentioned God and faith a few times, but we've always been interrupted."

He studied her expression. It was hard to tell whether she spoke truth or not. But then she peeled back a little of that armor covering her eyes, though her expression remained guarded. "I'll think on your words. It feels like...too big a decision to make without consideration."

Thank You, Lord. He eased out a breath. If she really would ponder what he'd said, that was the best he could ask for. Leading this woman to faith would make all this pain and confusion worth the trouble.

CHAPTER 5

*N*aomi Wyatt stepped out the door, adjusting her daughter, Mary Ellen, on her hip. The crisp mountain air enveloped her, a welcome respite from the stifling confines of the cabin. She inhaled deeply, the wild scent of dirt and horseflesh filling her nostrils. This ranch had become her haven.

Mary Ellen squirmed in her arms, so Naomi walked a little faster. "Let's go pet the horses." The corral beside the barn always held several. Four horses dozed there now, coats glistening under the late morning sun.

The black in the far corner of the pen caught her focus. Eric's favorite mare had been black. This horse even had the same quiet gaze as Eric's Gypsy, though their head shapes were different.

Too familiar pain gripped her heart. Every thought of Eric hurt. If only she didn't think of him so many times every day.

Shouldn't she be better now, a year and a half after he'd left?

She had to stay focused in the present. With this sweet baby who needed her.

Mary Ellen's tiny fingers gripped the wooden fence. "Ba, ba." Her other hand reached into the pen, grasping toward the animals.

Naomi smiled and sounded the word slowly. "Horses."

The black mare ambled toward them, and Mary Ellen squirmed with pleasure, nearly pulling out of Naomi's arms in her excitement. "Ba, ba, ba."

"Hold on, sweet one." She adjusted her grip to a more secure hold.

When the black reached them, it nuzzled Mary Ellen's tiny hand, drawing an infectious giggle. Naomi smiled. This was the medicine she needed to push away the melancholy.

She helped Mary Ellen pet the horse, her own fingers relishing the silky fur. She should come out to see the animals more.

After several minutes, Mary Ellen's happy cooing turned to fussing, so Naomi turned her away from the corral.

The spell was broken. Happiness never lasted these days, not in nearly a year and a half.

She sighed. Had Eric received the letter she sent with Jude? It had been three months since Jude left to take the sapphire shipment east, so surely her note had been delivered by now.

Would Eric reply? Would he even read it? He'd never answered the other letters she sent him in those first months after he left.

But surely learning he had a daughter...

She squeezed her eyes shut against the sting of tears. Tears she was so very tired of. How much could a person cry before the pain dried up? Surely she was nearing that point.

She started up the hill to the house, her gaze snagging on Dinah and Jericho as they rounded the side of the cabin. Jericho carried a bucket of berries in one hand and held Dinah's hand with the other.

Another twinge tightened her chest. This time the longing mixed with a bit of jealousy. Why couldn't she and Eric have been like that?

She was so incredibly happy her sister had found Jericho. *And* she was thankful she and Mary Ellen were here on the ranch...here in this beautiful haven in the Rocky Mountains. There was no denying the peace in this land.

If only the peace would seep inside her and heal the pain twisting her heart tighter every day.

Dinah and Jericho met her at the cabin's front door, and Dinah gave her a sweet smile. "Are you two out for a walk?"

Naomi nodded, turning the babe to face her aunt and uncle. "Seeing the horses. She's ready for a nap though."

Dinah moved closer to Mary Ellen, her tone brightening. "Are you tired, my angel?" She reached for the babe. "Why don't you let Aunt Dinah put you to bed?"

Naomi allowed her sister to take the babe, her arms thankful for the reprieve. Now that Mary Ellen was ten months old, carrying her always exhausted Naomi.

She followed her sister inside, but Jericho turned toward the barn. "I'll ride out to help Jonah and Miles."

Once inside, Dinah babbled to the babe as she carried her back to Naomi's room.

Naomi didn't follow. The rocking chair by the fireplace seemed much more appealing right now.

A few minutes later, Dinah slipped back into the room, closing the door to the bed chamber with a soft click. Would she busy herself in the kitchen? Or do some cleaning? Naomi hadn't kept up with her work around the house the way she meant to. Dinah had probably noticed, and her sister wasn't one to sit idly when there was work to be done.

But Dinah settled in the chair beside Naomi's, resting her

head against the tall chair back, then looking over to meet Naomi's gaze.

Those eyes.

Dinah always had a way of looking at her that stripped away any pretense, seeing everything she really thought and felt. What did those eyes see now?

Dinah reached out, her fingers slipping over Naomi's hand in a grip both gentle and firm. "What is it, Na? What's bothering you?"

The question raised a new tumult of emotion, but she swallowed it down. She couldn't bare her soul to her sister, not about this. Dinah knew about Eric, of course, but not everything. And that was the way things needed to stay.

So she gave a light shake of her head. "I'm just tired."

Dinah's eyes turned troubled, but she stayed silent. Naomi turned to stare into the fire. Maybe Dinah would leave her questions alone.

But a moment later, her voice sounded again. "I want to help you, Naomi. Can you tell me why you've been so sad?"

Once more, she had to swallow tears. Maybe she should say a little. It might give Dinah enough of an answer that she would stop pressing. She'd see she couldn't fix this.

Naomi swallowed again, pushing down the lump so she could speak. "I miss Eric."

Dinah's hold tightened around her hand. A quiet sigh slipped from her, but Naomi didn't look over to see the pity in her eyes. "I'm sorry, Na." Her voice held pain, tiny compared to the ache smothering Naomi. But they were twins, so it was natural Dinah would feel her hurt.

Naomi rested her head back against the chair. "I'll be all right."

A lie. But maybe if she spoke it enough, the words would become true.

Dinah's eyes held that mixture of pain and love she showed

34

so easily. "I had hoped your friendship with Jonah might help you forget Eric."

What could she say to that? Jonah *was* a good friend. He'd been injured when they first arrived on the ranch and had been forced to stay in bed until his badly broken leg healed enough for him to hobble with walking sticks. His bed had been placed in this main room of the cabin during that time, the room where she'd spent much of her days cooking and cleaning.

At first he'd needed her help, and maybe that was what had drawn them toward friendship. He was funny, and his wit ranged from sarcastic humor to silliness that made her giggle.

He also had a way of looking at her that seemed as though he could hear her thoughts and know what she was really feeling, just like Dinah could. Jonah was indeed a good friend.

But he wasn't Eric.

No one ever would be.

Dinah sighed. "The love of a good man can make everything better, Naomi. That's what I've been praying for you. You deserve that kind of love."

She tried to find the semblance of a smile for her sister. Dinah meant well. She was doing everything she could to help.

Unfortunately, nothing either of them did would bring Eric to her and give her the life she'd thought they would have.

The life he'd promised her.

CHAPTER 6

*T*he sun was almost directly overhead the next day as Jude and Angela followed the other passengers down the gangplank of the ferry boat onto the St. Louis wharf. The train had halted on the far side of the Mississippi, and they'd boarded the transport boat with the other passengers, moving like a herd of cattle, driven by men shouting and calling directions above the thrum of voices.

So much noise. It made his head throb. People flooded in a mass all around him, moving toward the line of wagons parked along the road. He needed to get his bearings, maybe find a memory or two that would help him determine what to do next.

"Why don't we step over here?" Angela's gentle voice pushed through the chaos. She slipped her hand around his arm, guiding him to the side, away from the river of pressing people.

He kept a tight grip on the carpet bag containing the money, but let her lead him. Their other belongings had been carried by laborers and would be stacked along the dock. The mass of bodies finally thinned, and with a few more steps, they stepped out of the crowd to a calmer spot on the dock at the edge of the water. A row of stacked crates shielded his view from most of the ships crowding the wharf as well as the men carrying boxes and barrels up and down the gangplanks.

He inhaled a deep breath. His lungs constricted against the thick scent of smoke and fish and who knew what else. Maybe this wasn't fresh mountain air, but at least he had room to clear his head.

After a few more steady inhales, his body finally settled, the pounding in his chest easing enough that he could think.

He looked down at Angela, her hand still wrapped around his arm. She was studying him, worry creasing her brow.

He'd not realized on the train how much shorter she was than he, the top of her head coming to about his chin. A reminder of how delicate she was. How much she was depending on him to protect her. To provide what she needed. To think of her needs before his own.

Just now, she probably wanted a place to rest and clean off the layers of coal smoke the train had coated them both with. Despite the grime that clung to her dress and face, she possessed an undeniable beauty.

He probably needed a good dunking himself, but he had much to see to before he could worry about his appearance.

He rested a hand on her fingers. "Let's find a room we can rent. I imagine you'll want to rest or...take some time for yourself." He might be rusty about how to speak to a woman, but he still knew better to mention anything about her appearance.

She shook her head. "I don't need to rest." She pointed toward the steamships lining the wharf, their smokestacks rising above the crates that blocked the rest of their large structures from view. "Should we book passage first?"

That made sense. Knowing where to send supplies and when they would leave would be the first step. But...would he have already made those arrangements when he came through the first time? If so, he would need to add Angela as a passenger now.

He couldn't have known for certain when he would return from New York though. He might have had an estimated date, but there were too many variables. Too many details outside his control to purchase such an expensive fare in advance.

Angela gave his arm another gentle tug, just enough to guide him forward. She must still think him too injured to make decisions on his own. He'd been that way when the sea of people pressing in had made him nearly want to curl into a ball until they all passed.

But he was better now. And he was a grown man who could handle a little headache—and a gaping hole where half his memories should be—and still carry on to make a few decisions. He stepped forward, guiding her as they wove around men unloading crates from a massive steamship, then a fisherman in a small dinghy tossing rope to another up on the dock.

Beyond them, double-decker boats lined the water's edge, chimney stacks rising from both sides like horns. Each ship had a large wheel on either side, at least those he could see. In addition to the vessels lining the shore, a few more loitered in the middle of the river, as if they were waiting for an invitation to join the party.

He kept his hand covering Angela's fingers on his arm as they walked. The touch felt right. Almost natural. Well, natural that a husband would stroll like this with his wife. But his skin touching hers brought all his nerves to life.

She'd worn gloves the first few days on the train, until they grew so grimy from the layers of smoke on everything she touched that she'd tucked them away in her satchel with an apologetic look. *He* certainly didn't care whether she wore gloves or not.

Women in the city might think covered hands necessary to

be socially acceptable, but out in the wilderness, that thin cotton would soil in minutes—and likely tear the first day on the trail. They wouldn't do much to keep her warm either. He'd have to get her some fur-lined leather gloves before the weather turned cold.

But what was he thinking? He couldn't take her to the ranch, not until he'd settled all the confusion around whether they really were married. She said they were, but so many things didn't add up to what he'd always intended. Not the least of them being the difference in their beliefs about God.

He might not know for sure until he had his memories back. But until then, he had a loyalty to his family to protect the sapphires. He couldn't take her to the ranch, not until he could fully trust her.

For now, he had to find a place he could help her get settled and know she'd be safe and happy. He didn't even have to look past the wharf to know St. Louis wasn't that place. Not only was it too big, too crowded, too smelly... It was also much too far away from the Coulter ranch for him to check in on her. He couldn't set her up, then abandon her. Whether that was his original thinking or not, spending these last few days with her made that option impossible.

Fort Benton was the best option. Two to three weeks' ride from the ranch, so he could see to her well-being. That town was busy enough she could make a decent living cooking or working as a seamstress. Would it be safe though? He would find a way to make it so. Perhaps he could pay a few men he trusted to watch over her.

And maybe he'd get his memories back long before they reached Fort Benton. *Please, Lord. Help me remember.*

Angela slowed as they neared a man who called out instructions to others loading crates on a boat. As the burly fellow finished his orders, Jude caught his attention. "Where can I purchase passage?" He motioned toward the steamboats.

The fellow nodded up the boardwalk. "That office there." Then he turned and followed his men onto the vessel without checking to see if they had more questions.

The building he meant was easy enough to spot. It looked like a warehouse perhaps, but the front corner held a door with a small sign overhead. His vision still turned blurry when he tried to read from a distance, so he couldn't make out the writing on the sign until they approached—*Fort Benton Transportation Company.*

The door opened when they reached it, and a swarthy, bearded man stepped out. Jude eyed him, then the chaos of boxes and desks inside. Men carried on loud conversations within. Would it be wise to bring Angela into an office like this? The idea of leaving her out alone among the sailors and dock workers appealed even less. He entered first, then kept her close with a hand at her back.

The men inside were an efficient bunch, and within minutes Jude had purchased passage aboard the *Marietta*, a two-story steamer leaving the following morning. The boat was bound for Fort Benton but would stop at various ports as it traveled up the Missouri. A faint recollection of being aboard a steamboat slipped into his mind, standing at the rail as townspeople waved farewell from land. That must have happened on his journey east.

With their travel plans secured, he should focus on finding a place to stay for the night.

As they stood outside the office, he scanned the street and the few buggies still lining it.

Angela pointed toward them. "Should we hail a hackney coach to take us where we need to go next? The drivers are usually savvy about the best places in a city. They might know where you would have ordered supplies."

Good idea. He motioned for her to proceed him. As they fell into step together, part of him missed her hand on his arm. He couldn't think of an excuse to ask for it back though. There weren't as many workers on this stretch of boardwalk, so there wasn't a risk he would lose her in the crowd.

When they reached the street where the buggies waited, the nearest driver straightened. "You need a ride? I'll take you anywhere you need to go." His words tumbled out fast, as hurried as Jude always imagined life would be like in a city.

Jude helped Angela into the conveyance, then climbed in too.

"Where to, gov'ner?" The fellow turned to look back at them as Jude settled beside her.

"Is there a place you recommend for lodging nearby? Somewhere comfortable." Angela deserved that and more after all she'd patiently endured on this journey.

"The Southern is a good one. They call it the finest hotel in the world, but you can get a plain room too if you've not got much to spend."

Jude nodded, and the driver turned back to guide the horse into the flow of traffic. As the clop of hooves on the cobblestone street took on a steady rhythm, Angela's focus locked on the buildings they passed. He should probably be paying attention, too, but her satchels stole his focus. There had been so many trunks unloaded from the ferry, he'd assumed one would be hers. Wasn't that what women usually traveled with? Trunks? Why had she brought so little? Surely she owned more than would fit in that small bag.

Regardless, she would probably like to have more dresses with her. He'd seen her in two that he could remember. Of course, he only had one change of clothes himself, but didn't women usually want more?

Too bad they wouldn't be in St. Louis long enough for a seamstress to make additional clothing for her. Maybe in Fort Benton. Or...if she was going to be a seamstress there, she would be able to sew for herself, right?

He slid a sideways glance at her. Did she even know how to sew? Did she like it? Would cooking be more her bent? They needed to have a serious conversation about her future soon.

The carriage came to a halt outside an imposing building, its facade rising six stories and spanning a full block. The murmur of voices and laughter drifted from open windows on the upper floors, mingling with the cries of street vendors and the ever-present scent of the river in the air.

After he helped Angela down and paid the driver, he gathered their bags and turned to the double front doors.

"This is nice." Angela's quiet words made him scan the front of the stone building once more, the carved touches that added the feel of elegance. Was she accustomed to elegance? She carried herself as though she was, but the story of her brother's death made him think she was working class.

But that had happened when she was a girl. Had her family's fortune changed since then? He knew so little about her still, though they'd talked some when his head wasn't pounding too hard to focus. Mostly she'd asked questions about the Montana Territory and the ranch.

One of the doors opened, and a uniformed man gave a slight bow. "Good afternoon, sir. Madam."

They stepped into the lobby, where a two-story ceiling rose high enough that he had to crane his neck to see the elegant designs carved on it. Columns covered in scrollwork stood everywhere, like trees in a forest lined up in perfect rows.

A clerk sat behind a desk in the center, writing in a ledger. "Welcome to The Southern. How may I assist you?" His voice was crisp and professional.

Jude stepped forward. "We need rooms for the night."

"Certainly, sir. We have several options available. Would you prefer a suite or a standard room?"

He glanced sideways at Angela. He'd planned for two, since he wasn't ready for the awkwardness of sharing one when he barely knew this woman—married or not. But in a suite, there would probably be a sitting room with a sofa or empty corner of the floor where he could bed down on. "A suite, please."

The receptionist consulted his ledger. "We have a suite on the second floor available. Would that be to your liking?"

"Fine."

They waited as the clerk scratched details in a leather-bound book. This would be a good chance to ask questions he'd forgotten to inquire of the buggy driver.

Jude cleared his throat quietly. "Would you be able to tell me names of the mercantiles or dry good stores in the city? I need to check on a few supplies."

The man nodded, not lifting his head or his pen as he wrote. "I can make out a list if you'd like."

Jude gave his jacket a tug. Not because this well-dressed man or this opulent hotel made him nervous. Not really. They just made him even more eager for his mountains. Getting the supplies was the only obstacle standing in his way now. "That would be helpful. Thank you."

"Of course." Then a few seconds later he asked, "Your name, sir? And how long are you planning to stay with us?"

"Jude Coulter. And one night. We'll leave out on the *Marietta* tomorrow morning." He shouldn't have added that last bit. He wasn't usually prone to mindless prattle.

The man looked at him for the first time since he'd opened his ledger. "Mr. Coulter?"

Jude's insides tightened. Did he know this man? He'd had no niggles of recollection. "Yes?"

He gave a sharp nod, as though agreeing with himself. "We've been receiving shipments for you, according to the agreement you made with our night clerk the last time you stayed with us." He motioned across the room toward a closed door in the back corner. "They're in our supply office. I can have the list sent to your suite after you're settled."

The knot that had been growing in his belly all day finally eased, releasing tension from every part of his body. "You have my orders? All of them?"

The clerk's expression turned uncertain. "We have everything that arrived for you. I don't believe you left a list of what you were expecting."

Jude fought to keep from grinning, lest the man think him daft. "Thank you. That's good news."

CHAPTER 7

*A*ngela sat at the dressing table, the dim glow of the oil lamp casting shadows across her reflection in the mirror. She could pull open the drapes for more light, but she only had a few minutes to finish her toilet in privacy before Jude returned.

She removed pins from her hair two at a time.

Jude had gone to the public washroom down the hall, leaving her the bed chamber to wash herself and refasten her hair. What she wouldn't give to have a clean dress to slip into. She'd brushed this one as best she could, and tonight she'd scrub her other skirt and shirtwaist, so she could wear them tomorrow.

He had been such a gentleman today. On the train, he'd been kind, even with his injury and the confined quarters. But his attentions today had been far more. He'd considered her needs first at every turn, even in his confusion.

She wasn't sure what to do with that.

Her own parents had loved each other, but theirs had been a life of hard work. Da was exhausted when he came home after long hours of labor, and A-ma was just as weary. They would

45

talk, but she'd rarely seen her father go very far out of his way for her mother. They both managed their own tasks.

Jude was quieter than most men she'd met. That seemed his nature, though at times his calm shifted into something like nervousness.

When they first stepped off the ferry today, panic clouding his eyes had sparked fear in her chest. Was there lingering physical damage from his head injury? Was he about to have an epileptic fit? But then she'd realized he might be struggling with his lack of memory. Maybe he'd simply needed a moment of quiet to breathe and think.

Watching him regain his peace had tugged at something inside her. In that moment, she would have done anything she could to help him smile again.

It turned out, a few helpful suggestions were all he needed.

Jude was...different. Gentle almost, yet rugged with the feel of something wild. His kindness always raised her guilt about deceiving him.

He was breaking United States law though, him and his family. She had to keep reminding herself of that. They were evading the proper paperwork and tariffs rightfully owed the American government.

Besides, she was so deep into this ruse now, she couldn't change the situation if she wanted to. Unless she told him the truth. That would change things, but not for the good. Right? She had an assignment to finish. She couldn't disappoint the entire United States Treasury Department. If she let herself be carried away by her personal feelings, she'd let down this country that had taken her and her family when they needed it most.

She ran a brush through her hair, untangling knots before braiding it, which would be quicker than trying to restrain her smooth strands in a coif.

A noise drifted from the sitting room. The door to the

hallway opening? Her heart picked up speed, along with her fingers.

"Angela?" Jude's voice sounded cautious.

"I'll be right there." She worked a ribbon around the end of the braid, then stood and straightened her skirt with a final glance in the mirror. This would have to do, but what she wouldn't do for a dress fine enough to match the richness around them.

When she stepped into the sitting room, she stopped short at the sight of him.

Damp hair slicked back from his clean and freshly-shaven face accentuated his rugged charm. His eyes were a clearer blue than she'd ever seen them.

Her mouth went dry, all the moisture moving to dampen her palms. The air between them seemed to crackle with tension. A tension she shouldn't allow. Somehow, she had to play the part of this man's wife and be convincing enough for him to believe it—without letting her heart be affected.

A bit of attraction was necessary, but only on his part.

She worked for a smile, something a little flirty, doing her best to ignore the heat flooding her face. "Hello." The word cracked as she forced it through her parched throat.

His eyes softened, crinkling at the edges. Did he see the affect he had on her? Thankfully, he didn't speak of it.

He took a small step back into the doorway. "I'm going down to inspect my supplies and make arrangements for them to be taken to the boat. I imagine you're hungry. Is it all right if I have food sent up for you? We can take the evening meal later tonight in the dining hall if you like."

The mention of food made her stomach tighten. She'd had a slice of toast on the train that morning, but it felt like days ago. Still, she didn't want to be troublesome. "Don't worry about me. I can wait until later."

He turned to step into the hall. "I don't know how long this will take. I'll be back when I can."

As he left the room, Angela sank against the wall, her knees weak from the surge of emotions coursing through her veins. If she had to sleep beside this man, it would be a long night.

~

*T*he steam from the boat's stacks billowed into the crisp morning air as Jude walked with Angela behind other passengers up the gangplank and onto the *Marietta*. He carried the carpetbag with the sapphire payment in his hand, but he'd allowed their other bags to be sent ahead to their room on the steamer.

The dock teemed with bustling activity, especially since this wasn't the only steamer setting out this morning. Workers loaded trunks and crates onto the boat. It wasn't hard to tell the laborers from the passengers—probably not unlike life anywhere else in the city, but he was far more aware of it here. Not just the difference in clothing either.

Most of the boat's workers carried themselves with a sense of purpose, their focused expressions sometimes edging toward disdain when passing the well-dressed travelers ambling about the deck, getting in the way of the massive amount of work loading this steamboat required.

When one of the men aimed a disdainful glance toward Jude and Angela, Jude's neck itched. *I'm not one of them, man. I know how to work for a living. I do it every day. This isn't my life.* But he couldn't stop the fellow to say as much.

And a glance at Angela, looking so lovely as she stared out over the water, the wind brushing loose tendrils around her face, made him want to endure any amount of scorn to give her the life she deserved. She was a treasure, this woman. Not just because of her stunning outer beauty, though he could see why that had surely caught his eye. But her kindness was undeniable. She could appreciate quiet, not needing to fill it with empty words. He had little tolerance for meaningless chatter.

If only she were a believer, he might be better able to believe he'd really married her, even on such short acquaintance. But she wasn't. And that left a gaping suspicion inside him.

He'd long ago made a commitment to himself and God that if he ever married, it would be to a woman who could be his partner in everything. Who encouraged him to deeper closeness with the Lord. Who hungered for righteousness the way Jesus spoke of in the Beatitudes. A woman he could truly be one with, in body, heart, and mind. His own parents had that kind of a relationship, and he'd promised himself he wouldn't settle for less.

He couldn't imagine circumstances that would make him to go back on his vow—not circumstances he'd allow himself to get into anyway. He'd asked Angela several times for more details about how they met and their courtship. She'd side-stepped the questions, telling him he would remember in time, and she didn't want to cloud his memories.

He needed to guard his heart where Angela was concerned. Until he had his memories back and knew for sure what was true. He tugged his gaze away from her, scanning the throngs of people around them.

A burly man with a grizzled beard was greeting a couple behind him, shaking the man's hand. "Welcome aboard the *Marietta*. I'm Captain Fisher."

The captain moved toward Jude, and he and Angela both turned toward him. His eyes twinkled, nearly hidden beneath thick brows and the grooves pressed deep in his leathery skin. "Welcome." He took Jude's hand in a firm clasp. "Captain Fisher at your service. Glad to have you both aboard the *Marietta*."

It was impossible not to respond to his exuberance. "Thank

you, sir. I'm Jude Coulter." He pulled his hand away and touched Angela's back as she shifted closer. "This is my wife, Angela."

"A pleasure to meet you, Mrs. Coulter." The captain dipped forward in a slight bow as he offered a warm smile. "You two were last-minute additions to our passenger list, if I remember right. Headed all the way to Benton?"

Jude raised his brows. "You have a keen memory." He'd never imagined the captain would take time to examine the register of travelers so thoroughly, nor commit those details to memory.

Once more the man's eyes crinkled. "Spending most of my life aboard ship as I do, I like to get to know the passengers. There're always a few on each journey whose presence is a pleasure, people I'd be honored to call friends." One side of his beard tugged upward. "Most folks are only heading up to the towns we stop at along the way, so I've learned to look for those traveling all the way to the end of the line. No sense in learning I like a man just in time to bid him farewell."

Jude couldn't help but grin. "That does make sense." This jovial fellow wasn't at all what he would have expected in a captain, but he'd likely make pleasant company.

Captain Fisher clapped Jude on the upper arm. "I'd better see to my duties now. It's about time to shove off." He turned and pointed toward the interior of the center of the boat, where the rooms appeared to be. "When you're ready to settle in, just waylay a porter and they'll show you to your chamber." He halted and looked back at them. "I sometimes host dinners in my personal dining room. I'll send an invitation around for you."

Before Jude could thank him or decline the offer, the captain was off, charging through the crowd with a bearing that parted the waters. He had a slight limp, but that didn't slow him.

Jude glanced at Angela. "Do you want to settle in?" He didn't plan to spend much time in their chamber. It could be *her* place to rest. He'd find somewhere else, maybe a hidden corner on one of the decks.

She gave a nod that felt more like a shrug. "All right."

Nearer the doors, more passengers crowded the space than before. Angela wove around the groups with ease, and he had to work to keep up with her, his carpetbag in hand. Coming from such a large city, she would be accustomed to crowds. They likely didn't smother her with a closed in feeling like they did him. Too, she was smaller and could slip into smaller spaces than he could.

When they reached the doors, a porter appeared before them as if he'd stepped from the woodwork. "May I show you to your cabin?" The man must be around Jude's age, but with his hair pomaded nearly flat to his head, he looked younger.

Jude stepped from behind his wife to answer. "Yes, thank you."

The fellow smiled. "It would be my pleasure. Your names?"

"Mr. and Mrs. Jude Coulter." The words nearly stung his tongue. So foreign. Not that such a concept hadn't ever crossed his mind. But he'd expected to remember the process of getting to the married state. The last thing he could clearly recall was nailing shut a crate of packed sapphires beside the storage building on the ranch.

Once inside, a long narrow hallway extended before them. Several lanterns mounted on the wall illuminated the route. The man stopped halfway down the corridor and opened a door on the left. "Your stateroom, sir. Madam."

A knot tightened in his belly as Angela stepped through the doorway first, and he followed her. How small would the bed be they would have to share? He still couldn't make peace with the idea that they were married.

The room was tiny. Barely twice the width of the hallway they'd just traversed. Straight ahead, a small washbasin stood on a stand, and above it, the only source of light in the room.

A small round window.

He moved toward it, drawn by the call of daylight. The view through the glass wasn't clear. Maybe because of the window's thickness, or perhaps due to layers of grime. He could make out the shape of the deck rail, then water stretching to meet the sky. Maybe the river changed to land before merging into the gray clouds, but he couldn't tell for sure.

Angela was thanking the porter. Asking his name. Jude forced himself to turn away from the light and be civil.

"...anything you need," the porter said, "just pull this cord." He tapped a rope that hung from the corner of the ceiling where it met the wall.

With a bow, the fellow stepped back from the entrance and closed the door.

Silence pressed over the room, and Angela turned to the bed.

Beds, rather. Bunks, one built above the other. Tension eased from his shoulders. This would work. He could sleep here without touching her in the night. Just the thought made heat flame up his neck.

Two months. He just had to get through two months in this walnut shell, then life would return to normal.

Of course, that reminded him of the fact that he needed to speak with Angela about his intentions. Soon. "I'll take the top bunk. I grew up sleeping in a loft, so being high won't bother me."

"Are you sure?" Angela turned to him, brows gathered. "I wouldn't want you to be uncomfortable."

He shook his head, not letting himself meet her gaze. "It won't bother me at all. Besides, these beds are so narrow, you might roll off. It would be a long drop."

They were about as narrow as the sofa he'd slept on the night before. When he'd finally returned to their hotel room after hours of seeing to the details of loading their supplies, he'd found Angela asleep in the bed. She lay on top of the covers, still in her dress, as though she'd only planned to rest a few minutes.

Yet her face had been peaceful, breathtaking in its beauty. Long strands of her dark hair had pulled loose from her braid to drape over the pillow like midnight streams of falling water. He let himself look for a long moment. But when the urge to step forward and touch her cheek grew nearly too strong to resist, he'd slipped out of the bed chamber and closed the door.

He'd planned to sleep on the sitting room sofa all along, but somehow the idea of sleeping beside Angela had taken hold of his body and mind...making the sofa cushions feel like the unforgiving rocks of the Montana mountains.

He loved those mountains though.

At least that was what he told himself through the long hours of restless sleep.

And now he had to endure two months sleeping in the same room with her. He'd be lucky if he survived this journey.

CHAPTER 8

"Careful there, cricket." A smile sounded in Jonah's voice as he captured Mary Ellen's fingers and stopped them from pulling his beard. They were seated on the floor in the cabin together. "You've got quite the grip."

Naomi watched the two from her rocking chair, letting the steady rhythm settle her. Jonah had ridden in mid-afternoon with an injured horse he placed in the corral next to the barn.

Then he'd come by the house to see Mary Ellen before heading back out. That babe seemed to have a piece of his heart, and the other way around too. Her daughter always reached for Jonah when she heard his voice.

As if he were her father.

Naomi pushed that thought aside, along with the reminder of Eric, her daughter's real father. For now, she should enjoy the pleasant view in front of her.

Mary Ellen was happy. Jonah was entertaining her, which gave Naomi a few minutes to rest.

A giggle sounded from the pair on the floor, drawing Naomi's attention back to them.

"Watch her when I do this." Jonah glanced up to make sure Naomi was looking, then tossed the child's worn quilt up in front of his face. As it drifted down to the floor, he popped his head up and said, "Peek-a-boo."

Mary Ellen convulsed in a fit of tiny giggles that stole her breath, sending out a snort with her laughter.

Naomi chuckled, her heart smiling too. How could anyone not adore that precious giggle?

Jonah's face stretched in a wide grin, and he raised the blanket to perform the trick again.

Mary Ellen's laughter overwhelmed her just as much this time, and that adorable snort made Naomi laugh again. "Are you my little piggy now?"

Jonah's sappy expression showed he was fully smitten with her daughter. That made two of them.

She watched them perform the show twice more, with Mary Ellen's response tapering to a chuckle the last time. Jonah finally straightened, stretching out his back.

She should take this chance to speak the words she'd been wanting to say for a while now. She swallowed, pushing down her nerves before they stopped her. "Jonah."

He raised his brows. "Yep?"

His casual reaction made it easier. Just like any of their other chats. "I just want to thank you. For everything you've done for Mary Ellen. For us both."

His eyes crinkled at the edges. "I haven't done much. I half expect you'd rather switch me than thank me."

She couldn't help a small grin. He had a way of making any moment easier.

He studied her for a minute, and she tried not to be uncomfortable with the scrutiny.

At last he tipped his head. "Something bothering you?"

Her chest tightened. How could she even begin to answer that? Most of the true responses included things she didn't plan to tell him. About Eric. About Horace.

She sighed and drew on the one topic that she could share. Jonah might even have ideas to help. "I've been thinking I need to decide what to do next."

His eyes were intent on hers. "What do you mean?"

She hadn't expected such a strong reaction. She shrugged. "I feel like I'm just marking the days. I need a focus, something that's mine. My responsibility to earn or achieve or develop." She nodded toward the babe crawling toward the front door. "And not just that little handful."

Jonah leaned sideways and scooped the tot up with one hand, bringing her back to sit on his lap. He placed both his pointer fingers in Mary Ellen's hands, and when she tightened her grasp, he bounced his legs the way he did when he gave her a "horsey ride."

She squealed with delight, but his focus wasn't on the play like it normally would be.

He still had that concerned gather in his brows. "Do you mean start a business? Maybe make things and sell them in Missoula?"

"Maybe. Or I could set up a shop in Missoula like Dinah and I planned once. I could do laundry and sewing." She could make a decent garment in a single day if she didn't have too many interruptions.

Jonah's brow lowered even more, but he didn't say anything.

He would stew on this for a while, then come back to her later with ideas.

The baby was growing restless on his lap, so he turned her around so they faced the same direction, then laid one of her small hands in his big palm. "Can you count the cricket's fingers?" He tapped each tiny digit as he spoke. "One, two, three..."

The sight of their hands—one so large and strong, the other so delicate and vulnerable—made the knot in Naomi's stomach twist. She couldn't remember when Jonah had started calling the babe Cricket, but it was his own private pet name for her. It made their connection even sweeter somehow.

When he reached number five on Mary Ellen's other hand, he lifted his brown eyes up to her. "Naomi, I've been wanting to ask you a question." Something in his tone caught her attention. Did he already have ideas to share?

"Sure."

He darted a quick look down to Mary Ellen before focusing on Naomi again. The knot at his throat worked down and up.

"I... I was thinking..." He stopped as though searching for words.

Worry crept into her chest. Why was he struggling with this?

He finally pushed out his question in a rush. "Would you want to marry me?"

The gust of words hung in the air.

She tried to take them in.

Marry. *Marry?* He was asking...? He was *proposing?*

She scrambled to school her shock, to keep her expression from anything that would hurt him. She'd never imagined this, though. Not really.

Sure, Dinah had suggested the possibility. And Naomi had thought about what it might be like married to this man. But only in a *This would never really happen* way. Never staked to reality.

She had to answer. No matter what, she couldn't hurt him.

"Jonah, I..." She couldn't find anything more to say. *Jonah, I'm shocked,* was what wanted to come out. Maybe, *Jonah, are you sure?*

Would either of those hurt him? He had to realize his question was unexpected. They'd not ever talked about marrying. For that matter, they weren't even courting.

"You don't have to answer now." He'd turned his focus back to Mary Ellen as the babe clapped her hand in his. His cheeks were shadowed, but the way his ears had turned red was hard to miss. "I just want you to know it's an option."

He lifted his head then, looking less the embarrassed schoolboy and more the earnest man she knew. "I'd be honored to take care of the two of you. We can have our own home. If you want to do sewing or what-not, or even have a real business, you'd be free to. Whatever you want." His expression turned a little wistful, as though the dream he painted sounded like something he might really want.

And she'd like to give it to him.

He was such a good man. As the second-oldest of the six brothers, he lived in Jericho's shadow. She'd seen how he struggled with that, struggled with being the invisible one, no matter how hard he worked.

She could help him feel seen. The leader in his own home. He would be an excellent father, maybe better than Eric would.

The thought brought a new stab of pain in her chest. Eric couldn't be a good father if he didn't care enough to open a letter to find out he had a daughter in the first place.

A sob rose up, but she pressed it down just in time. Still, she wasn't able to stop the burn of tears stinging her eyes. Hopefully they wouldn't turn red.

She needed to answer Jonah. Should she tell him *Thank you but no?* She couldn't do that, not with the way he looked just now.

And did she really *want* to say no?

The love of a good man can make everything better, Naomi. That's what I've been praying for. You deserve that kind of love. Dinah's words from last week slid back in.

The love of a good man. Jonah was a good man, no question there. Did he love her? Maybe not the kind of love that swept her off her feet like Eric's had. But she didn't want to be swept off her feet. She wanted a man who would stand beside her, not run off at the first chance.

That's what I've been praying for. Was Jonah the answer to Dinah's prayer?

God, what should I do? Even as she tried to pray the words, they hit a wall. Just like all her other prayers lately.

She'd disappointed God more than He could see his way to forgive.

She inhaled a steadying breath.

If Jonah was God's way of making things better for her, she should welcome the opportunity. She would be thankful later that she did. But...how long should she wait for Eric to respond to the letter she sent?

She swallowed another knot, then summoned a smile. "Thank you, Jonah. That means more than I can say. Truly. If you don't mind, I'd like to think about it a little before I give you an answer."

CHAPTER 9

September 1869
Missouri River

a week into their voyage, a porter brought the dinner invitation the captain had mentioned. Angela had been the one to open the door and greet Charlie, one of the staff assigned to their block of rooms. He'd extended the sealed note with a slight bow. "With the captain's compliments, ma'am." Charlie hailed from a small town in Virginia, he'd said, which must be where he'd picked up the relaxed cadence of his words.

Now, she walked just ahead of Jude in the dark hallway as Charlie led them to the captain's private dining room. She forced her breaths to come evenly, but the tension in her chest didn't loosen. She'd navigated a few dinner parties when on assignments, but this one felt different. The stakes were higher. If Jude saw through her ruse…

The lump in her throat soured. She couldn't even pretend her worry was only because of the damage a premature reveal would do to her work.

Jude had been nothing but kind to her. Even at cost to

himself. The last thing she wanted to do was hurt him. The pain she'd see in his eyes... She couldn't stand the thought of it.

She took in a deeper breath, then let out a shaky exhale as Charlie stopped at a door near the end of the hallway. He pulled the latch and pushed it open with a flourish. "Enjoy."

Jude touched the small of her back, a feeling that she still hadn't become used to. The way he settled the flat of his fingers on her dress didn't feel so much like an act of affection, nor of ownership. More like connection. A connection she couldn't let herself take to heart.

But she couldn't tense at his touch either. She stepped forward into the room, an action that made his hand fall away. How could she feel relieved and disappointed in the same moment?

The room was larger than she had expected, with a table at one end and an open area on the other. Polished wood adorned the bottom half of the walls and floors, and the upper walls were covered in elegant paper. Six other people already sat around the table—a man and woman on each of the long sides, the captain at the head, and the first mate beside one of the couples. She'd met Mr. Riggs the second day of their voyage when she nearly slammed a door into him as she stepped onto the deck during a windy spell. Since then, she'd learned to grip the handle with both hands as she opened it, lest a gust rip the wood from her hold again.

The men all rose as Jude led her to the table.

"Mr. and Mrs. Coulter. We're honored you could join us." The captain motioned to the two remaining seats. One at the other end of the table and the other to its right. Even she knew these were positions of honor, second only to the head of the table where Captain Rivers sat.

"Thank you for inviting us." Jude's voice held a steady warmth as they moved to their seats.

A footman stepped from against the wall to assist her with

her chair, and she willed her fingers to stop trembling as she settled beside her pretend husband. She didn't know either of the couples seated here, but the woman beside her sent a kind smile. From the lines marking her face and the mostly gray color of her hair, she must be about A-ma's age.

She edged close and spoke in a quiet tone. "I'm Margaret Drake. I don't believe I've met you yet." The same kindness that shone in her eyes softened her voice.

The men had struck up a conversation around them, so Angela leaned in to be heard. "I'm Angela Coulter." She'd introduced herself a few times that way, and it felt familiar now. As though she really *were* Angela Coulter.

The woman placed a hand on her arm. "It's a pleasure to meet you, Angela. There are so many people on this ship, I confess I want to hide in my room sometimes. I'm so glad I finally have a friend so I don't have to worry about talking to a host of strangers."

Angela returned the smile, though the words still ricocheted in her mind. A *friend*? They'd just met. No one in her acquaintance considered a person a friend so quickly. Of course, she didn't really have true friends, so how would she know? She knew lots of people, but there was no one she would turn to if she were in trouble, or even ask to borrow a wrap from. Her family was self-sufficient. If she needed something, she did what was necessary to get it.

She pulled herself back to the present to catch the end of Mrs. Drake's words as she introduced Angela to the woman across the table. Unfortunately, she'd missed the surname, but Mrs. Drake was still effusing. "Helen's children are such a delight. Wait until you see their precious babe, with her clear blue eyes and blonde curls, and those sweet dimples. You'll fall in love as surely as I did."

Helen's own dimples were showing as she offered an embarrassed smile. "She's a handful. But they're good children, all of them."

Angela offered a bright smile. "How many do you have?" If Mrs. Drake had said, she'd missed it. Hopefully she would be forgiven for asking a repeat question.

"Five." Helen looked even more embarrassed with the word. In truth, the woman didn't look old enough to have given birth to five babes, though the lines under her eyes attested to a bit of weariness.

"I heartily second Mrs. Drake's opinion of that baby." The captain's voice cleared aside any awkwardness from Helen's embarrassment. "An infant who can steal hearts so young..." He clapped a hand to Helen's husband's shoulder. "You'll have your hands full of suitors when she comes of age, Hugh."

Hugh gave a rueful smile as all the men chuckled. His fair features likely meant he'd had blonde curls and clear blue eyes as a lad too, though his hair had faded to a nondescript brown and the shadows darkened his eyes too much to make out their color.

As the captain began telling a story about his young niece, the footman returned with a platter of sliced meats. Then another appeared with a plate of cooked vegetables. Little by little, the table filled to capacity.

The conversation flowed as much as the food, with the captain's occasional questions prompting the others to share stories that revealed interesting details about their backgrounds. Mr. Drake proved to be as friendly and engaging as his wife, regaling them with tales of his time as a dentist. Mrs. Drake spoke of her travels abroad with her sister's family, and even the first mate, Riggs, she remembered, offered a story of the single voyage he worked aboard a spice ship that traveled to and from the East Indies.

"I've never seen so many bright colors on a piece of fabric as those they sold in the marketplace. All kinds of strange foods too. Made me so sick I couldn't stand for two days." Riggs splayed a hand over his middle. "I decided then I'd stay on boats that didn't leave sight o' the States." The lines around his eyes creased. "Figured sailin' up an' down the rivers fit that to the T."

The captain motioned toward the first mate. "I never was so happy as the day this fellow agreed to join the Marietta crew. He's the reason we run a smooth voyage, make no doubt of it."

Then he turned to Jude, and Angela's middle tightened. What would he ask?

"You've been quiet so far, Coulter. What takes you all the way to the Montana Territory? Business or pleasure?" His grin tipped a little. "Perhaps some of both." He raised his cup to his mouth, watching Jude expectantly.

"I have family in the Territory." Jude's voice held his usual steady timbre. Did the others realize how little he'd revealed?

"Your parents are there? I imagine they're past the age of mining. Maybe they've set up shop and are making their riches selling to all those flash-panners who don't know better." The captain chuckled. "I don't mean that unkindly, of course. I myself didn't hesitate to jump on the chance to turn a dollar in my younger days."

Jude smiled, though she knew those lines under his eyes meant he was having to force the expression. "My parents have gone on to a better place. My brothers still live in the Rockies though. Ranchers."

Mr. Drake's face lit. "I've long admired a man who spends his life raising animals. Not for the faint of heart, but I suspect the hard work is satisfying."

Now the sparkle in Jude's eyes rang true as he dipped his chin in a nod. "Some days."

Mr. Drake chuckled. "I imagine that's the case. Is it cattle they raise?"

"And horses. We started with horses, then added beef cattle about three years ago."

The men peppered him with questions for a few more minutes, inquiring about the count of the herds and where they sold the horses. She memorized every detail he offered. Did the sapphires come from the ranch property? Or was the mine in a different location, worked by laborers?

Mrs. Drake spoke up at the first opening, turning to Angela. "And do you love the mountains as much as your husband? I can hear his admiration in his voice."

Angela scrambled for the right answer. Should she say yes? She couldn't let them know who she really was. But Jude knew she'd never been there.

At last, the lies untangled themselves in her mind and she summoned the smile a new bride should possess. "I haven't..." She darted a quick look at Jude. "That is to say, I've not been there yet. We were just married in New York. I look forward to seeing Jude's family home. I have no doubt I'll love the mountains as much as he does." She didn't have to feign the heat flooding her ears.

"Newlyweds!" Mrs. Drake exclaimed. "Your wedding trip. Oh, my dears. I'm delighted to share in this special time." She gripped Angela's arm as she turned to her husband and the captain. "We must have a party to celebrate. I'll coordinate everything." She turned back to Angela and Jude, her grin taking over every part of her face. "I'm so happy for you."

Angela could only force another smile.

"How did the two of you meet?" Across the table, Helen leaned in, her smile shifting between Jude and Angela.

Jude didn't answer, probably because he had no idea. It would be up to her to create this fabrication.

"We, um..." She knew better than to use such filler words when creating a cover story, but her mouth had gone completely dry. As had her mind, apparently.

She cleared her throat. "We met in Bradford." It was the only town she could remember from those the train stopped at after leaving New York City. "We were both boarding a train to New York. We ended up sitting a few rows from each other, and..." She gave a little shrug so they would fill in the blanks themselves, then she turned to smile at her pretend husband. "Jude won me over with just a few words."

He returned her look, but his seemed to be searching. Not searching her eyes, but seeking something within himself. Trying to find the memory she described, no doubt. A weight pressed in her chest. *I'm sorry, Jude. I wouldn't do it if I didn't have to.*

"Those must have been some special words." Mrs. Drake patted Angela's arm.

Thankfully, the captain saved her from having to come up with a response. "Indeed. And what are your plans once you reach Fort Benton?"

Jude pushed back his plate, clearly finished with the meal. The conversation too, most likely. "I'm looking forward to seeing my family again."

"And I know they'll love you, my dear." Mrs. Drake beamed at her.

Once more, the captain saved her a response as he leaned back in his chair, settling in. "What I haven't yet told you all is that Riggs here has quite a hand with a fiddle." He lowered his voice and cupped his hand around his mouth as though trying to conceal the words from his first mate. "That's the real reason I'm so glad to have him around."

He lowered his hand and nodded, the corners of his mouth curving upward. "We always enjoy a bit of dancing after dinner." He motioned under the table toward his leg. "This peg won't let me take part, but I do enjoy watching you all enjoy a bit of fun."

Riggs pushed his chair back and stood, giving a slight bow before turning to crouch by the wall behind his chair.

Murmuring rose between the other two couples at the table, but Angela's middle had twisted in a knot tight enough to moor this massive vessel to a dock. She glanced at Jude. Was he as ill-prepared for a public dance as she? This was an art she'd not had the chance to learn as a youth.

She'd sidestepped dancing easily enough at various parties she attended on assignments. But this setting was far more intimate. If she made an excuse to stay in her seat—or even return to their room early—the others would try to change her mind, she had no doubt. And such a disturbance would embarrass Jude. She couldn't allow that.

But if she attempted to dance, especially if Jude's skills lacked as much as hers, she would embarrass him still.

He didn't look worried when he met her look. Just raised his brows in a silent query about whether she wanted to take part. He must have seen the fear in her own gaze, for his expression dipped into concern.

Could he dance, then? That seemed an odd skill for a man whose family owned a ranch in the remote Montana Territory. Maybe there was more society there than she'd expected.

The Drakes were already standing, Mr. Drake pulling the chair out for his wife. She grabbed his arm, chattering with excitement as he escorted her to the empty area at the other end of the room. The odd layout made sense now.

Even Helen and her husband were standing, speaking quietly to each other as they strolled to join the Drakes. That left her and Jude at the table, across from the captain.

Jude touched her hand, pulling her focus back to him. His brows tented over eyes so earnest, they made a lump catch in her throat. "Would you like to dance, Angela? I'll do my best not to embarrass you." He spoke quietly, leaning in closer so she could hear him as Riggs began testing out the notes on his fiddle.

She made sure to speak only loud enough for him to hear. "I've never learned any of the dances."

His fingers curved around her hand, giving it a gentle squeeze. "Just follow my lead. We'll keep it simple."

Her chest pressed so tight, air struggled to break through. Jude would regret that offer after the first two steps. She'd attempted to teach herself some of the dances she'd seen at parties, but her arms and legs never moved smoothly or with any kind of rhythm.

Yet he'd asked, and the weight of the captain's gaze was boring into her side. She'd have to give this her very best effort.

She nodded, and Jude's hold on her hand shifted as he rose. He didn't release her though, just turned his hand to hold hers more securely, then guided her to her feet and moved onto the dance floor as he drew her to him.

CHAPTER 10

$\mathcal{T}$he sudden closeness stole Angela's breath once more, the way Jude's arm wrapped around her back. He didn't give her a chance to get her bearings though. Or to back away.

His hand at her waist guided her to the left. She gripped his shoulder as women usually did, scrambling to move her feet as they were supposed to. She surely looked as clumsy as she felt, half stumbling, half scrambling.

Jude pulled her a little closer and leaned in to murmur in her ear. "Just relax. Slow and steady steps. Two right, then one left as we turn."

Her heart hammered, but she tried to do as he said. To find the rhythm. Two to the right. One left and turn. Two right. One left and—

"Relax if you can. Let me move you."

With his breath warming her ear and neck, there was no way she could relax. But she did her best, focusing on his arm firmly around her, softening into it. Feeling his guidance and making herself pliant as he moved her.

The other couples were swirling in a much livelier dance

than the two of them, but Jude had chosen well with this slower step.

As they moved, her head began to clear. Her pulse slowed, and the twist in her middle eased. The way Jude held her, she felt so safe. Protected. She closed her eyes and let herself be led, settling into the feel of his arms. The music slowed, then ended with a final draw of the bow.

She opened her eyes to find Jude watching her. For a few seconds, they stood there, the moment surreal, yet she could linger like this for hours.

The captain cleared his throat. "Thank you, Riggs. What a pleasure. All of you. How about another?"

As the fiddle stroked up a second lively song, she exhaled a long breath. Jude raised his brows once more, his mouth tipping in a grin that said, *Ready for more?*

With the thought of learning another dance, she couldn't quite manage a full smile. But she nodded, hoping he could see the gratitude in her eyes.

They started to the right. He leaned close again and spoke into her ear. "The music is a little faster, like a reel. You'll skip instead of stepping, but the same pattern as before. Skip two, back and turn."

This dance definitely moved faster. And took more coordination. But she focused on letting Jude move her, like before. It didn't take long before she was puffing from the exertion, but grinning too. She couldn't break her concentration enough to talk, but when she looked up at Jude, his smile matched her own. The twinkle in those dark eyes made pleasure well up inside her.

They were doing this. Together, they'd accomplished something she wouldn't have thought possible.

After that dance ended, Captain Rivers clapped his pleasure. "A slow one now, Riggs. Let the ladies catch their breath."

As the violin crooned a soothing melody, Jude settled Angela in his arms, pulling her a little closer. The simple three-step rhythm was so easy when he guided her. She was close enough that she could almost lay her head on his shoulder. She might have done so if this room were a little darker. And if the captain weren't watching them.

But he thought them newlyweds. Wouldn't such an action by a new bride be expected in a casual setting like this? Jude would think her forward though. Except...he thought they were married too.

Did she dare? The dance must be half over. If she was going to, she should do it now.

Without allowing herself to question the act again, she moved in and rested her head against Jude's shoulder. He was the perfect height. Her temple fit perfectly in the cradle of his neck and shoulder. She didn't have to tilt her neck or strain, just...relax.

She exhaled a long breath, her entire body easing as the tension seeped out.

Jude's arm around her tightened a little, protecting her, lending his strength so she could let down her guard.

She could stay like this forever, safe in his hold.

As he moved her in simple, easy steps to the loveliness of the music, she could feel the steady thump of his heartbeat. Her own pulse settled in, blending with his. The scent of him soaked through her, rich and masculine, with a hint of mint. She had never been this close to a man before, but with Jude, it felt natural.

The final strains of the song filled the room, and Jude drew her to a stop. She reluctantly lifted her head from his shoulder and found his warm gaze. Those blue eyes were dark, earnest. And held a hint of something more. A depth that made her heart skip a beat.

The captain clapped his hands, breaking through the

moment. "Magnificent, Riggs. All of you. A pleasure to see you enjoying yourselves so much."

Jude turned to the captain, and she did too. He kept his hand at her back. Or at her waist really, holding her close to him.

Captain Rivers stood, his movement more awkward than he'd seemed before. "Well done, everyone. What a lovely evening. I think I'm ready to retire, but feel free to continue if you'd like."

The other couples ambled toward the table, a host of "This dinner was such a delight," and "We'll turn in too," showing that the party had indeed come to an end.

Jude led her to their chairs so she could gather her wrap. Then they said their farewells. As she stepped through the door into the dim corridor, she permitted herself a final glance back into the room, the place where she'd felt peace for the first time in so many years—maybe even since she was a girl. She let herself remember the feeling for another heartbeat, then inhaled a breath and squared her shoulders.

The moment had been nice, but her job required focus. She had to remember the sapphires. The tariffs his family wasn't paying. Her duty to her country. She had to stay alert and not let herself be pulled so deeply into the role that she forgot what mattered most.

~

Jude stood at the railing of the upper deck with Angela at his side as the steamboat pulled up to the dock of Jackson's Ferry, one of the countless little towns along the Missouri. Joyful shouts and calls from the shore filled the air to greet them. They'd stopped nearly every day during the two weeks they'd been traveling from St. Louis.

Watching the bustle of unloading cargo and passengers provided a diversion from staring at the same scenery pass them by, but how much farther along would they be if not for these constant stops? Was it possible to book passage on a ship that traveled only to Fort Benton? Mayhap Jude would tell Jericho to search for that next time.

Jericho. His middle knotted with worry that had clung close this entire return trip. What had happened to him?

A flash of memory slipped in. His brothers gathered around him as he climbed up on the wagon's seat. They were happy, jostling for position to say farewell to him. Sean and Lillian, Lucy's children, were there too.

Along with two other women. He remembered now. They were called Dinah... He didn't know, but the other was her sister. The sister was holding a babe.

His focus homed in on Jericho. His bother wasn't hurt. Wasn't lying ill in bed. He looked hale and hearty. In the memory, he shook Jude's hand, then stepped back and wrapped his arm around Dinah.

The picture of the two standing there, arm in arm, they seemed so natural. Like he'd seen them posed that way a hundred times. Was it possible that Jericho had *chosen* to stay behind? That he'd willingly sent Jude off the ranch to handle the sapphire delivery?

The thought sounded impossible for the Jericho who was clearest in Jude's older memories. But something about this new idea rang true. God must have done a work in his big brother's life. Maybe around the time he and Dinah had grown close.

Jude let his eyes sink closed as he lifted a prayer. *You, Lord, are a healer of hearts. The only One mighty enough to redeem us when it seems impossible. Thank You.*

After lingering in the Lord's presence another moment, awareness of Angela's gaze on him slipped in. He opened his eyes to meet hers. She looked confused, perhaps a little worried. Maybe he should try to explain. If he spoke openly of his faith, it would help him gauge how willing she was to learn more.

But before he could do so, she turned to the town before them. "Jackson's Ferry is smaller than the others we've stopped at."

He studied the buildings lining the main road. They were haphazard in size and design. Built for function, not beauty. Just like most other frontier settlements.

Angela gasped, then pointed to the edge of the village. "Are those...Indians?"

His chest tightened as he followed the line of her finger. Would she be one of those easterners who disdained the natives?

The two men she pointed to were watching the ruckus of the ship's arrival, standing back a little from the hustle. From the way they wore their hair, they looked and dressed like braves he was familiar with, but he couldn't tell more from this distance.

"They've probably come to town for trading. I can't tell if they're Mandan or Osage, but both are friendly."

She glanced at him, something like wonder in her expression. "Have you met many Indians?"

At least she didn't show fear or disdain. Maybe she would be open to the truth about the tribes. "Some of my best friends live in a Salish village not far from the ranch. I've found the natives are just like the white people—their actions are a reflection of how they're raised and the conditions of their hearts. When they grow up around anger and violence, they become angry and violent. When they grow up learning to be kind and honest, that's usually reflected in their own actions. God made each of us, and he loves those two braves just as much as He loves me and you."

She studied his face for a long moment, her brows gathering as she considered his words. She didn't answer though, just finally turned back to face the town again.

The steamboat's horn sounded, echoing across the distance

as the crew prepared to depart from the bustling port. The mighty paddlewheels at the stern churned the murky river water into a frothy white wake, propelling the vessel away from the dock. Passengers waved their farewells to friends and loved ones left behind on the shore, their voices swallowed by the cacophony of creaking wood and groaning metal.

He and Angela stood quietly, taking it all in.

The wind whipped up as the boat navigated to the center of the river, the banks much narrower here than when they'd first set out from St. Louis. As the town receded into the distance, a strange sense of familiarity washed over him.

He'd been here. He'd seen this very sight before.

Or maybe not that exact image, but something very similar. Flashes of memories slipped in. They must be from his trip downriver on the way to New York. He gripped the rail, holding himself still as he let his mind take in each of the memories, exploring the outer edges of each vision, letting each settle clearly in his mind's eye.

"What is it, Jude? Is something wrong?"

Angela's quiet words hummed with worry, drawing him back to the present. He found a smile as he turned to her. "Nothing's wrong. Just a few memories coming back."

Her eyes widened. "Really? I didn't know you'd remembered anything. What was it?" Then she blinked. "I mean, if you don't mind my asking."

He shook his head. "I've just had the first bits come back today. A few minutes ago, the memory of saying goodbye to my brothers, and now riding on a steamboat, watching us pull away from several different ports."

Her smile brightened. "That's wonderful. I'm so happy for you."

Something in her voice felt tight. She'd likely wondered how his amnesia would affect her. It would, but probably not in the way she might imagine. He needed to speak of those details with her. It wasn't fair to let her think she would accompany him to the ranch when he had no plans for her to travel past Fort Benton.

Better get it done now. Was there a kind way to start the conversation, or should he be candid about the facts. He wasn't good at beating around the bush, but surely he could be forthright and kind at the same time. He steeled himself and started in. "Angela. I've been thinking through everything and..." He locked her gaze in his. "You know I don't have any memory of the train ride to New York. Which means I don't remember meeting you, or marrying you." He tried to soften those last words.

She nodded slowly as she studied him, her brows gathered in clear worry.

He plowed on. "I don't know exactly the reasons we married, but I know when I left the Montana Territory, I didn't have any intention of bringing a wife home. I think it will be a much better life for you—better all the way around—if you stay in Fort Benton when we get there. We'll find a place you like. A boarding house or your own home, if you prefer. If you want to have your own business—baking or taking in sewing or the like —we'll purchase all you need for it to be a success. Either way, I'll make sure you have plenty to live on. I'll check on you several times a year and be certain you never want for anything."

Her face paled, her wide eyes fixed on him as her jaw worked a few times. She seemed to be struggling for a response.

God, help me. Make this all work out. The knot in his gut twisted tighter.

At last, she managed to speak. "Jude. What are you saying? You don't want to be married to me? But..." She hesitated, her eyes rimming red as unshed tears glistened in the corners. "We love each other. We..." Her voice cracked, making his chest nearly do the same.

He had to fight to keep from stepping forward to pull her into his arms. He needed to stay strong though. "I'm sorry, Angela. I really think this is best."

"But how?" She threw up her hands, her voice rising. She must be realizing he wouldn't change his mind. "How can it be best to abandon your wife?"

He flinched, though he tried to stop the reaction. "I'm not abandoning you. I'll provide everything you need. I'll give you a way to reach me if you ever have cause." He couldn't tell her the real reason he couldn't take her to the ranch, and that left him with no good reason to give her at all.

She propped her hands on her waist, fire sparking in her eyes. "You're leaving me behind and riding off to who-knows-where. That's abandonment." Then her expression softened, and her hands fell to hang at her sides. "I'll be a good wife, Jude. Just give me a chance."

She stepped forward and gripped his arm. The touch nearly made him flinch again. He caught himself this time, but as her gaze implored him, those dark eyes glistening with hurt and hope, he could barely hold himself still.

Was he making the wrong decision? Was it possible he'd actually sworn to love, honor, and cherish her?

Yet staring into those eyes, his heart pinched. He might have already traveled halfway to the *love* part. It would be so easy to cover the final distance. She was beautiful, and more than that, her quiet steadiness at his side made him feel stronger. Made him feel like the man she seemed to see in him. They suited each other—that had been proved every day since he'd awakened on the floor of that train car.

But she didn't share his faith.

That reminder sunk in his belly like a stone in a pail of water, settling there to weigh down his insides. He couldn't become one with her as God planned unless she shared the part of him that mattered most.

Unless they'd already become one. The weight on his chest pressed impossibly hard. He had to get his memories back. That's the only way he could know for sure. And until then, he had to prepare her for this outcome.

He inhaled a steadying breath. "I'm sorry, Angela. You're a wonderful woman. I understand why I was drawn to you. But you don't share my faith. You don't know the Lord in the personal way that's so important to me. I made a promise to God and myself that I wouldn't spend my life with someone who didn't value the Lord's ways above all else, even me." He cleared the rust from his throat. "I don't know why I went against that back in New York City. All I know is now. And I have to keep my vow."

She stared at him another long moment, sadness darkening her gaze even more. Would she question why he wasn't keeping his vow to *her*? He'd not realized that hypocrisy until after he closed his mouth.

But she didn't call him on it. Just turned and stared out over the water to the woods covering the shoreline they passed. "I understand." The sadness in her tone tore at him. But was she giving in too easily? Wouldn't a wife—if she really was a wife— fight for her husband, even if he didn't remember her?

All this was making his head pound again.

Lord, why have You put me in this position? There's no way I can obey You without hurting her.

CHAPTER 11

*A*ngela followed Jude into their stateroom, the heavy oak door closing behind them with a soft thud.

Closing out her plans and hopes that this mission might actually succeed.

The dimly lit room smothered, pressing in around her. Surely it was only the possible demise of her assignment that worried her, not the fact the Jude felt nothing toward her. Her eyes stung just letting that thought form in her mind.

She was failing in her job. That was the only concern here. She couldn't let her emotions tangle in her work. She couldn't let herself actually care about this man. Besides, this didn't even have to be failure in her assignment. If he left her in Fort Benton, she could simply follow him to his ranch. Or maybe someone there could give her directions.

She simply had to keep strong now. If she could find anger toward him, that would clear away her disappointment and all the hurt his rejection had brought to the surface.

She knew rejection well.

It had been her friend every time she stepped foot out the door of their flat when she was a kid. No one looked past the races of her parents to see *her*. To decide if *she* was worth knowing.

A sting burned in her nose, and she turned toward the foot of the bunk so Jude couldn't see her eyes turning glassy. Not that he was looking.

The dratted man hadn't met her gaze once since he told her she wasn't good enough to be part of his life. That he felt nothing for her. At least not enough to see if more could develop between them.

A sob slipped out before she could stop it, but she tensed her insides and clamped her jaw against it. Maybe Jude hadn't heard. He was rummaging in the satchel he kept up on his bunk, making enough rustling noises that he probably hadn't caught her weakness.

She reached to adjust the blanket on her mattress. It was already straight, but she had to do something to show she wasn't curled around herself mourning him.

"Angela?"

She stilled, but then she reached for one of her bags, the one she kept her ledger in. "Yes?" She didn't turn, and thankfully, her voice gave no hint of her emotions.

"Can you look at me?"

Now he wanted to look her in the eye? She drew in a fortifying breath, swiped a sleeve across her eyes, then conjured anger as she stood and turned to face him. She needed to find something to fortify herself against weakness.

She pictured those boys, tormenting poor Chen. There was the spark she needed. It wasn't strong enough, though. She'd used that memory too much.

Papa. She brought up the way he looked when he'd come home that last evening, black eye and swollen lip. Exhausted and in pain, but still riled about the disgraces he'd been arguing against. Her father had been strong. And so was she.

Facing Jude, it wasn't hard to keep her shoulders squared,

her chin up, and her defenses fully secure. She could easily keep herself from caring about the tender worry in his eyes. The way they saw all the way to the core of her when he looked at her the way he was now.

"I'm sorry I hurt you."

A new rush of anger surged, fortifying any softness that might have found a crack. She locked her jaw to keep from spewing words in the tone she wanted to. Instead, she kept her voice controlled. As light as she could manage. "You didn't hurt me. I just..."

Ugh. She wasn't supposed to erect a wall between them. She was supposed to be convincing him that he loved her and couldn't live without her. That she would be the wife he needed. How could she possibly do that without losing control of her emotions?

A thought slipped in. What did a man really need in a wife? Cooking and keeping house, sure, but he could hire someone for that. The one thing he couldn't hire—well, she had a feeling Jude *wouldn't* hire for this particular duty—was...

She couldn't go all the way, but maybe she could give him enough of a taste that he'd rethink his plan. She inhaled a breath.

Yes. This was perfect.

She made her shoulders ease, and did her best to soften her gaze. To look wounded. "It's just, well..." She took a tiny step forward, met his gaze. Did her best to steel herself against the power of those eyes while showing him the hurt in her own. "I love you, Jude." She sniffed. "I don't want you to leave me. I want to be with you. I don't think I can stand being apart from you." She took another step forward, a bigger one this time. Close enough that she could reach out and press a hand to his chest.

His eyes turned wary though, so she didn't dare touch him yet. She felt dirty, playing on his emotions like this. But if she were honest, the other part of her couldn't wait to close the distance.

This man and his rugged handsomeness. That strong jaw with a couple day's scruff. The thickness of his neck that proved the muscle she'd felt in his arms. She'd already experienced the strength of his hold, the security there. And the night they'd danced had left her wanting to be held by him every moment since.

She couldn't push too quickly , or she'd ruin her chance. So she kept herself still. Held his gaze. Made her eyes as earnest as she could. "I know you don't remember your love for me, Jude. But you *did* love me. You..." She fought the blush surging up her neck. "You told me so every time we..."

The wariness left his eyes, replaced by a heat that gave her courage. She reached out and pressed a hand to his chest, over his heart. The thunder there matched her own.

She met his gaze once again. He'd not moved, not even a hair. His eyes were locked on her.

She inhaled a breath to steady herself, then took another step forward, resting her other hand on his chest too.

He still didn't move, save the pounding of his heart. She didn't think he was breathing. She allowed herself a tiny smile. Maybe she could remedy that.

Before she lost her nerve, she rose up on her toes, lifted her hands to his shoulders for support, and pressed her lips against his.

She'd never kissed a man. Why had she thought she'd know how to do this? The feel of his mouth against hers sent a tingle through her, but he never moved. Didn't part his lips. Didn't do anything to kiss her back. Was she supposed to peck his mouth the way she had her mother's cheek?

She stayed like that for several heartbeats.

This wasn't helping at all. She'd probably just proved to him that no spark existed between them. The impulsive act had sabotaged her, securing the demise of everything she was trying to do.

But as she eased back, their lips didn't separate. Was he...following her? A solid hand clamped against her back, locking her in place. His mouth finally responded to hers, his lips parting, his head tipping sideways, just enough so they fit together perfectly.

Now *she* couldn't breathe. Her entire body came to life, though she fought to keep herself still. If she succumbed to the heat inside her...

But his kiss coaxed her, drawing her in. Stripping away the worries that had seemed so important a moment ago.

This man. She could stay like this for days, completely absorbed by him.

The warmth of his breath mingled with hers, his hands securing her close to him. She could hardly breathe, her chest heaving with each ragged intake of air.

Jude began to ease the kiss, and she wanted to beg him not to stop. Not to break the magic of their connection.

When this ended, she would have to face...

She didn't want to think about what she'd have to face. But she'd already opened that door, and the memory of her assignment slipped back in.

What was she doing?

She couldn't let herself be drawn so fully into this. If she didn't stop the kiss now, she'd never find the ability again.

She eased back and didn't let herself think about how Jude's mouth followed her again. He didn't want the kiss to end any more than she did. She pushed that thought aside, moving her hands from the nape of his neck—a place that felt so intimate—down to his chest. That wasn't any better. Every one of his heaving breaths sent fire up her arms.

She dropped her hands to her sides. Then took a step back, putting air between them.

His brows gathered in worry. Those dark eyes. That mouth,

lips fuller now than she'd ever seen them. Who would have thought this rugged mountain man could kiss like *that*?

She had to get out of here. Away from him, before she charged back into his arms.

"I-I need to go to the washroom." Her voice came out shaky, but at least she'd managed coherent words.

The worry marking his expression deepened. "Angela, what's wrong?"

She couldn't answer that question. Not without completely giving away her lie. So she turned and aimed toward the door. "Nothing. Nothing at all."

She whipped open the door and fled into the corridor, pulling it closed behind her. She needed to stop and catch her breath. Maybe sit down before her legs buckled. But she didn't dare slow until she'd turned the corner in the dim hallway.

Then she allowed herself to halt and sink against the wall. Her heart still hammered, but at least she could slow her breathing now.

What had she just done? She squeezed her eyes shut, but that only resurrected the memory of being held in Jude's arms. That security, the sense of belonging, of being truly seen and understood by someone else.

By Jude.

His mouth had coaxed from her a passion within her she'd not known existed. Had she always been capable of feeling so much at once? Of craving so much more? Of being so consumed?

She'd been drawn to Jude from the start, though she'd tried to make herself think of him only as the critical part of her mission. But now...

She sucked in a breath, wanting to slip back down the hall to the stateroom where he likely waited, confused by her reaction to kisses that he must think they'd shared many times. She had to stay strong and separate her mind from these silly longings.

She had to keep her focus on the work. Somehow find a way to stay with Jude all the way until he took her to the source of the sapphires. Then she could submit her report, and she would be applauded. She'd prove that Winston's trust in her abilities hadn't been wrong. That her background and appearance didn't matter. That she was capable of any assignment they handed her. That she could be an asset to this country.

And prove America had not been wrong to accept her family.

CHAPTER 12

On the lower deck of the steamboat, stacks of wooden crates and barrels filled every available space except the narrow walkway around the rail. Passengers were discouraged from coming to this deck, but Jude needed quiet. To be by himself, away from the constant presence of others. And definitely not in that smothering tin box of a stateroom where Angela might enter at any moment.

He inhaled a breath, though it smelled far from clean. Scents of everything that filled the crates mingled in the air, tainted by the tangy smell of whisky from the barrels lining the center. And through it all, the smoky haze from the fire in the ship's boiler room added to the stink.

He meandered the thin path the crew had left between boxes and barrels, moving toward the rail so he could look out over the water as he prayed. He had to sort through this unrest inside him, and he desperately needed God's wisdom to know how to proceed.

That kiss.

He'd not meant to allow any kind of intimacy between them.

He would be leaving Angela in Fort Benton, and stirring up a physical connection would only make that harder.

But when she'd kissed him, his mind had begun to wonder if the two of them had done more than kiss in the past. He had no memory of it, but if they actually were married, Angela would have plenty of memories of their time together. Even though she knew he didn't remember, it would hurt her if he pushed her away as though she was disgusting to him. The last thing he wanted to do was bring more pain than he already had.

And she was the farthest thing from disgusting. In truth, it had taken everything in him to keep from responding to the kiss from the first brush of her lips.

He'd managed though...for a time. But when she started to pull away, his body had reacted without his consent.

And once he'd pulled her close... Sweet mercy. He'd never known it would be like that with a woman. Never realized he could feel so drawn. So...consumed. Thankfully, he'd kept an edge of control. But the way his body craved more...

At the rail, he lifted his gaze to the gray sky ahead of the boat. "Lord." His voice was barely audible over the splashing of the waterwheels. "I need Your guidance. What would You have me do with Angela? Show me Your will here."

Even as he tried to clear his mind so he could hear any silent nudgings, the memory of Angela's face after their kiss crowded in. She'd looked nearly panicked. Not at all the expression he'd expect from a new bride after a kiss like that.

Something wasn't right here.

"What's the truth, Lord?" He frowned into the tiny waves of river water the ship created as it plowed ahead. The ripples felt familiar. He must have stood like this before, watching the water from the lower deck of the steamboat he traveled down-river to St. Louis. What was that ship's name? No matter how he strained, he could find no memory of it.

He allowed a sigh. That wasn't an important detail anyway. There were so many other things he truly *did* need to remember. Maybe if he applied his mind to the task, he could start at the beginning of the journey and find more memories of the entire route.

He'd already remembered saying goodbye to his family, so he pulled that image back up. He'd been in the wagon with crates of sapphires stacked neatly in the back and covered with an oilskin. Buck and Belle stood in the harness, plenty stout enough to haul the load. He'd had to take the long way down the slope to the river instead of the new path the boys had been clearing directly from the house out to the Mullan Road. The weather had been pleasant, not too hot yet, though summer must have been nearing.

He could find no other memory until Fort Benton. There at the fort, was that a real memory of him standing on the dock, looking at the fort buildings behind him? He could remember turning to stare at a steamboat docked in the river. A smaller ship than this one. With only one waterwheel.

The smell of the muddy riverbank filled his senses, the stench of so many unwashed bodies coming and going from the ship. He'd been at the ranch so long, he'd forgotten how frontier towns could smell.

But as he tried to find a recollection of being on the ship, nothing distinct surfaced. Nothing of a stateroom similar to where he and Angela slept on this voyage. The memory he'd had of the boat pulling away from a village seemed more like a general feeling. Like it had happened so many times, he couldn't separate one specific occurrence.

Frustration swelled, so he moved on in his mind. St. Louis? He'd stayed at that same hotel, The Southern. Surely he could recall something of being there the first time.

He squeezed his eyes closed and took in a long breath as he focused on the lobby. The dark red drapes hanging on either side of each window. That high ceiling. Speaking to a clerk at the desk in the center. Yes, it had been a different man than the one who'd helped when he and Angela arrived there. Older, with only shiny skin on top of his head and short gray hair wrapping around the sides. He'd been helpful though. Agreeable and gracious, providing more accommodations for the supplies than Jude had expected, based on Jericho's instructions.

He exhaled. Good. Now for the ferry across the Mississippi to the train station. He couldn't summon a memory there, but the sensation of boarding the train for the first time sank over him. Smoke had hazed the air so thickly, he'd strode down to one of the cars farthest away from the engine. He remembered thinking the layers of soot covering the exterior of the car made it appear that not even this distance would protect him from the grime after days and days on this train.

Had he spent days and days on that one? When had he changed trains? He couldn't recall the answer to that even on the return journey when he'd been with Angela. His headaches had been so severe, much of that time was a blur.

A memory slipped in of himself disembarking from a train car. The station was small, so it couldn't have been New York. A woman and little boy were selling sandwiches, and he'd purchased one, slipping the lad an extra gold dollar before he walked away from them. He'd turned back to the train before he could see the lad's response. He didn't want their gratitude anyway, but hopefully it would buy the family food for a day or two. The woman's dress had been patched more than once, and the boy's trousers were nearly short enough to reveal his shins.

That must have been a train stop to take on coal in a small town. There would have been many, many others like it. He opened his eyes and squinted, shifting his mind to try to picture the seat he'd occupied on that train.

There was one in a car painted yellow. The bench had been wood with no cushion. He had a flicker of memory when he'd been wiggling, trying to find a better position where his back bone didn't dig into the wood. Had he used extra clothing as padding? Yes, his green checked shirt, folded in thirds for more thickness.

Had Angela been with him there? No. No one had shared his bench. He'd placed his carpet bag beside him. And on the seat across, an older couple had conversed a little with him. The man spoke of digging wells. Maybe that had been his line of work? Perhaps he'd handed the business to his sons, for a fellow with a full shock of white hair and plenty of crepy wrinkles couldn't still be expected to work a shovel.

So he must not have met Angela by that point. Later? She'd said they both boarded the train in Bradford, Ohio. Try as he might, he couldn't tie that name to any particular memory. He could recall more moments on trains though. More times disembarking to purchase food at various stops. Each time he could feel a sense of urgency. A feeling of tension. He had to deliver the sapphires safely. Without any loss or theft. Then he could get back to the Montana Territory. To the wide-open sky and soaring mountain peaks. To the ranch and his family. The place he loved. The place that was home.

Another train station slipped into his mind. This one much bigger. Was it New York City? It must be. He'd been focused on getting to the luggage cars. On setting eyes on the crates packed full of sapphires. Then he needed to hire a wagon to transport them.

Had Angela been there at all? Unease tightened in his chest. If they'd been planning to marry in the city, as she'd said, wouldn't he have a sense of that? Sure, he would have been focused on the sapphires too, but a wedding and his soon-to-be bride would have occupied a portion of his thoughts.

In fact...he did remember flagging a hackney coach at the train station. He'd climbed in—alone. He wouldn't have left Angela in the train station by herself. Wouldn't he have taken her to a hotel before he went on to finalize the sale of the sapphires?

And why had she been away from New York when they first met? Had she ever said?

And...if they were married, wouldn't he remember a hotel? A room? A church? But, though he'd found all the other memories, none of those came to mind.

She claimed he'd never asked if she was a believer or shared his own faith. At the time, he'd still been fighting the headaches, unable to think clearly. But he was thinking clearly now.

There was no way he would have married without talking about the God who was everything to him.

Which meant...

That unease turned to a gnawing in his belly. He'd wondered so many times since awakening on the blanket pallet on the floor of the train...

But now that he had scraps of memory, he was almost certain...

What Angela said about them being married couldn't be true.

Anger sluiced through him. She'd lied to him all these weeks?

And kissed him like that... And they'd shared a stateroom without being married...

He scrubbed a hand over his face, letting his fingers splay over his eyes. *God, what do I do?*

But why would she say so? She must be desperate. Running from something? Penniless and trying an unusual means to gain support? She was so beautiful, though. She would have a host of men lined up to wed her if she gave them a second look.

He let his mind examine the angles of each possibility. If they weren't married, he didn't owe her anything. He would see that she was set up with a way to provide for herself the rest of her days, but he didn't have to feel guilty about not taking her to the ranch as his wife.

Yet...could he be certain they'd never wed? Maybe she was lying about the timing. Maybe he'd met her in New York City and there had been a hasty ceremony.

No. That made even less sense. He couldn't fathom a reason he would make such a permanent commitment on a whim—marrying a woman he didn't even know.

There was something else going on, and he had to find out what.

Should he confront her? Demand to know the truth? But how could he know if what she told him really was fact?

Maybe he could catch her at her own game. Carry this marriage charade a little further and see what she revealed when she was caught in her lie.

But...if he attempted to kiss her again, to pretend he was ready to resume marital *activities*, would she go along with him? A woman not bound by the Holy Spirit as her conscience...

No.

Not Angela. His chest eased.

Their kiss had shaken her. She might not know and serve the Lord, but she'd not done anything that would make him think her immoral. Nothing immoral except lying, that was.

Help me, Father. Give me discernment to ferret out lies from truth. And give me wisdom in the conversation ahead.

CHAPTER 13

*J*ude hesitated outside the door of their stateroom, his heart pounding as he wrestled with the turmoil in his chest. The darkness of the corridor pressed in, the lanterns barely holding back the shadows.

He had not joined Angela for the evening meal in the dining room, sending word that he was tired and she should eat without him. In truth, it was not fatigue that kept him away, but worry about his plan. What if she didn't stop him? How far should he go before confronting her?

Taking a deep breath to steady himself, he pulled the latch string and entered their stateroom. The chamber contained little more light than the hallway, a single oil lamp casting flickering shadows onto the walls, swinging with the gentle sway of the boat.

Angela sat on her bed, a book in her hands, but her eyes were fixed on him. She looked like a wary deer, her dark gaze searching his face.

He closed the door behind him and stepped farther into the room, moving to the foot of their bunks where he kept his satchel containing his personal items. He forced a casual tone. "How was dinner?"

"They served roasted chicken and rice." A layer of tension hummed beneath the pleasant tenor of her words.

He sent her a smile. "Likely those freshly plucked chickens we saw them load at yesterday's stop."

"Perhaps."

Enough of these pleasantries, which were only making this harder for both of them. He pulled the chair to beside Angela's bed.

Her eyes widened, and she sat up straighter.

When he settled on the edge of the seat, she offered a bright look. "Yes?" Her voice was too chipper. Then her brows lowered in concern. "Is something wrong? Your headaches aren't back, are they? I should have thought of that when Charlie said you wanted to rest during dinner. But when you weren't here, I assumed you'd gone for a walk. I assumed you were all right. I never should have gone ahead without you."

He met her eyes, adding a bit of a smile. "Quite the opposite. I'm feeling much better." He paused. "I wasn't actually tired. Mostly, I needed to think." He leaned forward, a little closer to her. "And I couldn't stop thinking about that kiss."

He reached out and brushed his fingers over her cheek. The contact stirred something inside him. He'd actually intended to rest his hand there, but she pulled away, nearly hugging the wall, and his hand dropped to his knee. Maybe this wouldn't be as hard as he'd worried. She seemed close to the tipping point already.

He let his mouth tug in a secret smile, completely ignoring the worry clouding her eyes. She'd lied to him. He had to keep that fact forefront in his mind.

"Do *you* remember the kiss?" He let his gaze dip to her lips. Like a rogue stallion, his heart surged and his body heated exactly as it had when she'd been wrapped in his arms, when the taste of her had overwhelmed the rest of his senses.

He forced himself back to the present and gave her another suggestive look. "It made me remember other kisses."

Her eyes flared wider than he would have thought possible.

He pushed on. "And more." He reached for the cuff link on his right sleeve and worked the clasp open. "I think I'm fully healed now." He kept his voice as deep and smooth as he could manage as he dropped the strip of cloth on the blanket and moved to the other cuff. "I'm ready to be the husband you deserve." He reached up and tugged one string of his tie, loosening the noose.

Angela's breath hitched, her chest rising and falling rapidly. Her gaze darted to the door. Measuring how quickly she could escape? How far she could risk allowing him to carry this charade? Clearly, she didn't plan to make it easy. For that matter, being so near her and exercising full restraint wasn't easy on *him*.

He reached back to unfasten the cuff of his collar, but then a better idea surfaced. He tipped his neck and gave her a hopeful look. "Maybe you could unfasten my collar. I think I remember you helping me with that before."

Her chin trembled as she gave her head a quick shake. "I-I can't."

He almost hesitated. What was he doing, intentionally frightening her? He was no cad. Mum would box his ears if she saw him now.

He nearly huffed out a chuckle. Then she'd turn and box Angela's ears for lying to him in the first place.

That reminder gave him fresh courage, and he flicked open the latch on his collar, then tugged the cloth off. These blasted city clothes took so long to manage. He'd have been down to his skivvies by now if he'd been in his usual trousers and work shirt. Of course, he didn't actually *want* the charade to go that far, so maybe all this fuss was good for once.

He forced another smile, hopefully one that looked eager, not frustrated. "Have you missed me as much as I've missed you, my dear?"

Angela didn't answer, just stared at him with those impossibly wide eyes.

She'd moved over enough that he had plenty of room to turn and sit on the bed beside her, so he did. He eased his back against the headboard, turning to give her another slow grin. He had no idea if he was doing this the way a husband would. Most likely not. But as long as she gave up the ruse soon, it didn't matter.

She looked worried speechless, pressed against the wall with her mouth a thin line. Was she contemplating telling him the truth? Maybe he should add a bit more pressure.

He started to reach up and touch her cheek again, but she flinched before his hand traveled half the distance. He wouldn't force his touch on her, no matter what she'd done to him—or intended to do. So he let his hand settle on the bed next to her.

He made his voice take on that warm, intimate tone again. "Angela. Would you like to tell me about some of the things we've done before? Or maybe you could show me. We could take up where we stopped earlier...with that kiss."

Her nostrils flared, and her gaze flicked to the door again. She was getting closer. Like a wild colt he'd been trying to touch, she would probably bolt any minute. He'd be ready to catch her. Surely at that point they could speak candidly.

She didn't answer either of his suggestions. Not that he'd expected her to tell him about any non-existent intimate moments they'd shared. And if he tried to kiss her, he'd have to force himself on her physically, which he wouldn't do.

So he reached for the bottom of his shirt where it tucked into his trousers. "Think I'll just get more comfortable before we start." He tugged the shirt hem out of his pants and pulled upward, leaning forward to lift the cloth over his head.

As he'd suspected, this was the moment she chose to bolt. He'd barely gotten the hem up to his arms when she surged toward the foot of the bed, launching herself off like a deer clearing a creek.

Thank the Lord he was prepared, for he managed to lunge forward himself, landing his boot on the floor and grabbing for whatever part of her he could reach.

His hand closed on fabric and he gripped hard to the back of her skirt. Her forward motion halted like she'd slammed into a wall.

"No. Let me go." She struggled against his hold, but he was far stronger—no surprise there.

He grabbed her upper arm but was careful not to be rough as he secured his fingers firmly around her. "Angela." He had to grit his teeth to keep from huffing. It was more the tension that stole his air than anything else. The necessity of holding her tight without hurting her in any way. "I think it's time we talk."

She gave one more half effort to pull from his hold, then stopped fighting. She stood with her back to him, her shoulders dropping in a way that made something stir inside him. Something like sympathy.

He *didn't* want to hurt her.

Whatever made her tell such a falsehood must have been important. If she would simply tell him the truth now, he would do what he could to help her. After all, *she'd* helped *him*. She'd been his strength when he'd been injured and lost his memory. He would have flailed without her.

She finally turned to face him, and he released the back of her skirt. He loosened his hand at her arm, but only enough that she could pivot. He didn't trust her not to try to bolt again.

She didn't meet his gaze but focused somewhere on his chest. That brought the immediate realization that his shirt hem was still bunched up around his armpits, revealing far too much of the skin covering his belly. That wasn't the place she was looking, but still...

He used his free hand to jerk the cloth back in place. The shirt hung loose, a condition that might be considered intimate. But in truth, this whole situation was so untoward, well...

At least he was covered. He shifted his hands so he held her wrist instead of her upper arm, then led her toward the chair. She eased down to perch on the edge, though it was clear she'd rather be anywhere else. He could sit on the bed, but that would give her a free path to the door. Better he keep himself a barrier between her and escape.

He crouched in front of her, leaving enough distance to ease her worries about him accosting her. To confirm that fact, he released her wrist and met her gaze. "I won't touch you as long as you don't try to run again."

Even her focus was skittish, for she looked as if she might jerk her gaze away at any second. At least she gave a slight dip of her chin to show she understood.

He took in a breath to clear his head, then released it, letting out the muddle of distractions with the spent air. "Now. I think it's time you tell me the truth. Exactly why you aren't eager to participate in things married couples do." He allowed a bit of steel to creep into his voice and eyes.

Her expression turned wary. "Your memories are back." She spoke it as a statement not a question.

Not all of them, but enough. He nodded. "The truth, please."

She pressed her lips together, the moment stretching.

Should he mention he would go easy on her if she told him everything? That certainly wasn't how to negotiate with a man, but she was such a little thing. And she still had the scent of fear about her.

Before he could speak, she straightened. She inhaled a deep breath, her usual self-assurance returning, at least in part. She met his gaze, repentance shimmering in her eyes. "I'm sorry, Jude. I really am. I did it to help you." Another deep breath in. "And also to help me."

He didn't speak. Did his best not to show any response. But this felt more like the truth than anything she'd said before. More like the real Angela. Though did he really know who that was?

"I... I first saw you at the station in New York. You caught my notice, both because you're..."—She motioned toward him. "Well, you're not like most men. Not only are you...handsome"— her gaze slipped off his eyes, hovering somewhere around his ear—"but you obviously don't belong in the city. You look like you'd be more comfortable hefting logs in the wilderness. Or riding horses on a ranch somewhere."

She'd read him well that first meeting. Had he been so obvious to everyone? Or just her?

The lines of her neck flexed when she swallowed. "You stood and moved toward the corridor between the trains. You were right beside me when the crate came down on top of you. It was such a hard hit. You lost consciousness. And when you awoke..." She met his gaze again, sorrow and worry clouding hers. "You were talking so strangely, like you didn't remember...anything. I...well, I never meant for things to go this far. I knew you'd need help. You were traveling alone, and somebody needed to take care of you. When I stepped in to help, the people assumed I was your wife."

Her lower lip slipped between her teeth. " I thought it would help us both. I was worried about my safety. I—" She cut off her words and looked away.

This was the part he needed to know the most. What was her situation that she would so quickly cling to him. Had she nowhere to go? No one who would be looking for her?

"Angela. I want to believe you. I want to understand. To help even. But you have to tell me everything. No more lies, no more secrets. Just the truth."

Her gaze met his once more, a flicker of hope shining in her eyes. She gave a slow nod, and the tension in his chest eased. Whatever her situation, he would help her. They could work through the trouble together.

CHAPTER 14

*A*ngela's pulse thundered in her ears as she searched Jude's eyes for any sign of understanding or forgiveness. The shadows that played across his face, cast by the dim lantern light, made it difficult to read his expression. She gripped her hands together. How could she convince him not to send her away at the next port?

She hated lying to him, this man who'd proved over and over his goodness. His kindness. His integrity. But he and his family were evading tariffs. Right? That didn't seem like the man she'd come to know, but it was what Winston had said. Perhaps Jude wasn't aware of that end of the business.

Everything in her wanted to tell him the truth. All of it.

But she didn't dare. If she revealed her mission, she'd ruin her chance to accomplish it. That might mean the end for the Treasury's agents. The task of uncovering fraud would be given to the Secret Service. Not only would she be out of a job, but so would all the other agents. And Winston, the one man who'd believed in her enough to give her a chance.

The one man before she'd met Jude.

Why couldn't her target on this assignment have been a

beast of a fellow? Uncouth and completely unlikeable? She wouldn't have minded so much lying to *him*. But Jude...

Tears burned her eyes, completely unbidden. Yet even as she forced them back, Jude's expression softened.

"Tell me, Angela. Why would it help you to pretend to be my wife? When you left New York on the train, didn't you have a destination in mind? People waiting for you somewhere?" His voice was so gentle. Almost tender.

She didn't deserve this. Not his understanding or his kindness. She could answer his question though. Honestly.

She shook her head. "No."

His brow furrowed. "You boarded the train with no idea where you were going?"

Again the awful regret in her chest rose up as tears. She shook her head. "No."

He eyed her. "No what?"

He wanted her to state it in her own words apparently. She closed her eyes and took a breath for courage. If only she had Jude's God and could beg for a greater strength. But He wouldn't help her in a lie anyway. The God Jude had told her about would never want someone like her. Not after this. She'd proved herself just as awful as people had said through the years. A conniving coolie who only looked out for her own good.

She opened her eyes and met Jude's gaze, the hopelessness of her situation pressing in hard. "I didn't know where I was going, Jude. I packed a bag with enough to last a few days and purchased a ticket to Northumberland. That was as far as the Bloomsburgh line went. I figured I would see where I wanted to go from there." All of that was true, though she'd left out the main reason she'd had no idea where she was going—she'd been planning to follow Jude. She'd planned to buy whatever tickets he purchased. She'd planned to end up where he did.

His brows lowered again. "What of your mother? Is everything you told me about your family true?" His eyes narrowed. "Is any of it true?"

The knot that had been churning in her belly now rose up to her chest. "It's all true. I'm the daughter of Patrick and Lìlì Larkin. I was born in China, but there was so much unrest, so many people dying because of the rebellion against the Qing government. Da got us on a ship to America as soon as he could. America was a haven. It embraced us, even granting all four of us citizenship because my father was Scottish. We had opportunities in America we never could have dreamed of in China."

She sucked in a breath. "But then my brother Chen died at the hand of a gang of bullies when he was eight and I was six. I grew up selling the baked goods my mother made, mostly egg custard tarts. When the Civil War broke out, my father supported our country and the government that had given him a much better life than Ireland or China had. He disagreed with the other Irishmen protesting the draft. One day he was trying to stop the others from rioting. Shots were fired. He was hit by a man who'd been born in the very same county where my da grew up. I wasn't even with my mother when she learned the news. I came home from selling food on the street to find her sitting at the kitchen table, the room dark, her eyes a shell with no light."

Jude studied her, his gaze drilling deep inside. Weighing the truth in her words, no doubt. At least in this she'd not lied.

When he spoke again, his voice was measured. "And do you still sell your mother's baking? Is that enough to support the two of you?"

She shook her head. "A friend of my father's helped me get a job with the Treasury office in Manhattan. My mother still bakes for a few families, but they come to pick up their orders from the flat. We get by."

"And what made you set out on the train? Won't you lose your job at the Treasury because you left unexpectedly?"

Frustration surged in her chest. She'd said everything she could without veering from the truth again.

She straightened. "Haven't I bared my soul enough? I needed to get away. One of my superiors...didn't want me there. So I left. It's for the best." She turned away from him so he couldn't see the chaos in her gaze. He would make assumptions from her words that wouldn't be true. Winston *had* wanted her to leave— to set out on this assignment.

She turned back to face him, letting her regret shine through. "I'm sorry, Jude. I really never meant things to grow into this. I only thought I would help you during your injury, and I'd be safer if people saw I wasn't traveling alone. I didn't think the ruse would go on so far. I knew you'd eventually learn the truth. But then I came to care for you." A twinge of guilt struck her chest at the deception.

Except...those words were true, weren't they? She did care for him. The problem came because she let herself believe the fantasy that a man like him could want a woman like her.

She pushed that thought away and locked onto his fathomless eyes. "Please, forgive me. Please?"

His Adam's apple bobbed as he swallowed. "Where do you intend to go?"

She took in another breath, this one deeper because a little of the weight had lifted from her chest. "Fort Benton, I suppose." She shrugged, looking away. She couldn't hold his gaze any longer, and she needed to stop his questions.

But he didn't answer, and the longer the silence stretched, the tighter her nerves grew. She finally looked back at him.

He still stared at her, yet this time he didn't seem to see her at all. He must be deciding how to move forward. She shouldn't interrupt him.

But perhaps he felt her watching, for he snapped from his thoughts and rose to his feet. "I'm going to sleep on the deck. We'll talk again tomorrow."

He turned to the door, and before she could respond or tell him *she* would sleep on the deck so he could have the stateroom he was paying for, he disappeared into the dark corridor.

The soft click of the latch echoed in the hollowness of her heart.

~

*W*hen Angela opened her eyes, the dim light of morning seeped through the small round window of their stateroom. *Her* stateroom.

Jude wasn't in the bunk above her. Even without looking, she could feel his absence. It hurt in that aching place in her chest.

She lay there, letting herself grieve. Maybe she should tell Jude the truth. *All* the truth.

About her assignment. That she knew about the sapphires. That she'd been lying to him even as she "confessed" the night before.

She sighed, the tiny flame of hope in her heart snuffing out with the breath. He would never forgive her. Or even if he somehow did forgive her for his God's sake, he'd never trust her again.

But as she pushed the blanket aside and stood, bracing to gain her balance with the gentle sway of the boat, the seed of hope tried to poke its head once more.

What if by some chance Jude *did* forgive her? Surely he'd felt the connection between them, the one that had singed her mind and heart and every part of her.

If she was willing to cast aside her work for him, maybe there was a tiny chance he would forgive her awful lies and they could move forward together. She *would* have to give up the assignment, she knew that without a doubt. She had a feeling she wouldn't be able to convince him to share his family's secrets with the United States Treasury Department.

Maybe resigning from her work would be the act that allowed him to fully trust her. She would let him be part of every step. See her flaws and her worries and her complete devotion to him.

But...could she join Jude and his family in avoiding tariffs and smuggling sapphires into the country illegally? Maybe she could convince him to abide by the laws. Surely she could.

What was she thinking, even contemplating this? She couldn't leave her work, the job she'd struggled so hard to secure. She couldn't simply walk away when she'd worked so hard to prove Winston had been right to give her a chance, that she was strong and smart and capable enough to work as an undercover operative for the United States Government. How could she walk away from all she'd fought to attain?

And A-ma. How could she leave her mother behind in the city? A-ma had said often these past years that she didn't want Angela to hold back her own life for her. That if she found a young man worthy of her, she shouldn't let worry over her a-ma stop her from accepting his offer and building her own life.

A-ma had her friends. In fact, Yan Liu on the floor above them had offered an open invitation for A-ma to move in with her any time. A-ma wouldn't do so as long as Angela lived with her, of course. But the offer was there.

Just the thought brought a niggle of relief that Angela couldn't allow to settle. Just because A-ma would have a place to live should Angela ever marry didn't mean she should allow another thought about abandoning her job and riding off with Jude. Especially when he'd never want her if he knew the full truth.

She moved to her satchel and pulled out her brush. She wasn't hungry, but she would go to breakfast, just in case Jude was there looking for her. She owed him that.

As she pinned up her hair, her wayward mind drifted back through what would be necessary if she *did* resign from the agency. She would need to send a telegram. Would Winston accept a telegram? Or would he be suspicious that someone else had sent it? Or that she was in trouble and being coerced? He was a suspicious man, his wariness hard-earned after years of chasing criminals.

Would he send someone after her to find out the truth? An image of Lawrence and Martin slipped in. Surely he wouldn't send those two henchmen. Though he might, if he thought she was in trouble.

A new possibility slipped in, the thought making her fumble her last pin.

Winston would want the assignment completed. If he accepted her resignation, he'd send someone else to finish the job. Maybe even give it to Lawrence and Martin. Those two always worked as a pair, and when Winston learned she and Jude were headed to the Montana Territory, he would want to send men capable of rugged terrain.

Would she have to tell him where they were going?

She sighed and turned to the door. None of this would be relevant anyway. She had no future with Jude. He'd never trust her again, so she might as well continue with the assignment.

Then she'd return to New York City, to the life she'd once thought normal, even laudable. A job she'd been thrilled to secure. A supervisor who believed in her, at least enough to give her a chance.

Now that she'd met Jude Coulter, though, that life didn't look nearly so wonderful. It felt like a rope that would always pull her back. A noose she could never escape.

She stepped into the corridor and followed the familiar path to the dining room. As she turned the second corner, a door opened in front of her—a door to the kitchen, if she wasn't mistaken.

A porter exited, carrying a tray of food he must be delivering to one of the staterooms.

She shifted to give him room. "Good morning, Ronald."

The blonde man who'd helped them to their room that first morning sent her a lopsided grin. "Mornin', Mrs. Coulter. Headed to breakfast?"

Mrs. Coulter. She smiled past the lump in her throat. "I am."

The boat swayed more than usual, and Charlie shifted his hold on the tray as he spread his legs for a sturdier stance. The door to the kitchen swung and would have hit him in the back, but she caught it just before it struck him. A blow like that would surely spill the tea sloshing in the mugs.

"Thank you kindly." Charlie stepped forward. "Better get this delivered afore I spill it down my trousers."

She gripped the door handle and glanced into the kitchen as she prepared to close the door. A handful of people worked in the small space, standing at counters or sitting at the table in the center. Just as she was about to shut away the scene, one of the men sitting glanced up at her.

Her breath stalled. That couldn't be...

She squinted, moving close enough to peer through the narrow opening. He only looked like Martin because she'd been thinking of those two ham-fisted goons minutes before.

She wanted to believe it wasn't him.

But he locked eyes with her, and his were narrowing. *He recognized her.*

She pulled the door wider. If Martin was here, Lawrence must be as well. Had they been on the ship the entire time? Or maybe they'd boarded at the last stop.

But why?

Why would Winston have sent them?

Was she in danger? Maybe Winston had discovered a threat they didn't know about and had sent them to protect her.

She stepped into the kitchen to talk with Martin, but she'd

forgotten all the other kitchen workers were there, until they turned to eye her.

The man pouring something into a pot at the stove flapped a hand toward her. "Passengers no come'a in'a my kitchen." His accent clearly showed he wasn't an American by birth.

She sent him an apologetic smile. "I'm sorry. I just need to speak with this man. I'll only be a moment." She reached Martin, who'd stood to meet her.

"You havva problem wit him?" The chef turned his full body to face them, eyeing Martin like he'd added poison to the stewpot.

She shook her head. "No. I've met him before is all. I have a question for him." She couldn't say anything that would blow Martin's cover, whatever he'd established in order to be a kitchen worker here.

The man flapped his arm at them again as he turned back to the stove. "We work in'na my kitchen. Go outside to talk."

Gladly.

She stepped to the door, glancing from the corner of her eye to make sure Martin was following.

Thankfully, the corridor was empty when they stepped into it and she closed the door. Still, she turned and led them all the way down to the end of the hall, where the only door led to a supply closet. No one should hear their conversation here.

A lantern on the wall opposite the door and one just behind her gave enough light to see Martin's guarded expression well. His mop of loose brown hair was just long enough to curl around ears that stuck out. Just now, he seemed inclined to use those ears, waiting for her to speak.

She kept her voice low, though it came out more like a hiss. "What's going on?"

CHAPTER 15

*M*artin raised one thick brow, a trick Angela had never been able to learn. "That's a question for *you*. Why did you blow my cover?"

She frowned. "I didn't. I never said who you are. And what are you doing here? Winston said I was the only one assigned to this mission. Did he get more information? Is there another threat we didn't know about?"

Martin tipped his chin sideways, eyeing her. "I don't know. Is there?"

She wanted to huff and throw up her hands, or maybe use them to grip his thick neck and shake him. But she held in her frustration like a capable agent. "Don't talk in circles. Why did Winston send you?"

He studied her a long moment, like he was debating whether to tell her. Or maybe he was trying to come up with a cover story. Martin wasn't always the fastest thinker in the room.

"The boss was worried about you. Sent us to make sure the job got done."

She frowned. By *us*, he surely meant Lawrence too. But that wasn't the important point here. "Worried about my safety?"

Because that wasn't the feeling she was getting from Martin's tone.

He shook his head. "Worried about you doin' the job right. We're a bit of insurance, you might say."

Anger seared through her like fire, so hot that her chest burned.

Winston had lied to her? He'd told her she was the only agent assigned to Jude. That she'd earned his trust after doing her work so well. The tears that threatened her eyes were far worse than the anger, so she reached for that hotter emotion again. "Why would he do that? That's not what he told me." She bit the words through clenched teeth.

Yet even as she spoke them, another possibility slipped in. Were Martin and Lawrence acting on their own? Had they overheard Winston give her the assignment? Had they followed her to get the praise for accomplishing it themselves? Or to find the source of the sapphires and steal whatever they could get?

Martin didn't look concerned about her feelings. He was just cold enough not to care about who he hurt, as long as he accomplished his goal. Lawrence too. They wouldn't think twice about knocking her out of the way to earn the pay of the assignment and the advancement it would no doubt award.

She had to force herself to breathe through her fury. "You two came of your own volition, didn't you? Winston didn't send you. He doesn't even know you're here. You want to steal my assignment. Or better yet. You want me to do all the work, then claim the glory. You think they'll give you a better position in the agency? Winston will see through your lies. You can be sure of it." She shouldn't be saying all this to him. She needed to clamp a hand over her mouth. But she couldn't hold the words back.

She wouldn't let these two goons take the job she'd worked so hard to earn. Jude was *her* assignment. No matter that she'd been contemplating resigning just a quarter hour before. These scallywags wouldn't steal from her if it took her last breath to stop them.

Martin's chuckle grated on every one of her nerve endings. "You're precious, you know that?"

Maybe she could sock him right in the nose. She wouldn't have much strength compared to this overgrown lug, but she could draw blood.

He laughed again, this time chortling as though he found himself funnier than he found her. "You think we'd come all the way across the country just to snipe in on your deal? You must think you're somethin'." He shook his head. "We're not aimin' for better work in the Treasury. You can be sure of that. I'd say our days there are limited. If we can get the skinny on where these gems are comin' from, Winston has the contacts in place to overhaul the next shipment. That'll give us more'n enough to live on for the rest of our days. You too, if you keep yer nose clean an' do yer job."

Oh.

Oh.

Her mind scrambled to make sense of his words. Not just because she'd never heard him string so many together at once, but...

Winston *has the contacts in place to overhaul the next shipment?* "What do you mean by overhaul?"

His smirk grated worse than his laughter had. "Take the goods. Have them delivered to us instead of the buyer. We'll send the delivery boy back with some fake money an' that'll be the last job we pull. Ever."

He had the nerve to smile. These two cads were planning to steal from the American government? From Jude and his family? She glared at him, once more spitting her words at him. "You'll never get away with it. Winston will stop you."

Martin's eyes widened in contempt. "You're even dafter than

the average dame. Winston said you had smarts, but I never bought it. It must be only your looks he likes."

Her stomach roiled, and tears sprang to her eyes. Martin didn't know what he was talking about. Winston treated her like a professional. With respect.

"The boss is in it with us. That's what makes this a sure thing. But we have to pull this job right the first time. Won't be no second chances. The big fellows are startin' to poke their noses in, and Winston doesn't have much time left afore they start diggin' deeper. If he's forced out afore we get the facts on these gems, we won't be able to land next year's catch."

"Here's the thing. You got Coulter in hand. Keep him happy an' this thing will come together just fine. You'll get your share of the gems too."

She couldn't breathe, though her chest heaved.

This wasn't possible.

Martin and Lawrence were criminals—the fact didn't surprise her at all.

But Winston? Her mentor? Her friend? The only man who'd believed in her since Da's death?

He'd been using her, all this time?

She had to get away. Had to think through everything he'd said. Find the loophole. The point that would prove he was lying. He and Lawrence must've cooked up this scheme.

She took a step back. "I understand." Her voice sounded normal, though the words came to her ears as if someone else spoke them.

"Do you?"

The voice behind her made her heart lurch, and she spun to face Lawrence. He peered down his large nose at her, his blond brows raised. He stood so close—near enough to breathe on her —so she took a step back, which only put her closer to Martin.

Lawrence studied her with a scrutiny that looked far too menacing to be considered friendly.

She shifted sideways and backed up a step so she could see both men at once. Her foot touched the wall behind her, making her feel like a cornered child against a pair of bullies. She wouldn't have room to dart out of reach if one of them got riled.

She couldn't let herself be afraid, though. She took a breath, letting it lift her shoulders and raise her chin so she could meet Lawrence's gaze. He was taller than Martin. He probably had the same amount of muscle, but spread over the longer frame, he looked leaner.

She dipped her chin and repeated her previous words. "I understand." But she wasn't committing to anything. Certainly not to help these miscreants.

"And you'll play your part? Do everything you can to help us pull of this job with no problems?" Lawrence must have lived in England at some point, for his words tipped with a bit of the accent from that country.

Once more, she was having trouble drawing breath. She didn't want to lie anymore. Everything in her despised the dirty feeling that accompanied a falsehood. That had been the start of her trouble with Jude. And now to learn that she'd lied to a good man to help a group of traitors and thieves?

She was done with these men. And done with lying.

What could she say that wouldn't be a falsehood, yet would satisfy these two vagabonds so she could get away?

But that was the problem, wasn't it?

If there was one thing she'd learned about lying in all this, truth wasn't only in the words she spoke, but in the meaning the other person understood. If she technically didn't lie with her words, but she led Lawrence and Martin to believe something other than what she really meant, *she would still be lying.*

And she would lie no more.

Certainty filled every part of her, more solid than the bones supporting her.

She lifted her chin. "I don't think Jude trusts me anymore."

Not to mention she wouldn't go along with a plan that hurt innocent people or the government she'd worked so hard to support most of her life.

The air in their small corner had turned thick, and she could practically taste her own defiance—and her fear—as she waited for their response. Lawrence was usually the one who spoke between the two of them, so she looked at him.

He studied her a long moment, and the lamplight flickered off the anger in his eyes. She didn't let herself back down.

When he finally responded, a snarl rumbled from him. "You little twit." He stepped forward, closing the small distance between them. He loomed over her, and when his hand lifted, drawing back, she knew what was coming next.

His fist surged toward her. She ducked, flicking to the side. It kept the blow from landing square in her face, but his knuckles struck the side of her temple, flinging her neck sideways.

A thump was followed by his grunt of pain. She might have done the same, but she couldn't say for sure.

She narrowed her focus. Ignore the pain and not take her eyes off her opponent. The rules Da had taught her so she could defend herself against bullies.

Bullies like these two.

She stayed low, crouching so she would be ready to sprint away at the first opening. She barely had time to flick her gaze upward before Martin's hands landed on her shoulders, most of his weight bearing down on her body. It knocked her backward, her rear landing hard on the floor, the back of her head hitting the wall. Not hard enough to make her gaze go dark, but she had to struggle not to let the pain stall her.

The weight of his massive body still pushed hard on her shoulders, making it nearly impossible to breathe.

Her legs were free. Her hands, too, except their range was limited by his weight on her shoulders.

She swung her right foot wide and up, making contact with the side of Martin's left leg.

He didn't flinch.

She struck out with her other leg, trying to catch his knee. From the corner of her eye, she could see Lawrence drawing up for another blow. This time, she wouldn't be able to duck away. She could almost feel the impact of his fist in her cheek.

Suddenly, Martin's weight lifted off her, the man moving backward, almost like a massive hand was pulling him. As he tumbled onto his rear in the hallway, a third figure came clear.

Jude.

She gasped, relief nearly stealing her control. He had a revolver in his hand, pointed at Lawrence.

Jude stepped back beside her, where he could see both men well, though he kept the gun aimed at Lawrence. The taller ruffian had frozen in his fighting stance, right fist drawn back, ready to plow into her face.

He was focused on Jude now.

"Angela, get back to the stateroom. I'll be there once I see to these two." Jude's voice was hard, sterner than she'd ever heard him, even when he'd been demanding she tell him the truth.

The truth.

She would tell him *everything*, as soon as she could. Whether it made him turn against her or not. It would, no doubt. And she'd lose her job and everything she'd worked for. At least she would always have A-ma.

Quietly, she lifted to her feet and ducked under Jude's gun, keeping close to him as she moved between him and Martin, the thug still lying on his back where Jude had thrown him. He, too, was watching Jude, not even flicking a glance to her as she moved past.

At last she was beyond them all, the length of the corridor stretching ahead. She desperately wanted to escape through the door to the deck and suck in the fresh air. She was alive. Unhurt.

But she turned. She couldn't leave Jude with these two scoundrels. What did he plan to do with them?

"Get out of here, Angela." Frustration tinged Jude's voice. "I'm not letting them move until you're safe."

She couldn't leave him in danger. "What will you do with them?" Maybe she should get help.

Jude nearly growled his answer. "What they deserve. But not until you're gone." His voice turned to a bark with each of his next words. "Go. To. The. Stateroom."

"All right." She stepped backward and turned to obey. Though it took everything in her to leave him her trouble alone.

CHAPTER 16

*J*ude tightened his grip on his revolver, squeezing the cold metal as he held the two men at gunpoint. The dim lamplight flickered in the narrow corridor, casting shadows across their faces and shimmering off the sweat beading their foreheads.

His heart pounded as rage and frustration simmered within him. He'd heard enough of their heated argument with Angela to realize she knew these men.

Were they the reason she'd left New York with no plan of where she would end up? When she'd been arguing with them, she hadn't sounded like she was willing to go along with what they wanted her to do.

But the way she hesitated when Jude told her to get to safety made him wonder if she was trying to protect them.

That woman was more frustrating than any person he'd ever met, a tangled web of secrets. Every time he found one end and started to unravel the truth, more knots popped up.

He growled again, letting his frustration loose in his voice. "Down on your bellies, both of you. Put your hands on the back of your heads."

He received scowls from both, but he didn't back down. Just kept the gun aimed at the taller one, who was still standing.

Angela had called him Lawrence, the man on the floor Martin.

Lawrence finally dropped to his knees, grumbling something too quiet for Jude to understand.

He needed to check them for weapons, then hopefully Riggs would be here with help and some rope to tie these two up. He'd been having breakfast with the first mate but left the meal early to go pack his things. When he'd stepped into the hallway and realized what was happening, he'd slipped back in to get Riggs's help before returning to stop the squabble. He'd not expected it to escalate so much in those few short minutes.

Thank God he'd arrived in time to stop them before Angela was truly hurt. She'd been trying to stand on her own, but such a petite frame against these two seasoned thugs...? How in the world had she gotten mixed up with them?

It didn't matter. He'd see that they were placed in the hands of the nearest lawmen, then he'd get off this ill-fated boat and ride the rest of the way to the Territory. Before he left, he would pay for Angela's passage back to St. Louis on this same steamboat, and maybe even wire the hotel in St. Louis enough for her to sleep there and for them to see that she had train fare back to New York. She likely had no money for such a trip.

But then he would be done with her. She could manage her own affairs, and he could settle back into his quiet life on the ranch. She'd be only a wild, ridiculous memory, one he wasn't even sure he would tell his family about.

It wouldn't take long for his chest to stop tightening at the thought of not seeing her again. The attraction he'd felt for her would pass in time.

The two scoundrels finally moved into the position he ordered.

Where was Riggs? The man should have been here by now.

He couldn't move or tie either of them until the first mate came with ropes, but at least he could make sure they weren't hiding weapons.

He kept the gun pointed at Lawrence as he shifted forward, approaching Martin first. Jude lifted his boot to nudge the man's waistband and check for a knife or handgun.

A spark flashed at the corner of his eye. He jerked his focus back to Lawrence as a boom rang through the corridor.

The noise pushed him back a step, but he caught his balance and refocused his aim on Lawrence.

That man was already on his feet, a pistol pointed at Jude. He must have been hiding it in a sleeve.

Jude wouldn't have thought he could move so lightning-fast.

A burn at Jude's thigh tried to press through his focus, but he ignored it. The bullet might have creased him there, but it hadn't broken a bone. He could worry about the pain later.

He and Lawrence stood in a stalemate now, both aiming at each other. The other man's gun looked to be a Cooper revolver, which would be just as deadly as Jude's Colt '49.

"Thought you had the upper hand, didn't you?" Lawrence snarled.

Jude had no doubt of his own aim. If he pulled the trigger, his bullet would hit the other man's chest.

But these two appeared to be seasoned thugs. Lawrence would shoot him at the same time.

Which meant they'd both die.

And this other scoundrel, Martin, would be free to hurt Angela. Maybe she'd be smart enough to stay away from him now. Riggs and the captain could help protect her.

But Jude's family... His brothers and niece and nephew. They would mourn him, and they'd already been through enough grief. With Mum and Dat's passing, then Lucy's.

So he didn't shoot, but he kept his pistol aimed. *God, let Riggs get here soon with help.*

"Toss your gun here, then lay on your belly with your hands on your head." Lawrence's words curled with dark satisfaction. He must like getting revenge already for what Jude had made them do.

Jude's jaw clenched. He lowered his revolver and tossed it lightly, not far enough that it would reach the taller man. Even Martin would have to shift to grab it.

Jude would comply, but he didn't have to make it easy for them. With a deep, measured breath, he lowered himself onto his stomach, the cold wood pressing into his cheek.

Lawrence's footsteps approached, the sound as menacing as a rattlesnake's tail. Martin followed him. Were they going to attack?

Lord, help me. Give me wisdom and strength to respond how You would have me.

But the men didn't stop in front of him. No blows struck his ribs or head.

The footsteps moved past him, and he dared to turn his head so he could see.

They were running, sprinting down the corridor.

Escaping.

New fury filled his veins, and he scrambled to his feet, running even before he caught his balance. The searing in his leg slowed him.

Voices sounded ahead, and he rounded the corner in the hallway to meet a cluster of men entering from the deck. Riggs was among them, but not the two ruffians.

"Coulter. What's happening?" Riggs stepped to the front of the group.

Jude tried to push around him. "They're getting away. Two men attacked Angela, but they ran. Quick." He pointed out the open door, and finally the men blocking the path turned and poured outside.

"After them!" Riggs called the command to his men—sailors

from the looks of them. "What do they look like?" That last part must be for Jude, but he didn't stop to answer.

He'd already pushed through the clog and caught sight of Lawrence and Martin sprinting toward the rail. They might jump, and if they did, it would be so much harder to catch them.

The moment he had a clear path, he lunged forward, running as fast as he could to catch the thugs before they climbed over the rail. Even ignoring the fire flaming in his leg, he didn't reach them in time. Lawrence hung from the rail, then his hands disappeared. Martin swung his second leg over so he was sitting on the rail. He didn't look eager for the plunge—more than two stories down to the water from this top deck—but after a glance back to see Jude coming, he gripped the rail beside him and twisted, lowering so only his hands could be seen gripping the wood. Then they disappeared just like Lawrence's had.

Jude slammed into the rail as he reached it, his breath coming in heaves as he peered into the water below. No sign of the men. They would surface any minute.

The sailors crowded around him, peering into the water too. He relayed what had happened while they watched, but still, there was no sign at all of Lawrence and Martin. Had they struck their heads on a rock and drowned? That didn't seem likely for *both* of them.

"They might 'ave got sucked under the boat an' come up the other side." Riggs spoke from beside him, then pointed to some of his men. "You three, go aft an' watch for 'em." Three fellows trotted off to obey.

As Riggs assigned locations for the others to search, Jude continued to study the water. What should he do if they never found out for sure what happened to those two? Could he abandon Angela without knowing for sure she was free from them? Trouble like those two had a way of reappearing down the line.

But she *wasn't* his responsibility.

Some might argue he'd already done more than right by her, especially the way she'd lied to him.

But he couldn't see it that way. She had cared for him and helped him through every obstacle of their journey. She never made him feel uncapable, despite the fact he'd been weak while those headaches lasted. She'd not stolen a dollar from him either. He'd counted the money in his bag, and not a penny was missing. In fact, there was more than Jericho usually brought back from his deliveries.

Jude let out a long sigh. He didn't know what to do, but he needed to check on Angela. While Riggs and his men continued the search, he had a few questions to ask her.

Lord, let her tell the truth. The entire truth this time. Please.

CHAPTER 17

*J*ude stepped into the dimly lit stateroom, his shoulders sagging with weariness. It couldn't be later than half past nine in the morning, but exhaustion already pressed hard on him. That and a lingering sting on his leg. Someone had brought him a wet cloth from the kitchen to clean the blood away. Thankfully, it had just been a surface scrape as the bullet rushed by him.

Maybe this fatigue was compounded by dread of what Angela was about to tell him. Would she finally speak the truth? *All* the truth?

He was pretty sure he'd put together the basic facts of her story—either she owed these men money or they thought she did. Or maybe she'd agreed to be used in *other* ways. The thought made bile churn in his belly, and he steeled himself not to react, no matter what awful details she laid bare.

The flickering lamplight cast shadows on the walls, but his gaze quickly found her standing beside the bunks. She looked so slender and fragile, like a strong wind might push her over. She had one hand on the upper mattress to steady herself with the rocking of the ship, and the other gripped a fold in her skirt.

She might be dreading this conversation even more than he was.

Her dark hair had been pinned up in its usual elegant style, but strands now hung loose around her face and neck, giving her an air of vulnerability that tugged at something in his chest. "Jude." Her voice came out soft and sad. "I owe you an apology and an explanation. I'm truly sorry for everything." She was speaking the right words, but his frustration rose again. She may just be trying to prepare him for another lie.

He shook his head and motioned toward the chair. "Sit."

She settled, and he perched on the edge of the bunk. He had to lean forward with his elbows on his knees so his head didn't hit the upper cot. The position wasn't comfortable, but it would do.

She spoke before he could. "I'm so sorry, Jude. I didn't mean for it all—"

He raised a hand to stop her.

She ceased speaking and sank against the chair back, her shoulders sagging and her chin dipping. He braced himself not to feel sorry for her. Not to be manipulated. "I'm tired, Angela. I'm tired and I'm bleeding. I just want the truth. All of it. Don't try to play mind games or soften the facts. Tell me who those men are and what you have to do with them."

She frowned when he spoke of the blood. "Are you hurt?"

He waved away her concern. "I've already tended it."

She nodded, and it looked like she was gathering her courage. "All right. No more lies. Not even twisting of the truth. I made that promise to myself." She finally met his gaze, her eyes glimmering. "And I make it to you now too."

Don't let her manipulate you. But she was doing too good a job, even before she started. He stayed quiet so she would keep talking.

She inhaled a breath that made her chest rise. "Those men... Lawrence and Martin. They were sent to watch me."

She paused, either giving him a chance to respond or gathering nerve to continue.

Finally she did. "They were watching me because...We're all agents for the Treasury Department."

Jude stared at her, the words settling in his mind like lead. An agent? Of the US Treasury?

What in the dynamite-blasted hills was she talking about? Her words were already surging forward again, so he scrambled to catch up.

"I was sent to follow you. To learn the location of your family's sapphire mine. We didn't know it belonged to your family, just that a huge shipment of sapphires was delivered and sold in New York City every summer. I was to follow the delivery man back to the mine to find the location. I was told you were bringing the shipments into the States illegally. You weren't following the proper procedures and weren't paying the tariffs. I—"

"Stop." He needed to think, to catch up. He still couldn't quite wrap his mind around everything else she'd said, but this he could speak to immediately. "We *do* pay tariffs, both on the import and on the sale of the gems. And all the government's paperwork and procedures are followed to the very last detail. I'm in charge of that myself, and I always handle it before the crates leave our ranch. Whoever you're getting your information from is wrong." Or lying.

She took in another breath, her shoulders sagging a bit more. "I guess I shouldn't be surprised." She looked so blasted miserable that he almost felt sorry for her.

He worked to make sense of the other details she'd said. She'd been assigned to follow him? Why would the Treasury question his family's integrity or the legitimacy of the documents they submitted? "Do you know why we were under suspicion?"

"I do now. I didn't know when I left New York, but Martin

let me in on a secret." Those last words were spoken with a bitterness that gave warning about what she might reveal next. As if what she'd revealed so far hadn't been shocking enough.

"I guess I should start back when I first joined the Treasury."

Right. Because he needed her life story to get the facts. But saying so probably wouldn't keep her talking.

"Da had just died, and life was...hard. A-ma was worried about me going to the market to sell her baked goods, what with all the riots still happening there. We were both worried the food sales wouldn't be enough to cover our rent. I went to one of my father's friends, Mr. Stewart. In truth, he was one of the few friends we had left. The war tore apart so many families, and those who didn't go to fight were often split by convictions or loyalties."

She cleared her throat. "Anyway, one day when Mr. Stewart came to check on us and bring a slab of pork castaways he'd picked up from the butcher, I asked him if he knew of any jobs with the government. He held a position with the Department of Agriculture, and he was always well-respected. He thought for a minute and said I just might be the kind of person Winston needed. We made arrangements for me to accompany him to the office of a friend of his who worked in the Treasury, Marcus Winston.

"Winston asked a lot of questions, then told me I'd start the next Monday. I was thrilled with the regular paycheck. At first I was mostly doing errands, picking up paperwork or notes from contacts around the city. He gradually told me what his office did—mostly undercover work to investigate concerns of fraud and other illegal acts that fell under the Treasury's jurisdiction. As I proved I was capable, he gave me more challenging work. I attended teas and dinners to gather information. I followed the wives of certain men on their shopping days to overhear details and see how they spent money."

She sighed, sinking deeper into the chair. "I got to know

some of the other agents, including those two." She pointed toward the hallway. "I never liked either of them." She managed a weak smile. "They made me nervous, I guess, and they didn't seem very upstanding. Not law-abiding and willing to fight for justice like employees of the United States government should be." She huffed. "Turns out my judgement was correct about them, but not so accurate when it came to others."

Her eyes glimmered, and she swiped her fingers beneath them quickly to hide her tears. "Winston was the first person besides my parents who seemed to really believe I had something to offer. He saw my strengths and gave me the opportunity for advancement." The delicate lines at her neck flexed as she swallowed. "I guess just because someone sees your abilities doesn't mean they'll always do the right thing with them."

"I shouldn't have trusted him so fully, but even now as I look back, I'm not sure I ever saw signs he was using the Treasury as a cover for his own schemes. He called me in and said I'd earned a larger assignment, one he was allowing me to handle on my own. He told me how important this was, that there had been errors made by some of our other agents, and the higher ups were starting to ask questions. Even the Secretary of the Treasury, McCullough. Winston said I had to do this well and make sure I brought back correct information. One more significant error and the higher-ups might pull fraud investigation away from the Treasury and give it to the new Secret Service. If that happened, not only would we all lose our jobs, but we would disappoint our country's leaders, who relied on us to protect our economy."

She looked at him with eyes so bleak, it took everything within him not to reach out and squeeze her hand. "America has been so good to our family. Giving us a haven when we had to escape China. Letting down the Treasury when it truly matters... I was determined to accomplish this assignment, whatever it took."

She seemed to be sinking into her sad thoughts, so he prompted with a question. "So in the New York train station when I first spotted you, was that the first time you saw me, or had you been following me before that?"

She gave a sad smile. "Winston told me he'd received word that a shipment that was likely yours would be arriving that Wednesday. I watched you unload, then followed you to the Tiffany offices. When you left, I was in a hack nearby. I heard you say you were going to the train station, so I had my driver take a shorter route. That way I could be in position to hear you when you purchased tickets."

Wow. As far as he could tell, she'd done everything an undercover agent should do. Not that he would have expected less from her. She'd proved herself intelligent and thorough, long before he'd realized anything was wrong with her story.

Surely many people before Winston had realized her cleverness and innate talents—if she had allowed anyone close enough to see them.

"How did you plan to proceed with the assignment once we boarded? Did you intend to keep yourself a stranger?"

She gave a slight shrug. "I didn't have a definite plan. I've learned to look for opportunities, openings I couldn't have known would come, then slip into them."

Misery clouded her eyes. "I'm so sorry, Jude. I never meant to hurt you or your family. When you fell and I could tell you weren't remembering anything about your situation, I saw what seemed like the perfect opportunity to travel with you without suspicion. I didn't have a plan to get out of it later. I guess I supposed I would find another opening when I needed it. Or maybe I would uncover everything I'd been tasked with learning and could simply slip away. But then, as I got to know you, as you recovered and we talked, and I saw who you really are."

His insides churned. "That's why you wanted to know so

much about my family and where the ranch is, in case I recovered my memories before we got there."

She gave a pained nod. "That was all I cared about, at first." She brushed the wayward strands of hair away from her face, her hands trembling.

That little tremble told him she cared about what he thought.

Or...or she hoped he was buying her latest story.

"But by then I was in too deep, trying to do right by the country I love, the department that gave me a chance, and the superior I thought believed in me. And not hurt you in the process."

He understood.

In truth, he did see why she'd done the things she had. She'd grown up in the midst of such animosity and turmoil, probably desperate for someone to appreciate who she really was. The first time she'd finally received that approval and recognition, she'd committed herself to do everything she could for the person who offered it. Maybe both to help her boss and the Treasury department, but probably also to prove they weren't wrong for believing in her, though she may not have thought of it that way.

This woman was worth so much more than her experiences had taught her to believe. She was strong and capable and smart and giving. If only she could see herself the way he could. The way God did.

"I was so shocked to see Martin this morning," she said, "working in the ship's kitchen. I'd had several interactions with him and Lawrence back in New York and knew Winston used them as henchmen sometimes. At first I thought maybe he'd sent them for my safety." Her eyes turned glassy again. "What a surprise to learn that he'd really sent them to make sure I did the job fully. The greater shock though was learning this job wasn't for the Treasury at all.

She squared her shoulders. "Whatever you think of me... You need to know this. Winston plans to redirect your shipment next year so the sapphires will be delivered to him. Or maybe to a contact he'll sell them to. Anyway, he's thinking he'll be able to leave the Treasury and live off the funds from your sapphires for the rest of his life. Those two goons are in on it, too, and they wanted me to keep playing my part—stay with you as your wife—until I learn the source of the sapphires."

A tear slipped down her cheek.

A tactic to soften his defenses? But something deep inside him knew she spoke the truth this time.

Lord, is that Your *guidance? Show me truth from lies. Show me how to lead her to You.* He weighed her story , doing his best to hear the Spirit's direction on what he should believe.

The unrest inside him finally settled. Maybe she really had finally told him the whole story.

So what do I do with this, Lord?

Her red-rimmed eyes met his gaze. "What about Lawrence and Martin? What will happen to them?"

Disappointment shoved away the relief he'd felt a second before. He heaved out a sigh. "Nothing, unfortunately. At least not yet." He told her the sorry tale of how they'd gotten the upper hand, then took off and disappeared into the Mississippi.

Her face paled. "So they're still loose? Can someone go after them?"

"The first mate has men spread around the boat, searching for them in the water. If they haven't already drowned, they won't make it to shore without us seeing them. I wouldn't be surprised if they've caught them already. I think we're supposed to dock soon, so they'll get the authorities involved there if they need to."

Another tear slipped down Angela's cheek, but she swiped it away impatiently. She didn't often show weakness, and crying must feel that way to her. In his experience, it took strength to let yourself cry. Most people didn't understand that.

An urge slipped through him, but even as he started to push the thought away, a nudge in his spirit prompted him. Was this God's *next step* he'd been asking for?

Without letting himself reason his way out of it, he stood and reached for Angela's hand. "Come here."

She rose, her eyes questioning him. There was no sign of worry there though.

Good. When his mind had replayed the fear twisting her face as he'd touched her the other night—was that only *last* night?—he'd almost lost the contents of his stomach. How had he thought it acceptable—to himself or God—to do something to her that brought such fear? God had forgiven him the moment he'd asked, but forgiving himself was proving harder. He'd apologize to Angela for pushing so far when he had a chance.

But just now, he met her red-rimmed gaze, letting his eyes soften as God's would if He were in Jude's place. "You look like you need a hug."

A sob shook her chest, and her eyes pinched closed, more tears slipping through her lashes. She let him pull her close, and as he wrapped his arms around her, her body seemed to finally release its clamp over her emotions. Little by little, deep racking sobs broke loose. Sobs that shook her body and fractured his heart more with each one.

Had she *ever* allowed herself the healing of tears like these? She seemed to be releasing years of hurt. Maybe even grieving her father's tragic death, too, though that had been four years ago.

Her hands gripped the back of his shirt as though she needed the support to keep from falling in a heap on the floor. He'd hold her as long as it helped. At the moment, this was all he could do for her.

Give me wisdom, Lord. Show me how to be Your love to her.

Showing her love wouldn't be hard at all. If he were honest with himself, she'd become far more important to him than any physical treasure. He still had to guard his heart, though, for until she accepted the life-changing love of the Lord, nothing more than friendship could grow between them.

CHAPTER 18

*A*ngela's eyelids didn't want to open, but she forced them apart. Her face felt swollen, like she'd been sleeping for days—yet she still wasn't rested.

This lethargy probably came from crying so long in Jude's arms. The memory of that should embarrass her, but she could still feel the strength of his hold. The steadiness. The gentle way he'd stroked her back, occasionally murmuring words she never would have expected from a man. *Let it all out. It's good to cry. You've needed this.*

She should no longer be surprised by Jude's gentleness. His intuitive ability to read her and speak the very thing she needed to hear. He was a wonder. A gift she never could have expected.

A gift from God?

She glanced at the underside of the bunk above her, where Jude's steady breathing still sounded. She'd never really given thought to the possibility that God played a part in the everyday lives of people.

She didn't question whether God existed, though maybe she should have, given the beliefs of her mother's family. It had always been easier to accept the Catholic faith her father subscribed to. The United States as a whole believed in Christianity, after all, which maybe wasn't Catholic exactly, but close. Anyway, it seemed likely there was a God up there Who'd created the world.

But did He actually see her now? Jude seemed to know Him well. Jude was such a good man, it made sense that God would want to speak to him. That He would do good things for him.

But her? Did God even know she existed? That she was on this steamboat traveling up the Missouri River? Was it possible He'd sent Jude as a gift to her? But why? She'd done nothing to deserve such a gift.

A rumble in her middle broke through her wandering thoughts, and she slipped out from her blanket to stand. As she took a moment to grip the bunk and find her sea legs, she allowed herself a glance at Jude. He was turned away in his sleep, so she couldn't see his face, but those strong shoulders sent a longing through her.

He'd been as exhausted as she was after she finished blubbering in his arms. He'd said he would ask the captain for an extra stateroom—even a closet with a hammock—so she could have her privacy, but she'd assured him they could continue sleeping in these separate bunks as they had before. He'd agreed to worry about it later, that this would do for a nap.

It seemed they'd both slept the rest of the day, if the dusky light through the window could be believed. Dinner was probably just being served in the dining room. It might have even been the bell signaling the meal that woke her.

After repairing her hair and appearance as best she could in the small mirror on the wall, she sent a final glance to Jude. He needed sleep more than food right now. She could have a tray sent to the room for him later.

The corridor was mostly empty, a few voices came from around the corner. A woman speaking, then a man's quiet murmur. Other passengers going to the dining room, likely.

When she reached the corner, the other couple had already disappeared into the dining room, and the door leading to the outside deck called to her. She needed fresh air more than food. She could enjoy the breeze and the scenery for a minute, then come back to eat.

She pushed open the door and stepped onto the deck, the heat immediately wrapping around her. But a cool breeze ruffled her hair, brushing her skin and soothing away her lingering sadness. The deck seemed to be empty, so she strolled to the spot near the front corner where she could lean over and have a clear view of the water's ripple as it moved aside for the massive ship to pass through.

She gripped the rail, relishing the stronger breeze. Trees blanketed the land on both sides. Not a glorious view like the prairies they'd passed by yesterday, but this thick foliage provided life for so many animals. Who knew how many birds lived among those branches and vines? Probably even species that hadn't been recorded yet.

She leaned forward, letting the rail press into her middle as she studied the water just below them. The Missouri wasn't a particularly clear river, but she could see a foot or so past the surface. The way the water built a small wall in the wake of the ship always fascinated her.

The sounds of the crew at their work drifted from the deck below. A shouted word in the distance, something that sounded like "Four!" Maybe a response to a question one of the others had asked. She'd heard calls like this so many times in the weeks they'd been aboard, the voices mostly faded into the background unless she homed her senses to hear them.

Another man was speaking in a normal voice, somewhere closer on the deck below, though not loud enough she could make out the words. The tone sounded familiar. Riggs or the captain? She'd not had opportunity to speak to any of the other crew except in passing. They all seemed to prefer keeping to the lower deck than mingling with passengers on this upper level.

She leaned a bit farther over the rail. From this spot, she could see a small portion of the lower deck. When she'd looked the other day, it had seemed to be overflowing with cargo—crates and bins and barrels. There didn't seem as many now, which made sense since they'd been unloading at stops along the way. She could just see a man sitting on the floor, leaning against a barrel. Something about him struck a chord within her. It wasn't Riggs , and certainly not the captain. One of the others she'd watched from a distance? Maybe a porter, taking a break?

But when his voice drifted up again, realization clutched at her throat, nearly pressing the air from her chest.

Lawrence.

It couldn't be him. Maybe just a crewman who looked—and sounded—like that scoundrel?

But then he laughed, his angular face tipping up a little and offering a better view. The sound and the appearance matched.

It was him. No question about it.

How could he have climbed out of the Missouri and up onto the deck without anyone spotting him? The man must be a cat, with lithe climbing skills and as many lives as any feline could claim.

He was quiet now, but another man was speaking. She strained to hear, to decipher the voice and words. It had to be Martin. She couldn't hear the tone well enough to say for sure, but it certainly didn't *not* sound like him.

Martin was surely the only person on the ship who would speak with Lawrence in such a casual setting. Jude had told her that the crew members had been given a detailed description of the two reprobates and were on the lookout for them.

He'd said they were watching the river and planned to ask about the thugs when the ship docked at a little settlement that day. The stop must have happened while she was sleeping. Had these two somehow crept back onboard during the commotion that always accompanied a docking? But would they have been able to reach that town as fast as the boat had? Surely a steamer traveled faster than two men on foot.

Regardless of how they'd managed to board, she had to tell Jude these two were back. He would know how best to finally stop them for good.

She spun and strode as fast as she could, taking care to keep her footsteps quiet on the deck in case they could be heard below. As soon as she slipped into the corridor, she ran to their room.

She must have pushed the door open louder than she'd intended, for Jude sat up quickly in his bed, nearly knocking his head on the low ceiling.

"What is it?" He spoke before he'd turned fully to look at her. He blinked, his hair still sleep-tousled.

Even with the urgency pounding in her chest, warmth slipped through her at the sight of him. This was an image she would love to see every day for the rest of her life.

She had to push that away, though, and focus on the emergency at hand. "Lawrence and Martin are on the ship." She nearly blurted the words, then stepped all the way into the cabin so she could close the door. "I saw them on the lower deck, but they didn't see me."

Jude had already swung his legs over the side of the bunk. He dropped to the floor and reached for something on the upper mattress. A gun, it turned out. He pressed it into his waistband and slipped on his jacket, then turned and strode to the door. "Are you sure they didn't see you?"

"They gave no sign of it. I was on the upper deck, leaning over the rail. I heard Lawrence's voice, then saw him on the lower deck sitting beside a barrel. I heard another voice that I think was Martin's."

Jude had paused in the doorway waiting for her to finish. He nodded and looked ready to pull the door closed—with her still in the room. "Stay here. I'll get Riggs and some men, and we'll make a plan to catch them."

"I'll come help. I need to show you where they are."

He hesitated. "I don't want you anywhere near them. They won't hesitate to kill, and if they found you, they might try to take you with them by force."

Just hearing the words aloud—the truth that it was—made her want to shrink back. But she forced her shoulders to square. "Let me at least show you where they are. If there's nothing else I can do to help, I'll come back here." She wouldn't be foolhardy, but nor would she hide away when her knowledge could make Jude's work easier.

His lips pressed closed. She was sure he was going to deny her, but he said, "Show me the place then."

She led the way down the corridor, and when they stepped onto the deck, Jude's long stride kept him beside her. She walked softly, and so did he. How could he make his steps so soundless? Maybe he'd learned that skill in his precious mountain wilderness. Sneaking up on animals when he hunted or some such.

At the rail, she took up the spot where she'd been before, and as she leaned forward, she strained to hear any sound of their voices. All was quiet below, not even shouts from the crew.

The rail pressed into her middle as she strained to find the spot.

Lawrence wasn't there.

She scanned the area slower. That was where he'd been sitting. It had to be. But only empty deck lay where he'd been moments before.

"They're not there." She straightened to allow her middle relief from the pressure of the rail and met Jude's gaze. He too had been leaning over to see. "They were there right before I ran to get you."

She pointed down, and they both leaned again to see the place. "There." She kept her voice low in case Lawrence and Martin were still close by. "Do you see that crate with an empty spot beside it? That's where Lawrence was sitting, leaning against the barrel."

Jude scanned the open deck behind them. "I'll find the captain and Riggs. We'll do a full search of the ship." He turned and met her gaze. "We'll find them, I promise. While we do that, I need you to wait in the stateroom. All right?"

In truth, she'd rather be locked away and let Jude deal with those two overgrown bullies. For once, there was someone capable who was also willing to stand up for her. Someone to protect her.

CHAPTER 19

he midnight moon cast a pale glow through the stateroom's narrow window as Jude stepped inside. He hated the news he had to give Angela. He and the captain's men had searched every crevice and corner aboard the steamboat, but the henchmen remained as elusive as spectors.

Angela stood by the window, shadowed so he didn't even see her until she moved toward him. "How did it go?"

He closed the door, then eased out a breath as she stood in front of him. Her face was still concealed by the dark, but she could probably see the frustration on his with the moonlight shining on him through the porthole.

"We didn't find them." The words tasted bitter, like defeat. "The second mate is in charge through the night. He and the crew will watch for them, then do a full search again at dawn."

Angela nodded but didn't speak. He still couldn't read anything in her shadowed expression.

Jude backed away and removed his coat. He was more frustrated than tired, but he should sleep while he could so he would be sharp tomorrow. He wasn't moving to a different cabin until he knew for certain there was no more threat to Angela.

As he slid the jacket from his shoulders, Angela's voice broke the quiet. "Jude?" Something in her tone made his muscles tense.

He turned back and saw that she'd moved so the light illuminated the side of her face. "Yes?"

"Is there a way to get to Fort Benton without riding the steamboat?"

Interesting question from his little schemer. He kept his answer simple. "A person could buy a horse and ride, following the riverbank."

Her brow furrowed. "Would it be safe?" Was she worried about the elements, the wild animals, or the tribes living near the river?

He could only give his best answer considering what he suspected she was aiming for. "Nothing in the west is without danger. But if a person is careful and decent to those they meet, it wouldn't be an especially dangerous trip. Not more than any of the roads between towns in the Montana Territory. It's a little slower going than the steamboat, though."

Angela's lips pressed. He could nearly see her mind working through the details, forming a plan.

Come to think of it, getting off the ship might be their best course of action, removing her from the threat of these two blackguards. But, if he and Angela slipped to shore at the next stop, shouldn't he take her to the next town and wait for a steamer going back to St. Louis? He could send her home to her mother, then ride on by himself toward Fort Benton. And the ranch.

But his insides twisted at the idea of sending her away. Completely out of his life. Was it just the fact that Lawrence and Martin might find her again? They would be after *him* though, right? So sending her the other direction might put her in a safer situation even. He could hold his own if those two misbegotten weasels found him. He'd have to.

Angela's voice interrupted his thoughts. Probably a good thing.

"Jude, is there any way the two of us could slip off the ship and take a rowboat to shore tonight? Could Riggs help us?"

He stared at her, considering the twist in her request. "Tonight?"

Her eyes held a determination that showed she would do what she must to carry out this crazy notion. But maybe... As the idea took shape in his mind, the wisdom in it shone clearly.

Riggs would help them, he had no doubt. He could have a rowboat lowered quietly without any fanfare, so it wouldn't wake any sleeping scoundrels. A few hours later, he and Angela could slip down and climb a rope ladder to the rowboat. After rowing to shore, they could walk until they reached the nearest town. He could buy a couple horses, and they'd be on their way.

He'd have to eventually face the decision of which way to travel—east to send Angela back to New York, or west to take her to Fort Benton.

Maybe he should ask her. Now, there was a thought he should have had before this moment. She was capable of making her own decisions, after all.

And she wasn't his wife. He needed to stop thinking like she was his to protect and provide for.

A knot in his chest twisted. Whether he wanted to protect and provide for her or not, he had no right to, not more than the God-given command to do good unto all as we're given opportunity.

He only had to face this next step for now. "We probably could slip away without them knowing. Once we get to land, we'll need to walk quite a-ways before I can buy us horses. We'll be sleeping on the ground—under the shelter of trees if we're lucky."

She gave a firm nod. "That won't be a problem for me. I can do whatever I need to."

Not even a flicker of hesitation. She might think herself capable now, but if she'd never maneuvered the wilderness—whether it be forest or plains or mountains—her eyes would be opened soon enough. He'd be there to help, though.

He turned to the door. "All right then, I'll talk to Riggs." He paused, then turned back. "Have your things ready to leave the moment I return."

Her expression took on a hint of smile. "Don't worry. I'll be waiting."

~

The moon had moved several hours past the midnight mark by the time Jude knelt in the rowboat, reaching to help Angela descend the rope ladder hanging down the ship's side.

She wore the green dress that didn't have as many frills, but it's skirt still ballooned around him as he reached for her waist to lower her to the center of the boat. His hands finally found that slender hold, and the feel of her nearly waylaid his concentration. He wanted with everything in him to pull her against him, maybe even onto his lap. He could imagine her side curled into his chest. He'd simply hold her.

Pushing that longing aside was one of the hardest things he'd ever done—or at least it felt so in the moment—but he managed to simply guide her into the boat. "Come down to your knees instead of standing, so you don't tip the dingy." He kept his words to a whisper.

He was fairly certain they hadn't alerted either of those two rogue agents, who seemed to have an uncanny ability to pop up everywhere they weren't wanted.

Only one crewman stood at the rail above them, pretending

to be at his regular work as he helped lower them down, then pulled the rope ladder back up. Jude would have liked to call up a thank-you to the man, but that might wake the two sleeping henchmen, ruining all their efforts. Instead, he offered a wave he hoped conveyed his gratitude.

The crewman nodded and stepped away.

As Jude settled with the oars, he met Angela's gaze in the moonlight. *Ready?* He mouthed the word, and she returned a smile and a quick nod.

They'd done it. Slipped away from danger and started a brand-new adventure.

He moved the oars as soundlessly as possible through the water, taking his time and letting the current carry them to shore at an angle. Since the steamboat was moving against the current, he and Angela were drifting the opposite direction from that massive vessel. Once they hit land, that would change.

The second mate had said the nearest settlement was to the west, farther upriver about twelve miles. If they started at first light, they might be able to sleep there tomorrow night.

His oar snagged in underwater reeds, and he adjusted the boat's angle so they could approach as near the bank as possible. Angela had turned to see the land nearing behind her.

"We'll need to take off our shoes to wade to shore." He'd been hoping the water would stay deep enough against the bank that they could step onto dry land, like in the rivers that cut through the mountain canyons. But the bottom of this boat was already running up on sand, so they'd need to traverse the shallows.

"Unless you want me to carry you to dry ground." He couldn't help a grin with that option, which probably made her more likely to decline the offer.

Angela frowned at him even as she leaned forward to unbutton her boots. "I can walk."

After running the boat hard into the sand, he reached down and tugged off his left shoe. His would come off much easier than her delicate boots with the heels and the buttons up the side. He should have just carried her, not given her the option to walk.

These worries would clog his head if he let them, so he focused on rolling his trouser legs and gathering an armload of luggage. The porter had brought them a bundle of food, blankets and a few cooking supplies while they'd waited for word that the second mate was ready for them to board the rowboat. Thankfully, he and Angela had been able to divide the goods between their existing bags, so they still only had two satchels each.

He would take Angela's on this first trip so she didn't try to carry the bags herself. He could come back for his own after he helped her to shore.

He eased out of the boat to keep from tipping it. "Stay seated until I come back for you." Thankfully, the steamer was long gone, even the lights no longer visible, so they didn't have to worry anymore about being quiet.

He splashed through the muddy water, letting his toes dig into the slippery muck before he reached the rocky section at the bank. After dropping his load on dry ground, he turned back to help Angela.

She gripped her skirts in one arm and took his hand with the other. But when she stepped from the boat, the vessel tipped precariously. He grabbed her arm with his free hand to steady her and the craft. He tried not to show his nervousness. His satchel with the payment for the sapphires was still in the boat. If water surged in over the side, what would it do to all the paper bills mixed in with the coin?

But Angela, with a quick, "I've got it," stepped from the dinghy, released his hand, and trudged through the water.

He let her manage the last steps on her own, securing the boat and those precious bags. He reached for the hull and tugged, dragging it through the shallows. This vessel was much stouter than the skiff he and his brothers had used when they were youngsters back in Kansas. The hind end had stuck on something—a stick maybe—so he gave an extra hard jerk.

The dingy snapped loose from its snag, surging toward him with all the strength he'd put into the pull. His feet lodged in the mud, not lifting nearly as quickly as the boat was coming at him. He stumbled backward, his backside landing in the water with the front of the rowboat in his lap. Cold surged around his belly as the river's surface rose up to the base of his ribs.

"Jude!" Angela's cry sounded behind him, accompanied by splashing.

"I'm fine." He raised a hand to wave her off, spraying droplets of water as he did so. Every part of him would be soaked by the time he climbed out of this river. The Missouri couldn't let him go without a final memory, it seemed.

Angela was at his side now, helping him shift the boat off his legs. She reached a hand to pull him to his feet, but he shook his head. "No sense in us both getting drenched."

He turned onto his hands and knees, then used the boat as support to push himself up to standing. By the time he had his balance, Angela was pulling the skiff the rest of the way to the shore. He trudged forward to help, and the two of them managed to finish the job, pulling it all the way onto land.

He straightened and blew out a long breath. Water dripped from his clothes, streaming down his ankles and feet.

Angela was eyeing him from across the boat, her mouth curved and her eyes sparkling in the moonlight. She thought this was funny?

An urge slipped in, one he would almost never have given in to before. He needed to shake off this grumpiness though, and a little chuckle would be good for them both.

So he raised his brows. "You find it funny to laugh at a man when he's down?"

Now her pert mouth spread farther, flashing her teeth in a true grin. "I helped you up, didn't I? You're not down anymore."

He stepped forward, slipping around the boat so he could reach her. With his every movement, droplets fanned the air around him. "I should have given you a dunking then so you'd know what it's like to be so wet. You wouldn't be laughing so much." He kept a teasing tone in his voice and reached out for her as he spoke.

She arched sideways, away from his grasp, giggling as she did so. "Don't you dare."

He lunged forward, his waterlogged coat restricting him from easy movement. Still, he caught her sleeve as she scrambled away. The fabric slipped through his fingers, leaving the tinkle of her laughter in its wake.

He couldn't stop his own grin. This was what they'd needed.

She faced him with two strides between them and a massive fallen tree at her back, its branches rising up higher than either of them could reach. The river ran on one side of them and the dark woods stretched on the other.

Did he have her cornered?

What he planned to do with her exactly, he couldn't say. Tug her into the river mayhap? Pull her into his arms and kiss her breathless? That sounded like a much better idea.

His breathing came harder just thinking about it, so he focused on their play. This was simply an innocent way to lighten the heaviness they'd been under these past days.

He gave a mock growl and advanced another step forward. She giggled again and stepped backward, her feet crowding against the fallen trunk.

He eyed the brush behind. "You back any more and you'll topple into those branches."

When she glanced backward, he lunged the final step to reach her. She squealed as he grabbed her wrist with one hand and wrapped the other around her waist. Her giggles turned to full laughter, and a snort even slipped out when he tugged her to him.

One of her hands pressed on his shoulder with a tiny bit of pressure, as though she was trying to feign resistance. In truth, she was nearly doubled over from laughter.

He pulled her flush against him, letting out another growl as he wrapped his arms all the way around her, saturating her clothing as fully as he could manage. "That's the way. Now you'll get your due."

"No." She puffed the word between laughs. "You're wet." She'd half-turned in his arms so the side of her shoulder was against his chest, probably so she could bend forward to catch her breath through her gaffaws.

He let himself chuckle too, mostly from the pleasure of seeing her succumb so fully to her mirth. She was beautiful any time, but this joy lit her face more than the moonlight.

He allowed his hands to slip to her back, then held them there as her laughter slowly ebbed. Her eyes had filled so fully with joy, they'd begun to leak, and she wiped away the droplets he couldn't bring himself to think of as tears.

Her laughter finally faded, and she relaxed in his arms, letting her head rest against his shoulder, both hands flat to his chest.

She eased out a long breath, her body sinking further against him as the air slipped out. "Oh, I needed that. I don't think I've ever laughed so hard."

She sounded spent, like releasing so much emotion had worn her out. Between yesterday's heart wrenching cry and this session of laughter, she seemed to be letting herself feel and express a depth of emotion she might never have allowed before. At least, not in many years.

And he'd been blessed enough to be here for both moments. He'd held her, both during each experience and in the aftermath.

She swayed a little in his arms, and he secured his hold. *Lord, let her feel Your security now too. Let me be an extension of You to her.*

For long moments they stayed like that. His heart lifted up frequent prayers—that she would feel the Father's love and acceptance. That she would know she was treasured by them both—by Jude and by the One who'd fashioned her with magnificent detail.

At last, she let out another breath. Probably a sign she was ready to return to normal life. As he released her and they both turned to walk back to the boat, he sent up special *thanks* for these moments he'd carry with him always.

He should get them back to practical matters now before the silence became awkward. "I was thinking we could bed down here, just inside the tree cover where we won't get wet from dew." He motioned toward the edge of the woods.

Then he gave a soft chuckle. "I hadn't planned to start a fire, but I can do so if you want to dry off."

She shook her head. "I don't need a fire, but I'll help if you want one."

A new dose of weariness pressed on his shoulders. "I'll dry off while I'm sleeping. The night's warm enough." He had a blanket if he needed it. Hopefully, he'd not made her so wet she would take a chill while she slept.

Within minutes, they'd spread the blankets the second mate had sent with them. He tucked their belongings under the over-turned skiff so dew didn't soak them, then they both settled into their bedding.

He stretched out on one blanket but didn't pull the other over him yet. It was good to be back on solid ground, back in the wilderness where he knew how to manage.

Captain Rivers had said they were in Nebraska Territory, about a quarter day's travel in the *Marietta* away from a little settlement called Mary's Crossing. They were probably at least two weeks' ride from Fort Benton, assuming they could get horses at Mary's Crossing. Maybe longer than that if he had to go easy for Angela's sake.

A new thought slipped in. Had she ever ridden a horse? He could ask her now before she drifted off, but that might start her worrying over it instead of sleeping.

So, he let out a long breath and allowed himself to sink into his weariness.

"Good night, Jude." Her sweet voice drifted from her bedding, farther than arm's reach away from him. A good thing.

"G'night." It felt so different saying that to *her* than to his brothers when they snuffed out the light in the bunkhouse.

As the nocturnal sounds settled around them, he closed his eyes and tried to push all thoughts out of his mind. Hopefully all the trouble was behind them now. From this point on, the main thing he'd have to worry about was getting her to safety.

And protecting his heart so that, when the time came, he could let her go.

CHAPTER 20

*E*ven before Angela opened her eyes, the ache in her neck made itself known. And the hard bump pressing into her hip.

She adjusted her legs to take the weight off of whatever rock she was lying on. Why was there a rock in her bed? She opened her lids enough for daylight to creep through. Daylight, and the realization that she was outside.

Memory swept in—sneaking off the boat, Jude rowing them to land, him falling in the water, joy and laughter filling her up as she tried to escape his drenched hold. Resting in the strength of his arms as her body and mind and emotions acknowledged her utter exhaustion.

She forced her eyes open the rest of the way, then lay still as she took in her surroundings. Birds twittered in the trees around her. The scent of a campfire and...was that ham?

She turned in her blanket to see Jude kneeling beside a fire, working with something in a pan. Pleasure and guilt warred in her chest. She shouldn't have slept late and forced him to do the cooking. He had already done so much for her. She needed to bear her own portion of the work.

She pushed up to sitting and brushed a hand over her hair to push down any loose strands. She probably looked a sight. Hopefully Jude was still too tired to notice. She cleared the sleep gravel from her throat before speaking. "Good morning. I didn't expect you to cook for us."

Jude glanced up at her, his eyes softening as he took her in. That warmth always felt like a hug. "We'll have a long day ahead of us. I figured it'd be best if we start off with full bellies."

Even as she smiled, a burn crept up to her eyes. "Thank you, Jude. I appreciate it." This man was so good, so...good to her. How could she possibly keep from falling in love with him? Whether she'd already reached that place or not, loving him seemed inevitable. No woman could see the man he truly was and not lose her heart. If only she could make him feel the same.

Now the sting rose to her eyes, but this time not from gratitude and love, but from the awful truth that she would lose him. She would lose her heart at the same time, and after meeting Jude, no man would ever measure up.

She pushed up to her feet. "I'm going to take a short walk. I'll be back soon." She needed privacy for morning ablutions, and that would allow her a moment to clear her mind and find a smile again. She couldn't let thoughts of the future ruin these days she still had with him.

When she returned to their camp, Jude had a plate waiting for her. The fried ham and biscuits the ship had sent with them looked marvelous, making her middle rumble with the sight.

Jude gave her an easy smile, then pushed to his feet. "I've already eaten. When you're finished, we'll pack up these last things and start out."

He turned to roll up his blankets. He must be eager to get moving.

She ate quickly, then packed her own bedding while he washed her plate and stored it in his bag with the other food and cooking utensils.

As she fastened the last buckle on her satchel, he stood and hoisted a pack onto each of his shoulders. "I'm glad we were able to keep it all down to four bags. If you can carry that one, I'll get these others."

She shook her head. "I can carry both of mine." Neither was overly heavy. She stood and took up a bag in each hand.

"Angela." Jude sounded frustrated, but she started walking upriver. "Let me carry those."

"I'm fine, Jude. Let's get going." She didn't slow down.

He followed, his long stride catching up to her right away. He settled in to her pace and she shifted her focus to take in the land around them. They were leaving the woods behind, moving into a grassland that stretched as far as she could see.

The vastness of the land was far greater than she'd thought possible, a seemingly endless sea of golden grasses rippling under the deep blue of the morning sky. The air started off cool, but as the morning progressed, the sun rose higher and hotter.

By the time Jude called their second rest, heat bore down on them like a heavy, suffocating blanket. Sweat beaded on her forehead and soaked the back of her dress. Jude had asked several times to carry one or both of her bags, but she always refused. He was probably just as miserable. She couldn't add to his load.

She'd long since switched to carrying her satchels on each shoulder as Jude did, but they weighed her down more with each step. Was this what saddle horses felt like? How cruel of people to inflict such misery on any creature.

Now she sat on her bags, letting her head hang under the burning sun. She had to gather another fragment of strength to keep going.

"Here's some water." Jude handed her the flask they'd been drinking from.

She took it and gulped, letting a little spill down the sides of her chin to her neck. Blessed cool.

At first, she'd hesitated to drink much so she didn't have to find an "outhouse" on this barren prairie with no tree in sight. Maybe she could walk down to the river? The low bank would only allow a small amount of privacy. Even so, her body seemed to crave every drop she drank, so she let herself quench her thirst.

When she could finally bear the thought of walking again, she looked at Jude.

He met her gaze with lifted brows. "Ready?" His sweat-dampened hair curled at the edges, adding a roguish charm to his already handsome features. He looked hot, but not miserable. Did he simply wear the exhaustion better than she, or was he really not as tired?

She didn't waste energy on answering his question, simply pushed to her feet and hoisted her satchels.

"Can I carry one of your bags now? Please?" Jude stood beside her, holding out an empty hand. His expression didn't look like he expected her to hand one over, but just the fact that he asked must mean he had energy to manage it. That was more than she could say for her own weary body.

She let the handles of her floral satchel slip down her left arm. She tried to catch them, but the bag fell to the ground with a thump.

Jude scooped it up and started forward. "Good."

Walking wasn't quite as hard with the lighter weight, and Jude adjusted his pace to hers, no matter if she pushed herself to stride faster or let her steps lag.

Sometime around noon, they reached a cluster of three scrawny trees near the river's edge. She sank down on her bag as before, relishing the shelter from the sun's intensity.

Her mind felt too thick to think. She didn't have the energy to form clear thoughts. Every fragment of strength had gone into marching forward, one step at a time.

Jude pressed the flask into her hands. "Drink. We can eat here too."

She obeyed, letting the cool water soak through her. Little by little, the liquid cleared her mind, bringing her senses back to life.

"Here. Splash this water on your face and neck." Jude crouched in front of her, the pan he held full of river water.

She did as he said, nearly dipping her face into its cool depths as she scooped the liquid onto her skin. When she finally looked up at him, water dripped down her chin and onto her dress. But she'd come alive again, and she could manage a smile for him.

A grin was already playing at the corners of his mouth. "Want me to pour the rest on your head?"

She nodded. "Please."

He chuckled and stood, then rained the half-pan of water onto her hair. A wonderful shower.

She wiped the liquid from her face and looked around for the food satchel. It was high time she be useful.

Within minutes, she'd put together a simple meal. Biscuits and smoked ham again, though she'd not been able to fry the meat to a golden brown as Jude had done that morning. But she added in dried apple slices, seasoned with cinnamon powder. Whoever had prepared their food package in the *Marietta's* kitchen had done an admirable job gathering foods that would last well outside of an icebox, remaining delicious and filling.

As they ate, the silence was only broken when a small steamboat floated upriver, headed toward Fort Benton. This one wasn't nearly as large as the *Marietta*, but she couldn't help imagining who the passengers might be and what was bringing them west. It must be mealtime on board too, for only a few figures could be seen on the deck. The ship was small enough to only have one deck instead of an upper and lower.

"I have a question for you." Jude sat on the ground, back against one of the trunks.

"Yes?"

He kept his focus toward the river, and something in his tone made her insides tighten. "Now that you've learned your assignment wasn't"—he seemed to search for the right words—"official Treasury work... Maybe you want to get back to New York?" He finally looked at her, his gaze searching. "Your mother is there, after all. And I imagine your department needs you. You might even need to let your superiors know about this Winston's actions, if they aren't aware already. They may need you to testify in court."

The more he spoke, the more a desperate sensation pressed hard on her chest. Not to New York. Nothing in her wanted to go back to the city. How could she stand the smothering mountain of people and buildings and...chaos everywhere? Now that she'd had a taste of this wide-open country, even when she was miserable in the scorching heat, this was better than being packed in so tight she disappeared in the mass of hundreds of thousands of other lives.

Jude was still speaking, so she forced herself to listen. To hear him out and measure her response.

"We can watch for a steamboat headed back to St. Louis. We might be able to flag one down on the river today, or at least we can wait at the next settlement for one to dock." He finally stopped talking and looked to her for an answer.

Did he *want* to be free of her? She slowed him down, there was no doubt of that. But did he feel nothing for her? No attraction at all? That thought mixed with her exhaustion to bring tears to her eyes, so she squared her shoulders a little.

She had to leave her hopes for more with Jude out of this. If he never loved her, what would she want to do with her future? The idea of Fort Benton still held a curious glow. That place was known as the gateway to the Montana Territory, the last stop of the steamships and the place people came daily to trade and restock supplies. There had to be needs there she could fill.

She could set up a baking business like her mother. She might not have to take her wares to a market to sell them. She could bake in her kitchen, then hang a sign out and allow customers to come into a front room to buy her treats. Surely such a place would thrive in a frontier town—fresh-baked bread and tarts and cookies. If all went well, she could send for A-ma and they could work together.

The idea solidified, giving her the confidence she needed to answer Jude without doubt.

She shook her head. "I'm not going east. I want to go to Fort Benton, like you'd planned before. I'll start a business selling fresh-baked goods. Like my mother does. "

Jude's brow furrowed, his expression unreadable. "Are you sure? The life there won't be easy. There are hundreds of men and very few women. I'll try to help you find a safe place and people I trust to help you, but it will still be far rougher than you're used to."

He must not have ever faced market day in the square, where hordes of housewives crowded in, arguing and bargaining until she couldn't hear herself think.

She didn't mind a challenge. Her entire life had been one obstacle after another, some of them feeling insurmountable. She'd overcome each of them so far, surely she could manage whatever Fort Benton threw at her.

"I'm certain."

Jude's eyes searched hers, his face still betraying no sign of his thoughts. "If that's what you want, I'll see you safely there."

Though he'd not tried to talk her out of her decision, his response left a hollowness in her chest. Once they reached that town, what would he do next? Leave her for his ranch, no doubt. She might never see him again.

As the tears sprang once more, she turned back to the scraps of her meal remaining in her lap. "I'm ready to continue when you are." She needed something—anything—to keep her body busy so the tears would fade.

She had to come to terms with the fact that Jude would never be more than a friend, no matter how much her heart wanted far more.

CHAPTER 21

*T*he settlement was much smaller than Jude had expected. Dusk had nearly darkened to night by the time he and Angela approached the simple log building nestled in a small clearing among the trees. The sign nailed to a post by the door proclaimed it to be *Walker's Trading*.

At the river, a rickety dock jutted out into the slow-moving current, its waters reflecting the crescent moon like a shimmering ribbon. Hard to believe a steamship would waste time stopping at a single trading post, but they must do a fair amount of business. Perhaps settlers had spread out around this spot, where there'd be plenty of land for each family to farm or hunt.

Woodsmoke hung in the air around them as Jude knocked on the plank wood door. A faint murmur of voices sounded inside, then footsteps moving toward them. The door swung open to reveal a man about a decade older than Jude. He was stocky, though not tall, and the curly red of his beard and hair made it likely his ancestors came from Ireland or Scotland. Perhaps the man himself hailed from there. Did he look at all like Angela's father had? Jude slid a quick glance to her to see if her expression showed anything.

But the man was speaking, so Jude turned his focus back to him. "Evenin', folks. What can I do for you?" No hint of a brogue in his words.

Jude nodded a greeting. "We're looking to buy a couple horses and saddles. A few supplies too. Do you have any stock for sale or know of some around?"

Motion in the room behind the man caught his attention. A single lantern cast flickering shadows about the room, illuminating another man seated at a rough-hewn table, his legs stretched out before him. A woman stood near a cast iron cookstove, a wooden spoon in hand as she stirred something that filled the air with a savory aroma. The scent made Jude's stomach rumble, a reminder of how long it had been since their last meal. The fellow at the table seemed a generation older than the curly-haired man and the woman. Maybe a father to one of them?

"Sure. Got a few head to spare." The man motioned outside. "My name's Walker. I'll take you around to see 'em."

Jude stepped back to allow the fellow to exit and lead the way. Before he could supply his and Angela's names, the woman called from inside. "Your missus can come in and visit a while if she wants."

Jude glanced at Angela to see if she wanted to rest there while he negotiated. The flash of panic in her eyes made her answer clear.

He turned back to answer the woman of the house, taking Angela's elbow as he did so. "Thank you for the offer, ma'am. That's neighborly of you. I think she was hoping to see the horses, too, though. She has an eye for a good mount."

That last bit might not be true, but it made Angela straighten a little. " Thank you, though. It's a pleasure to meet you."

"Of course, dear." Her eyes showed understanding even as she returned to her work at the stove. "You both come in for a bowl of stew when you're finished." His belly rumbled at the thought, especially with the savory smells drifting from the cabin.

As they followed their host around the side of the building to the corral, Jude let this hand rest on Angela's back. If felt right, and she leaned a little into his side. She must be nearly asleep on her feet. He'd finish the trading as quickly as possible so they could make camp for the night. He'd hoped there might be a boarding house or someone willing to let out a room, but that no longer seemed a possibility.

A half dozen horses milled in the corral, and the man stepped forward to lean on the fence. Jude stood beside him, studying the animals inside.

"That chestnut gelding would work for someone who knows how to take a strong hand. He was gelded late so gets a bit hard-headed at times." The man motioned toward a stocky horse, maybe the tallest in the pen.

Then he pointed to the darker-colored, angular horse beside the gelding. "That mare might be good for your lady. She just weaned a colt so she's ready to get back to work. Handles nice. I'd also be willing to let go of the bay." He nodded toward a handsome horse that looked half asleep, despite the interruption of their presence. "He's been my own riding animal for years, but I've been workin' on that three-year-old there. The bay's been a good horse. We've traveled a lotta miles together. Never had a complaint about him."

Jude slipped between the rails and approached each of the horses the man mentioned. He didn't have the keen eye that Jericho or even Miles did, but he could get along with an animal about as well as any of his brothers. He'd rather not have a mount that required constant convincing or a heavy hand like the chestnut, but both the bay gelding and the black mare seemed to have steady temperaments.

He returned to the fence where Walker and Angela waited,

and within a few minutes, he and the trader settled on a price for the horses, as well as saddles, bridles, halters, and packs. Walker said Jude could pick out the food, blankets, and other sundries in the trade room inside.

They followed him back to the front door, and this time Angela gripped his arm as though, seeming to need his help to hold herself upright.

Once inside the main room, Walker motioned to the wall on the left, a spot Jude hadn't been able to see through the open doorway. Shelves lined part of it, then barrels and crates extended out in two rows with a narrow walkway between them.

It didn't take long for him to gather what they'd need for the rest of their journey. Smoked meat, cornmeal, salt, coffee and a kettle to brew it in so they could continue to use the other pot for cooking. Oilcloths to cover them in case of rain, another blanket each, and a few more items he'd not thought to put on his list, including a knife for Angela, as she probably didn't have one with her. At least, not the kind she'd need out here for cooking and such.

Once he'd gathered everything and made Walker an offer, the man agreed readily enough. With the horses included, this was probably a larger-than-average sale for him. Jude handed over payment, and the fellow took it with a grin.

"Now you can all sit down an' eat." The woman called from where she was scooping stew into bowls. "I'm Mary, by the way. Harold's wife. And this is my pa, Martin."

Jude moved to the table where Angela was already sitting. "It's nice to meet you all. I'm Jude and this is Angela." Perhaps he should have let her speak for herself, but her eyelids were drooping closed, and he wasn't certain she heard what was spoken around her.

She'd pushed so hard all day long, never complaining,

despite the heat and exhaustion. Hopefully, riding would make their travel easier from here on out, but if days on the trail proved too much for her, he could always flag down another steamboat bound for Fort Benton.

Mary pushed bowls of warm stew in front of them, then settled in her chair to pepper them with questions while they ate. He answered as politely as he could manage, but he didn't feel up to giving these folks the entire sordid story of this journey.

Angela managed to eat half her stew before her chin dipped down nearly into the bowl.

"Poor dear. She's fully tuckered." Mary rose. "You two sleep in our back room tonight. There's only a small bed, but I reckon you can make do."

He reached to slide the bowl from under Angela's chin. "We don't want to put you out. I'd hoped there might be a boarding house nearby, but we can make camp in the woods."

"You can't make that sweet girl walk a step farther." Mary's voice sounded from within the dark room where she'd disappeared. "You just carry her in here. I'll put extra blankets out for you both."

Jude looked to Harold Walker, then Martin, to see if either of them objected to Mary's plan.

Harold nodded. "You'd best do as she says. We can do without that room for a night."

He'd never accept for himself, but having a real bed for Angela—with a roof and floor—would be a comfort they weren't likely to find again until Fort Benton. "Thank you. We appreciate the kindness, and I'll pay you for the room."

As he scooted Angela's chair out, bracing her so she didn't topple to the side, he leaned close to her ear. "Angela. Can you wake enough to walk?"

She gave no answer, and her head flopped over.

He slipped one hand around her back and another under her

legs, then lifted her into his arms. She was lighter than he'd expected, maybe because she snuggled into his chest, helping his balance as he maneuvered around the table and into the dark room.

Mary had lit a lantern, the light casting dancing shadows on the walls. A small cot stood in the corner, its counterpane dipping in the middle. Maybe he could tighten the bed ropes before they left in the morning to help repay the kindness of whoever they were casting out of this chamber for the night. He'd thought it was Mary and Harold, but after seeing the size of this bed, he guessed Mary's father slept here.

Mary pulled the blanket back, and he eased Angela down onto the frayed wool blanket covering the tick.

"I'll leave you two ta get settled. Open the door if you've need of anything." Mary spoke quietly as she backed away, then pulled the door closed.

He eased the quilt up to Angela's shoulders, and she didn't move more than the fanning of her lips with each steady breath. He allowed himself a moment to watch her in the flickering light. His insides ached as he took in the perfect lines of her face. *Only You could create something so beautiful, Lord.* Beautiful inside and out. Her spirit, her determination, her kindness. Her quiet wisdom. She was remarkable, this woman. Watching her like this brought physical pain in his chest. *Will You never bring us together?*

No answer quieted his spirit. And the longing...

He turned away. He must be a glutton for punishment to let himself long for something he couldn't ever expect to have. He'd made a commitment—to himself and to the Father. God was his priority over anything or anyone else. And He couldn't unite himself with any woman who didn't also have that same desire. Surely God would take away this longing for her if it wasn't His will for them to wed.

Soon, Lord. I don't know how much longer I can be around her without her taking up root in my heart. What had Jesus said when He was preparing to face death on the cross? *Father, if Thou be willing, remove this cup from me: nevertheless not my will, but Thine, be done.*

CHAPTER 22

*A*ngela's gloved hands tightened around the reins as she guided her mare, Shadow, through the tall grass. Jude rode beside her on Thunder. When she'd asked what he would name the gelding, he'd given her that warm-eyed smile. The one that said she amused him, but somehow the gaze made her feel treasured, not teased.

Then he'd raised his brows and said he'd not thought about a name. He'd looked thoughtful, and that was the only reason she'd ventured a suggestion. She'd offered Thunder, since the horse's heavy hooves sounded like thunder shaking the ground when he trotted.

Jude had turned to pat the gelding and said, *You like that Thunder? You finally have a name.*

Two days had passed since that morning they left the trading post, and she'd settled into the rhythm of their journey more with each passing hour. The land they'd been riding through was so vast, so different from the narrow streets and rigid buildings of New York City.

Out here, she could truly breathe. Though her limbs ached by the end of each day, working alongside Jude as they set up camp each night always made her weary body come back to life. He was such a patient teacher, and though she awoke each morning with new pains, an easy smile from Jude soothed her weary body. Each day she could spend with him was a gift, and she wouldn't take any moment for granted.

She'd been nervous about riding Shadow at first, having only been around cart horses in the city. Jude must have realized it, for that first morning he'd taken the mare's reins and motioned for Angela to approach and stroke the horse's soft neck. From there, he'd showed her how to place her foot in his hands, then hold the saddle as she bounced up from his palms and swung one leg over Shadow's back. This certainly wasn't the way the elegant ladies rode side-saddle in Central Park. But she'd never been one of those ladies. She might have occasionally dreamed of what it would be like to live their lives. But now, riding next to Jude in this wide open expanse of freedom, she couldn't bring herself to want that restricting life.

They were riding up a low hill now, and she leaned forward as Jude had taught her to help Shadow balance on the uneven terrain. When they crested the top, Jude jerked back on his reins and threw a hand out to stop her. She needed only a heartbeat to see why he'd halted.

A massive herd of cattle. No, these must be buffalo, like they'd seen in small groups over the past few days.

Yet so many... Hundreds, if not thousands, of the shaggy beasts covered the land in front of them. Massive wooly creatures grazing peacefully.

"That's a big herd." Jude kept this voice low.

She nearly choked on her laugh. "Yes. Big. How many do you think are there?" Maybe he had more experience estimating when there were so many. The animals stood close together, and still the herd extended nearly as far as she could see, like a great brown blanket spread over the land.

Jude gave a soft chuckle. "Well over a thousand. Maybe closer to two. Haven't seen a herd this size in a long time."

She glanced at the edges of the group. A few were wading into the river on their left, and to the right, they stretched all the way to a distant border of trees. "How do we get around them? They won't let us ride through, will they?" That idea felt far too dangerous for two lone riders among so many massive beasts.

"We'll have to ride around." He nodded toward the trees. "They're usually not dangerous, but if we get between a cow and her calf, or if they spook and decide to stampede, things might get hairy."

He nudged Thunder down the slope and toward the right, and she followed with Shadow. Both horses seemed bored of the buffalo now, plodding forward as though this was the same sight they'd seen all day.

Jude kept them a few strides out from the stragglers fringing the herd. Most of the animals ignored them, but one smaller buffalo jerked its head up to eye them as they passed.

Jude motioned toward him. "Looks like a yearling bull. Once he grows full size, he'll likely break away a few of these cows and start his own herd."

The young bull studied her and Shadow as they passed. His oversized head looked odd with his gangly body, but once he grew into that skull, he'd be an impressive animal. He huffed at her as they left him behind. Just like a cocky youth, eager to prove his abilities.

When they finally passed the herd, Jude slowed for her to ride up beside him.

She eased out a long breath and soaked in the wonderfulness of it all.

Jude slid her a glance, the corner of his mouth tugging. "What's that smile for?"

She sent him a sheepish grin. "It's so pretty out here. The way the land stretches forever. The rich blue of the sky. I never knew there were places like this." She hesitated, but Jude might appreciate this next part. "It makes me understand how you can believe God is up there, looking down all the time. That what happens on earth matters to him. If he took the time to make all this, it's easier to believe that he might be watching over the edge of a cloud to see what we think about it." She'd meant that *watching over a cloud* part to lighten the rest of the words, but as it slipped out, she regretted the disrespect in it.

Something flashed in Jude's eyes—pleasure maybe? But it passed too quickly to be certain. He tipped his head. He didn't look upset at her irreverence. Still, sweat gathered on her back as she waited for him to respond.

At last, he spoke. "You know, God isn't just up in heaven looking down on us. He's here with us, too."

She blinked, and had to catch herself before she glanced around for a great beam of light descending from heaven to the ground beside her.

The edges of Jude's eyes crinkled. "His Spirit is. He's everywhere, all at the same time." He motioned toward the land around them. "I think sometimes it's easier to feel Him when you can get away from other people. That's one of the reasons I love wide open country so much."

He slid her a grin. "The best place to feel the Lord, though, is in the mountains. Wait till you see the Rockies. The way those peaks rise up into the clouds. When you're standing up on a peak, staring at the mountains stretching in every direction, it's a feeling you can't ever forget."

He straightened a little in his saddle and looked up at the sky. "Lord, thank you for the mountains. For the chance to feel Your power in Your creation. Thanks too for these plains. For the wide open sky. For the river that makes our path easy to follow."

She didn't dare speak, or even make a sound. Was that a prayer? Had he actually been speaking to God in such a casual way? It felt intimate, as if she were privy to a conversation between two close friends. As if God were riding on a horse on Jude's other side. And was Jude finished with his prayer, or would he start into another round? He'd not ended with *Amen* as her father always had.

She slid a glance at him from the corner of her eye. He was grinning at her, so she dared a real look and fumbled for the closest thing to a normal smile she could manage.

Those warm eyes soothed away her nerves. "Not only is God with us all the time, He wants us to talk with Him. He wants to be our Father, and us His children, adopted into the family because Jesus died on the cross to take away our sins. To make us worthy of being in His family. Because of that, we can talk to Him freely."

So many notions she'd never heard before. She didn't have to wonder whether Jude really believed all this. He spoke so easily about it, this understanding was part of his daily life. He considered himself a son of God, adopted into God's family.

Jude, yes. He was truly good enough to be a son of God.

She swallowed down the lump in her throat. *She* wasn't good enough. Not that she'd done anything particularly bad in her life but...she simply wasn't good. Not the way Jude was.

Memory surged, all the lies she'd told when she pretended to be his wife. Her cheeks burned, but even more than that, her chest ached. She needed to apologize again, and perhaps this was a good time.

She shifted her focus back to land ahead so she didn't lose her nerve. "Jude, I'm really sorry for how I pretended to be your wife for all those weeks. I'm sorry for lying to others. I'm sorry for lying to you. I'm sorry for not seeing the truth about Winston. For putting you in the path of those two scoundrels."

She swallowed again, but this time it didn't ease the tightness inside her. "I'm more sorry than I can say if I've put you and your family and your mine and anything else in danger. If there's anything I can do to make it right, I promise I will." Tears blurred her vision, but she ignored them, keeping her focus locked on the grass in front of Shadow.

Jude didn't answer at first, and that only made the tears push harder at her defenses. She couldn't let them flow, couldn't let his sympathy get in the way of him having the chance to say all he wanted to. He could rail at her and tell her the full extent of how she'd messed up. There was probably much more at stake than what she knew of—his family's mine and livelihood. Maybe even a family legacy. If Lawrence and Martin somehow succeeded in locating the mine, or if Winston sent someone else to accomplish the assignment he'd originally given her... Would Jude's niece and nephew go hungry because of her?

"Angela." Her name on his lips was a sweet sound, gentle as the man who spoke it. "I've already long forgiven you. You don't need to ask again." He paused, but the weight in the air made it clear he had more to say.

She couldn't let herself put stock in these first words until she heard the rest. It would start with *but*, of course, clearing away this olive branch.

"You might want to ask forgiveness of God. And you can be certain that after you do, He'll forgive and forget those things completely." He let out a long breath. "I know from personal experience, the hardest part can be forgiving yourself. I don't think there's an easy way to accomplish that other than to know you've done everything you can to make it right, then choose to put it behind you." His voice warmed. "That's what Dat told me once. It takes time, but eventually you let go of the weight you've been carrying."

It didn't seem possible Jude could have ever done something so wrong that he struggled to forgive himself.

Maybe he heard her thoughts, for he looked at her with a sadness in his eyes that made her want to reach out and squeeze his hand or give him a hug, anything to ease that pain.

"When I was eight years old, we still lived back in Kansas. Everyone was in an uproar about whether Kansas would be a free state or not. The politics always seemed like endless talk, and I never liked to be around it. But there were these men...the Freedom Brothers, they called themselves. They were like heroes to me. They spoke of freedom, of fighting for what was right. I liked what they said, and I liked the stories they told about how they were making a difference for people. Making Kansas a better place. I believed them, and sometimes I would give them food from our farm. I never told anyone else, because Dat and Mum had warned me against them. I couldn't understand why, since they sounded like the kind of people Kansas needed more of. Once they said they needed more gunpowder and bullets, so I snuck them some of Dat's."

He fell quiet for a moment, and a lump formed in her middle. When he turned to face her, the pain in his eyes twisted in her chest. "But they weren't heroes. They were monsters. A few days later, I saw what they did with those bullets..." His voice cracked, and he looked away. "I saw them attack a family. Our neighbors. Innocent people who never harmed a soul. They burned their house down, and..."

Angela's heart clenched at the torment in his voice. "Jude, you couldn't have known."

He shook his head. "I should have. I should've seen the truth behind their words. If nothing else, I should have obeyed my parents. Because of me, because of what I gave them, they destroyed that family. They tortured innocent people—a father, a mother, and children—and killed every one of them. I ran for help, but they were long gone by the time help came."

He paused, the knot at his throat dipping as he swallowed. "That family's cabin was still billowing smoke, and the fire had spread through their fields to ours. Before we could stop the blaze, it burned up all our crops, everything but the garden beside the house." He was struggling more now, and she was tempted to tell him to stop. How could something so awful have happened to him, yet he still turned out to be this remarkable man she knew?

He seemed to need to tell this story, so she kept herself from interrupting.

"My family nearly starved that winter. Other neighbors brought food, even gave us a milk cow. I couldn't bring myself to eat any of it at first. I wanted to starve for what I'd done. For helping those men commit so much awfulness."

Angela's eyes burned for the little boy who had born so much guilt. "You were a child, Jude. They manipulated you. You meant your help for good. It was those men who turned the outcome into a tragedy."

He took in a long breath, his shoulders rising as the air filled him. Then he exhaled, nodding slowly. "I can see that now. I cried out to God for forgiveness. It was years later when we were building the ranch in Montana that I finally worked up the nerve to tell Dat and ask him to forgive me." He turned a pained gaze to her. "Honestly, I was so miserable with guilt, even after five years. I thought telling him would finally make me feel better."

A sad smile curved his mouth. "He said there was nothing to forgive. He'd become a Christian by then, and so had Mum. He asked if I'd prayed for the Lord's forgiveness. I told him I had, but I thought God must still be angry with me. What I'd done was so awful. Dat reached out and pulled me into a hug, even though I was thirteen years old and already stood as tall as his nose. He said God had forgiven me the first time I asked. That forgiving myself was the hardest part, and I had to make the decision to put it behind me. Not to live in its shadow, but to embrace the clean slate God had given me."

Finally, the pain slid out of Jude's features, and the clear blue of his eyes met hers again. "It was hard, but living in that freedom is so much better than carrying the weight of guilt.

"So that's my challenge for you. *I've* forgiven you. God will forgive if you ask. He'll forgive you of this lie and anything else. All you have to do is ask Him. Then choose to accept His forgiveness and walk in the fresh start He gives. He'll even help you as you move forward. He'll help you forgive yourself. All you have to do is ask."

It was all so much to process. So much to ponder. And she needed time for that.

Jude seemed to understand, for he shifted his focus forward again, settling into a quiet as easy and companionable as all the others she'd treasured these past days. One more kindness among a river of them flowing from this man.

After another few hours of peaceful riding, the sun began to dip toward the hills ahead of them. The landscape they rode through now contained more clusters of trees than before, as well as mountains that rose up in a dark red color.

When she pointed them out, Jude chuckled. "These are more like hills than mountains, at least compared to the Rockies. We'll see a lot of bighorn sheep and goats through here though."

The reddish color of the stone drew her eye more and more as they wove between peaks and through valleys. What she'd assumed was rock actually turned out to be a thick, clay-like covering.

At last, they reached a section that contained thicker tree growth, and Jude motioned toward a patch of woods. "Let's camp there."

She scanned the area as they approached, mentally preparing herself for the tasks ahead. There should be plenty of wood for the fire. And the cloudless sky hopefully meant there wouldn't be rain, so they wouldn't need to tie up the oilskins for shelter.

Jude had taught her how to start a campfire last night, with the flint and steel in his tinderbox. Maybe she could manage it herself this time.

After they dismounted, she turned to untie her packs. "I'll work on the fire and food while you tend the horses."

Jude glanced up at her, then the corners of his mouth tugged as he nodded. "All right."

They finished unsaddling, then Jude gathered dry kindling and helped her position the wood before he turned back to the horses. "If you have trouble, I'll be back in a few minutes."

She was already kneeling by the wood to open the tinderbox. "If I can't manage it, I'll wait for you."

But she would build this fire the way he'd showed her. Then she'd have a warm meal started by the time he returned from tying out the horses.

The more capable she became in Jude's world, the more likely he would see she really fit here.

CHAPTER 23

The sun cast a dusky, golden light on the land as Jude led the two horses out of the trees to the grassy area he'd spotted when they first rode up. He'd already taken both animals to drink at the river, and this would be a good place to hobble them so they could graze through the night without wandering far.

Both horses dropped their heads to the grass immediately, and he took a moment to stroke them. "You both did well today."

Thunder snuffled his boot before returning to the grass.

Jude gave him an extra rub. "Good boy." Maybe back at the ranch, he'd keep this gelding as his own riding horse. He'd not had his own mount in several years, not since Ginger grew too old to carry him up and down the mountains. She was pastured with the weaned foals now, a solid presence among all those youngsters.

He gave them both a final pat, then crouched beside the mare's hooves to fasten the hobble. "You've been a good girl, Shadow." He couldn't have picked a better horse for Angela if he'd searched for weeks. The mare was steady and calm but had enough pep to satisfy Angela's determination to keep moving.

He grinned as the image of Angela, when he'd tried to stop early yesterday, slipped into his mind. He'd realized how weary she was when she'd climbed back into the saddle after their mid-afternoon rest, so he'd tried to make camp an hour after that. She'd frowned and called him on it.

She wouldn't be coddled, that was for certain. He loved that about her, although it would be nice if she'd let him help a little more than she did.

And stopping early a night or two would be a relief, for it meant more time before they reached Fort Benton. A little longer before he had to leave her.

He pulled the hobble secure with a sigh, then straightened, patting the mare once more. He should be happy to end this journey. No need in prolonging the agony of being around her when she was so far out of reach.

Lord, why can't You just draw her to You so I can marry her?

Right. That wasn't how it worked, but it sure would be nice if God wouldn't have given people so much free will.

God was working in her heart, he could tell that by some of the questions she'd asked today. But Angela had a keen mind and strong determination. She'd have to come to grips with her need for God herself.

Maybe, if he hung around Fort Benton a while, she would come to that understanding, and he'd be there to celebrate her adoption into God's family.

Then he'd sweep her into his arms and ask her to join the Coulter family too.

Even as he pictured it, his chest tightened. He was putting his own desires ahead of what was best for her. He shouldn't want her to come to the Lord just so he could marry her.

Purify my heart, Lord. Cleanse my motives so they align with Yours.

Peace eased into his spirit again, and he inhaled a steadying breath. *Thank you.*

Something in that breath tickled at his awareness, drawing him back to the present. The scent of woodsmoke?

He glanced back toward their campsite. Angela must have succeeded in starting their fire.

No trickle of smoke drifted above the trees that surrounded their campsite. The fire likely wouldn't be strong enough yet to create that much smoke though.

And he wouldn't have thought the odor would have reached him yet.

He sniffed the air, turning to study the landscape around him as another possibility slipped in. In their camp that morning, he'd thought he saw a stream of smoke to the east. After he'd finished his morning ablutions and looked once more, there had been no sign of it. Angela had awakened then, and he'd shifted to his morning work to get them ready for the day —him checking and watering the horses while she prepared their morning meal. Then saddling the animals and packing up the last of their camp.

But now...could this smoke be from someone else who was also traveling alongside the river? If so, was it a stranger? Or might it be two *someones* they already knew and didn't want to cross paths with again?

His chest tightened as he studied the sky and hills in the direction they'd come from. Dusk had settled too strongly for him to see smoke from that far away. But he could smell that faint scent of it.

He had to go investigate, but would it be better to ride Thunder or go on foot? Probably the latter, so he could move quietly and climb the red rock easier to stay hidden. But first, he should retrieve his rifle and let Angela know what he was doing.

As he turned, Angela stepped from the trees, frustration marking her expression. That look shouldn't make him want to smile, but she was so blasted pretty with that hint of anger flashing in her eyes. She was angry with herself, he had no doubt from the way her chin was dipped, not lifted high. He guessed she'd not succeeded in starting the kindling burning.

He met her partway, and she faced him with her hands braced at her waist. "I need your help with the fire." Frustration radiated from her voice. Maybe she should use the sparks in her eyes to start the flame. She'd have a blaze in minutes.

He reached out, intending to touch her shoulder to lead her back to the fire. But she came to him, pressing against his chest as though she needed a refuge more than a friend.

He wrapped both arms around her as a sob shook her back. *Oh, Angela.* So much emotion and fire existed inside this woman. A person would never know at first glance how much she cared. How much spirit she possessed inside the lovely outer package she presented.

"It's all right." He murmured the words as he stroked her back. Would this be a full onslaught of tears like that time in their stateroom? The fact she was allowing herself to succumb to them again was a good sign. The more she let her emotions flow as they wanted to, the more she'd be able to release them in less...monumental ways.

But she stiffened, then released a growl that might have come from a bull buffalo. Her hands that had been pressed to his chest now gripped his shirt.

He loosened his arms to let her pull back. She only leaned away enough to look at him. The swirl of emotion in her eyes squeezed his throat. Anger, frustration, disappointment...they were all there. All aimed at herself. How could he help her see what an amazing woman she was? More talented and capable than anyone he'd ever met.

Though she was looking at him, her chin was still dipped low, like she was ashamed of herself.

He brought one hand up to tip her face toward his. "You,

Angela Larkin, are remarkable. More savvy and accomplished than anyone I know—man or woman. It's all right to be disappointed, but don't ever forget how capable you are. How talented God made you."

She searched his eyes, her own glassy. He did his best to show the truth in his gaze.

Heavens, she was pretty. Staring at her so close, those dark expressive eyes, the way all her features came together so perfectly. The feel of her petite waist against his arm. The softness of her chin, still between his thumb and forefinger.

Those lips...right beside his hand. His body flushed with the memory of how those lips felt against his. How could he be so near her and not taste them again?

When Angela's eyelids dipped, he realized how close he'd shifted. Her breath warmed his face, his mouth near enough to move in and meet hers.

He closed the distance, taking those soft, full lips in his own. *Sweet maple syrup.* Her intake of breath made his blood surge, and he let himself dive in to the kiss. She was so much more than he remembered.

She was sweetness and intensity as she met his mouth with her own. Her skin soft against his palm as he slid his hand up her jaw, weaving his fingers through her hair.

His other arm tightened around her, drawing her nearer. He couldn't get enough of her. This woman who'd claimed his heart so deeply, he wanted to give her everything.

He *couldn't* give her everything...

In the back of his mind, that reminder tugged. Tapping like an irritating knock on the door.

Angela. Now that he finally had her in his arms, how could he let go?

But he had to. This wasn't right.

Squeezing his eyes tight, he called on every bit of his self-control, pulling back, putting space between their mouths.

His chest heaved as he sucked in air. He still had her pulled tight to him, his fingers jumbled in her hair. He eased that hand free first, then took a step back. He had to let go of her waist, and the emptiness of his hands felt too strong as he dropped them to his side.

She had that dazed, half-sleepy, half-confused look. So innocent and vulnerable, he wanted to pull her close again. Instead, he stepped back.

Her brow gathered as she started to come out of the stupor. She stared at him, a hint of hurt creeping into her eyes as her mind worked to decipher what happened. Probably, she would think *she'd* done something wrong. He *couldn't* let her think that.

He shook his head, both to clear that thought from her mind and to shake the fog out of his own. "I'm sorry. I shouldn't have kissed you. I shouldn't have let myself..."

She straightened, her shoulders lifting as she took in a deep breath. She looked a bit more like herself now, fully in control. She shook her head. "It's all right."

She didn't meet his gaze, instead turning to look at the horses.

Should he say more? Make sure she understood that he hadn't pulled back because of anything she'd done?

But she spoke first, taking away his chance. "Can I finish the horses while you start the fire?"

The fire. Right.

She'd been upset because she'd not been able to light the kindling.

Smoke. His mind finally clicked into full awareness, his body tensing with the reminder of the possible danger.

"I need to check something first. I smelled smoke, and I want to see where it's coming from." He sniffed the air again. The scent was even stronger now.

Dusk had thickened, so he could barely make out the hills to the east he'd be searching. He turned back toward their camp. "I'll get my rifle."

He spun and strode into the trees, his heart slamming with each beat. He shouldn't have kissed her. What had he been thinking?

He'd *not* been thinking. He'd given in to his own weak impulses. *Sorry, Lord.*

It wasn't fair to Angela when he couldn't give her the future a kiss like that promised. *Bring her to You, Lord. Please!*

That circle of thoughts would put him right back in the tumult of frustration he'd swirled in before. And it would distract him from his focus when he needed all his senses alert.

At their camp, he scooped his rifle out of the scabbard still attached to his saddle, looped his new shot bag over his neck, then spun and headed back the way he'd come.

Angela was waiting for him by the horses. He wanted to sprint past her, but she looked like she wanted to say something, so he kept to a walk.

"Do you think it's Lawrence and Martin?" She studied his face with worry clouding her expression.

He focused on the distant outline of red rock hills instead of looking at her. "I don't know. It could just be another traveler. I need to make sure."

Angela shifted, drawing his focus to her against his will. She wrapped her arms around her middle, an act that made her look so vulnerable.

He softened the shield he'd been trying to place over his heart, letting himself look her in the eye. "Stay here. Either with the horses or back in the camp. I'll return as soon as I know something." Would she push to go with him?

She finally gave a simple nod. "Be careful."

He let out a breath. "I will."

As he started forward, he focused on keeping his steps quiet, his senses tuned to any sound, any smell or shadow that would alert him to the presence of another. Surely those two thick-headed thugs wouldn't be able to hide their presence from him. Especially if they didn't know he was nearby, searching for them.

Even as he homed his focus, memories of that kiss slipped back in. Flashes of the feel of her in his arms, the passion she returned in the kiss. He pushed each reminder away as quickly as it came. Yet they pursued him, haunting like a ghost that refused to be banished.

Clear my mind, Lord. Give me focus so I don't miss anything important.

The scent of smoke was growing thicker as he reached the first hill. He started up the base, but his boots slipped in the mud-like texture. He'd forgotten how hard it was to maneuver these slopes. He shifted his hold on his rifle to use both hands for the climb.

As he neared the top, he slowed to see what lay beyond without revealing his presence. In the valley below sat a small campsite. Flames leapt in the center, and packs and supplies were scattered around the edge of the light.

He focused on the shadows around the fire. No one was there that he could see. Should he get closer? Where would they have gone? Maybe to get water. Or to tie out their horses.

He should wait.

He shifted to a more secure and comfortable position. Then adjusted his rifle so he'd be ready to shoot if needed. *Let it be a stranger. Please.*

The last thing they needed was to face Lawrence and Martin again. At least now they were in the wilderness, where he could manage far better than he had on that floating jail.

Out here, they'd be on equal footing. He could finally stop those too so they wouldn't endanger Angela again.

CHAPTER 24

*A*ngela's fingers worked quickly with her new knife, cutting the dried meat Jude had purchased at the trading post into chunks and dropping the pieces into the water in the pot.

She had finally coaxed a spark to life, and now flames licked the wood around the pot.

She glanced through the trees surrounding their camp, but darkness had mostly settled in, and she couldn't see anything through the trunks. Had he found whoever was camping nearby? Were they strangers? Or Martin and Lawrence?

Worry gnawed at her insides. But that was better than remembering Jude's rejection during that kiss. Even now, the memory made emotion rise up to clog her throat. Why wasn't she good enough?

She sliced the last piece of meat and threw it into the water. She'd sloshed out half the liquid when she stumbled on the way back from the river, which meant she needed to go get more.

After another glance at the dark trees in the direction Jude had gone, she pushed to her feet and scooped up the kettle. She made her way through the shadows, keeping her steps light and her ears open, straining for any sounds that might indicate Jude's return.

Away from the shelter of the trees, the dim moonlight shimmered on the Missouri River ahead. She approached the water's edge, the murmur of the flow soothing her spirit.

She crouched at the edge of the bank, where the water lapped the muddy ground. She would have to reach out into the river to scoop water clean enough to use for cooking. Instead, she moved downriver a few steps, searching for a less muddy area.

There. She placed a tentative foot on a rock near the edge, then crouched and scooped clean water.

Once she moved her foot back to solid ground, she stayed crouched, closing her eyes to let the river's melody soak through her. Not only the water's flowing, but the chirrup of crickets and the croak of a frog nearby.

An iron grip clamped over her mouth, and a hand grabbed her arm.

Her eyes jerked open, but the palm covered her scream. A third hand grabbed her other arm, and she was lifted off the ground and carried backward.

Martin and Lawrence. It had to be.

She struck out with her legs, twisting her neck to get away from the hand smothering her. She caught a quick breath before they clamped down again.

"Thought you could run from us, did you?" Lawrence's voice sneered in her ear.

Martin chimed in with a wicked laugh. "You're a trapped rat now."

She writhed against their hold, but their grips were like metal clamps. She didn't stop fighting though, not until something hard slammed into her right temple.

Light flashed in her eyes as pain ricocheted inside her head.

She couldn't breathe. Not with the throbbing and the light and the hand closing out air.

Blackness seeped in, smothering everything. She gasped for one final breath, but nothing came.

～

*J*ude stayed concealed behind the crest of the hill, his gaze fixed on the deserted campsite below. The flickering campfire danced eerily, casting long shadows that stretched to the darkness around.

His body was clenched tight, and the tension was only growing stronger with every minute he waited for the owners of this campsite to return. It felt like he'd spent hours crouched here—though it couldn't have been more than thirty minutes—watching and waiting, his senses heightened, alert to any sudden movement or sound.

A faint sound drifted through the darkness. A man mumbling. He squinted to make out movement in the shadows, then a figure emerged, shifting into the circle of firelight.

Martin.

A chill ran down Jude's spine as he took in the sight of the man, his burly frame illuminated by the flames. But it wasn't just Martin that caught his attention—there was something else, something large and bulky slung over the man's shoulder.

Realization slipped in. That wasn't a bag or bundle of clothes. As the figure moved, the fire illuminated a flash of blue dress, sending a wave of panic coursing through him.

Angela.

The sight of her, draped over that scoundrel's shoulder, sent a surge of anger and fear coursing through him. She needed help.

Lawrence must be out there, too, lurking in the shadows. Would he follow them into camp? How had they found Angela?

And what did they plan to do to her?

He had to stop them. Before they hurt her.

Yet...was this a trap? Had they taken her to lure Jude into the open? He would be no good to her if he was also bound. He couldn't risk charging in blindly, not without knowing where Lawrence was. He had to know where both men were before he showed his hand, or else he might lose one of them and the threat would still be out there.

But if Martin hurt one hair on her head, Jude *would* intervene. His fingers clenched around his rifle as he aimed at Martin, the cold metal of the barrel digging into his skin. He would have the gun ready in case he needed to act quickly to protect Angela.

Martin managed to tie Angela to a small pine at the edge of their camp, despite her struggling the entire time. She was a fighter, that was for certain. Though pride swelled his chest— this woman was a fighter— she might be making her situation worse. If she stopped fighting, she might be able to lull Martin into going easy on her.

He scanned the darkness around the camp, especially in the direction Martin had come—from the river. The flickering campfire cast long shadows, making it difficult to discern anything outside of the fire's light.

In the camp, Martin paced back and forth, muttering to himself. Jude couldn't make out what he was saying, but he could see the anger on his face. Then, the man stopped short, staring back toward the path.

Jude followed Martin's gaze, his grip on the rifle tightening. The darkness seemed to grow thicker, suffocating him as he strained his eyes to see what had caught Martin's attention.

Was it Lawrence? Had he finally arrived, lurking in the shadows like a predator?

The soft nicker of a horse sounded, and Martin's posture

relaxed. He stared into the darkness for another moment, then turned away. They must have their horses hobbled close by.

But Martin had seemed reassured a little too easily. His reaction to the sound of the horse too casual, too relaxed. As if he'd been expecting it.

Had the nicker been a signal from Lawrence? Two Stones had taught them a game when they first met him, using animal calls as signals. Mostly they'd been bird sounds—a raven had been Two Stones's favorite. A horse's nicker could serve a similar purpose.

Jude adjusted his position, trying to peer through the night in search of some sign that would reveal Lawrence's location.

Nothing stirred beyond the campfire's reach. Keeping his finger steady near the trigger of his rifle, he scanned for the outlines of shapes that didn't belong in the natural landscape, for anything out of place.

Suddenly, something slammed into him—knocking him sideways onto the stone slope. The weight of his attacker pushed hard, but Jude writhed to flip over. To throw the man off his back. He'd lost his grip on his gun, but it couldn't be far.

This had to be Lawrence.

He must have seen Jude watching the camp. No matter what, he couldn't let him get the upper hand.

He heaved the man sideways, gaining enough space to elbow him sharply in the ribs.

Lawrence grunted, loosening his grip.

Jude scrambled to his knees, out of the man's hold. His rifle lay just out of reach. He lunged for it, his fingers brushing the cool metal just as a solid grip clamped down on his shoulder, dragging him backward once more.

Jude's instincts screamed as he was yanked away from his only means of defense. He twisted, using his captor's momentum to swing his free arm in a wide arc, aiming for any part of Lawrence he could reach. His fist connected with something solid, and a grunt of pain that told him he'd struck true.

Lawrence faltered, and Jude seized the opportunity to break free, rolling away and scrambling to his feet. The world spun for a moment from the abrupt movement, but Jude forced himself to focus. His survival—and Angela's—depended on it.

Lawrence recovered quickly, a dark silhouette against the night. They were close enough that Jude could hear the man's heavy breathing, could see the rise and fall of his chest as they faced each other.

He needed to grab his rifle—lying somewhere behind him—but he didn't dare take his focus off Lawrence. He eased backward, searching each foothold on the uneven mud-like rocky slope.

Without warning, Lawrence lunged forward, his bulky form swifter than Jude had expected.

Jude sidestepped down the slope, but his left foot slid downward on the slick red rock.

He caught himself just before tumbling over, his hands reaching out to brace against the ground. In the half-second of chaos, Lawrence struck him—all heavy breath and determination.

But Jude had grown up in the mountains. He knew how to move on treacherous terrain. With a twist, he redirected Lawrence's momentum, sending the man stumbling past him.

Except Lawrence had a double-fisted grip on Jude and jerked Jude with him. The two of them tumbled, rolling one over the other, down the slippery slope.

Lawrence's body pressed on him each time around, though Jude tried to break loose. To catch himself.

But the mountain was unforgiving, and their descent seemed endless, a chaotic spiral of limbs and grunts, the world a whirl of sky and stone. Finally, with a jarring thud that forced the air from his lungs, Jude landed at the bottom of the slope.

Lawrence's weight crushed him.

For a moment, everything was still. Jude's head buzzed with the impact, and warm liquid trickled down his forehead. He blinked to clear his vision as Lawrence pushed himself up to straddle Jude's chest, his knees pinning Jude's arms.

Anger flared in Lawrence's eyes as he raised his fist.

Jude braced for the blow, working to get his legs up to either kick the man or roll him off.

A fist slammed into his temple, sending a surge of light through his vision. Pain exploded in his head, flashing with light and stars.

Another force struck the same spot, though he barely felt it amidst the agony already pulsing.

This time the light faded, darkness dimming the glow. Then black took over, so thick it pressed in to smother his awareness to a tiny gray circle.

Then, nothing.

CHAPTER 25

*F*ear clawed at Angela's chest as she struggled against the ropes binding her arms to the scratchy pine behind her. The tree wasn't large—more of a sapling, really—but its trunk was just sturdy enough that she couldn't push it over.

Martin stood on the other side of the fire, his rifle cradled in his hands like he expected to use it any minute. Darkness surrounded the camp, and the fire cast dancing shadows around their space.

A shout sounded from the other side of the hill bordering the camp, and Martin jerked to face that direction as more noises came. Men's grunts. Rocks skittering. A thud, then another.

Her body clenched. That sounded like men fighting. Jude must have come for her. Did he get the drop on Lawrence, or had that thug surprised him? She could barely breathe as images of what might be happening on the other side of the hill filled her mind.

Martin was already scrambling up the slope, rifle in hand. Loose dirt and rocks tumbled down as he struggled for traction.

She had to get free. Two against one wouldn't be good odds for Jude, especially when at least one of those opponents carried a rifle.

She pulled harder at her ropes—both around her wrists and ankles. The tree branches seemed flimsy enough that she might be able to get her arms up over the top of it if she could stand. But the way he'd tied her legs, she couldn't get them underneath her with enough balance and strength to rise.

Her arms grew weak from pulling so much with them locked at such an awkward angle. But she must summon whatever strength she could to get away. She had to help Jude.

Desperation surged through her. Fear for him. The hopelessness of their situation. Tears stung her eyes, and she nearly screamed with the frustration welling up in her chest, except her gag wouldn't have let much sound out. She lifted her face heavenward, squeezing her eyes closed as more grunts and thuds sounded from beyond the hill.

They needed help. A strength much greater than her own.

Jude's words from earlier that day prickled her skin like rain. *Not only is God with us all the time, He wants us to talk with Him....All you have to do is ask Him.*

She opened her eyes, staring up at the few stars sprinkling the night sky. *If You're there like Jude says You are, help us. Help him. And help me help him.*

No voice boomed from heaven. No flash of lightning crossed the sky. Not even a blinking star to let her know God had heard. That He would consider answering her request.

But something inside her felt...stronger. Lighter maybe. A little less desperate.

She dropped her gaze to the fire as her mind worked to settle again. Maybe God would help them. She had to watch for an opportunity if He sent one.

A log in the fire shifted, sending sparks into the air. *The fire.*

Could she use it to burn the ropes? The ones around her ankles maybe.

She stretched forward but couldn't reach far enough to place her ankles over the flame. She could grab a log with her boots though—the log that had just shifted—and pull it closer to her. One end still blazed, and she clenched her body tight to lift her feet high enough to place the ropes in the flame.

The heat grew strong through her leather boots, but her binding jerked free after only a few seconds.

Yes! She might have shouted her victory if she didn't have this fabric tied around her mouth. She didn't have time for a celebration yet though.

After only a few thundering heartbeats, she pulled her legs free of the coils and worked them underneath her, then shimmied her hands up the tree behind her as she pushed up to standing. The first branch slowed her, and the rough bark scraped her arm as she twisted to tug the rope over the obstacle.

The second branch was smaller, but she had to bend at her waist to raise her arms so far behind her. With a final grunt, she rose up on her toes, bending lower as she pulled the top of the tree with her.

Her hands finally cleared the tree, and she tumbled forward to her knees. Her *oomph* stayed lodged in her throat as her body begged to collapse from pain and exhaustion.

No time to waste.

All had grown silent on the other side of the hill. Jude might need her more than ever.

She shifted on her knees to turn her hands to the dwindling flames on the log she'd pulled from the fire. It would be a trick to place the ropes over the flame without being able to see them —and without burning her skin or catching her sleeves on fire.

With each try, she managed a little better, twisting as much as she could to see the shadow of her arms in relation to the fire.

At last, the tension on the ropes eased. The fire must be eating up the threads of the rope a few at a time.

With a snap, her hands broke free, sending a rush of pain up her arms to her shoulders. Once more, she ached to lean forward and rest her forehead on the ground, let her arms work their way back to her sides to quell the pain pulsing through her.

Instead, she rose to her knees and jerked the gag off her mouth. It was too tight to pull upward over her nose, so she tugged it down around her neck. She scrambled to her feet and paused a moment to listen.

No sounds came from beyond the hill. That wasn't right. She tuned in and heard the quiet hum of voices.

She searched for Jude's tenor among them, but he wasn't speaking, she was fairly certain. That had to be Lawrence and Martin. What had happened to Jude?

Panic rose again, and she scanned the camp for a weapon. She had to get to him, but she couldn't go empty-handed.

Two saddles lay at the edge of the camp, and she sprinted to them. No rifles protruded from the scabbards, but a knife handle stuck up from a holder.

She reached for it and pulled out a blade longer than the cooking knife Jude had bought for her. This would do little to protect her from flying bullets, but might be better than facing the men defenseless. She would have to be careful about how and when she made her presence known.

She eyed the hill. She would be spotted easier if she went up in the same place Martin had.

So she crept along the base, moving out of the firelight and into the shadows. She walked as softly as she could, each scuff of her shoe on unseen sticks and rocks intensifying her anxiety.

Maybe this was far enough. Especially since there seemed to be a gap in the brush that would allow her a place to climb. A faint dip in the ridge line above might be the indentation of a heavily trod animal trail.

She started up, keeping her breathing measured despite the panic swirling in her chest. The incline was steep, and loose soil threatened to send her sliding back down with every step. She used scrubby bushes as handholds, pulling herself up bit by bit with her free hand. She kept a firm hold on the knife with her other.

At last, she reached the crest of the hill. She lay flat for a moment, catching her breath and scanning the scene around her. The moonlight cast an eerie glow over the area, illuminating silhouettes against the dark backdrop.

The voices grew louder, and a coarse laugh pierced the night air. Lawrence.

There, in a small clearing below, both scoundrels stood near a clump of bushes.

But Jude—*her* Jude—was nowhere to be seen.

Or...was that him on the ground beside the bushes? The way the shadow shifted, it had to be a person.

It had to be Jude.

It was impossible to make out his condition from this distance and in the dark, but her gut clenched at the sight of him lying mostly still. Was he hurt? Or tied up?

Frantic thoughts jumbled together as she formulated a plan. She had to get closer. And move without alerting them.

Angela took another steadying breath and focused on the ground and shrubs ahead of her as she crawled forward.

As she did, the men's conversation became clear. They were arguing about something—money, it sounded like—and their focus was entirely on Jude and each other. She still had to be quiet though.

When she reached a place where she could see Jude's form in the moonlight, about ten steps away from him, she paused to get a better idea of the situation. He lay still, his body unmoving, but his chest rose and fell with shallow breaths. One arm was stretched away from his side, the other draped over his belly. He must not be tied.

Which meant...he was hurt. Otherwise he wouldn't be lying so still.

The movement she'd first seen must mean he wasn't unconscious. Had he broken a bone?

The men had fallen silent. Martin was glaring at Lawrence, even though he had a rifle trained on Jude. "I don't like it. That wasn't the plan."

Lawrence turned away from him. "You dim-witted jackanape. You'd never be a really good agent 'cause you can't adjust when you need to." He waved a hand toward Jude. "When the blasted target drops himself neat as a pin right in yer arms, you get to change things up a little."

"We're takin' him on without the girl. There's no need to let her foul things up again. We've got other ways to make him do as we want. Ways that aren't nearly as risky."

She couldn't draw breath as she listened, her middle balling in a tight knot. They planned to kill her. At least, that's what Lawrence was arguing for. They must have first thought to use her to lure Jude into taking them to the sapphire mine. But Lawrence thought they'd be safer with her out of the picture.

You're right, you scoundrel.

She tightened her grip on the knife. She had to make a move, but how could she stop both of these men with only a hunting blade?

If You're here, help us. Help him. And help me help him. She sent up the same words she'd prayed when she'd been tied to the tree, except this time she was fairly certain God *was* here. He'd shown her how to get loose from the ropes. He could show her how to take down these two villains too.

As she ran the prayer through her mind once more, fresh courage seeped through her. *Thank You.*

The men continued to argue. Martin had his rifle, still aimed toward Jude.

Lawrence didn't hold a weapon that she could see. Did he still have the pistol he'd used to get the upper hand over Jude when they were fighting in the ship's hallway? She would have to assume he did.

Martin took a step back, lowering the gun. "I won't do it then. I'll turn an' walk outta here. You'll have yer hands full an' more, and I'll be a free man." His voice was low but firm.

A line drawn in the sand.

Lawrence's sneer sounded in his voice. "I say good riddance to ya. I can handle this one." His voice lowered. "The girl won't be a problem no more."

The two stared at each for a long moment. A stand-off that might turn the course of this battle one way or the other.

She couldn't see Lawrence's face, but the determined lift of Martin's chin was clear.

She wanted to cheer him on—he was fighting for her life, after all. But she couldn't let herself forget what he'd already done, nor what he'd been intending to do. He wasn't fighting to set her free. He wanted to use her as a pawn to steal a fortune from Jude and his family.

Fresh anger surged, propping up her intentions.

The stalemate continued another moment, then Lawrence chuckled. The sound rang with a hard edge but seemed to hold a thread of nervousness. "You're bluffing. I can see it in yer eyes." He motioned toward Jude. "Stay here an' keep the gun on him. I'm going back to take care o' the girl."

He waited a breath, but when Martin slowly turned the rifle back toward Jude, Lawrence started up the hill. He moved at half his regular speed, looking over his shoulder several times at his partner. Maybe making sure the man wouldn't do something to stop him. He must have been satisfied at last, for he faced forward and climbed faster, his long legs covering twice as much ground with each step as they had before.

Martin stood for another moment, the gun pointed in the general direction of Jude, but his gaze locked on Lawrence's retreating form. Something about his posture made the fine hairs on her arms raise on end. He didn't look ready to back down. But what would he do?

Her answer came in a movement so swift, she didn't even have time to scream.

Martin swung the rifle toward the hill, raised it to his shoulder, and aimed. Light flashed from the weapon just before the boom echoed off the mountains around them. Powder clouded in the air, framing Martin's form. He stood motionless, gun still aimed.

Angela turned toward the other man

Lawrence's body hung for a suspended moment before toppling forward to lie face down on the slope.

She couldn't breathe, yet her lungs scrambled for breath. He'd done it. He'd really killed Lawrence. His own partner. His friend.

Before she could grasp what was happening, Jude surged up from the ground, launching at Martin. The smaller man, though he was stout as an oak trunk, tumbled forward under Jude's weight. He didn't seem to be fighting, not at first.

Jude knelt on the man's back, reaching for one hand and yanking it behind him.

Then Martin roared. He tried to fling Jude off, twisting sideways.

Jude had a solid grip on the wrist twisted behind Martin's back though. At least solid enough to keep Martin from writhing out from under him.

The two strained, Martin squirming to flip Jude off, and Jude holding tight to that arm with all he had as he sat on Martin's back.

A weapon. Jude needed a weapon to get him under control.

She lurched to her feet, glancing up the slope to make sure Lawrence hadn't moved as she ran toward the melee.

Lawrence's lifeless body hadn't moved.

When she reached the struggling men, she stayed just out of reach. "Jude, here's a knife."

He was straining with everything in him. Maybe he couldn't free one of his hands to reach out and grab the weapon. Where was Martin's rifle? She'd have to load it again, but she could hold it on Martin while Jude took control.

She caught sight of the stock poking out from under Martin's leg. Not much chance she could grab it without being drawn into the fray.

But Jude shot a quick look at her. "Here." He threw out a hand for the knife.

She darted close enough to place the handle in his palm.

He moved as fast as a cat, gripping the weapon and placing the blade on the side of Martin's neck. "Stop fighting or I'll slice the first vein I get to."

Martin stilled, then slowly lowered his free hand to the ground, laying it flat.

Jude stayed in that position, his chest heaving. He might just be trying to catch his breath, but he was probably also planning the best way to secure this scoundrel without him breaking away.

She took a step forward, slow enough that Jude could see what she was doing, and pulled the rifle out from under Martin's leg. Once she straightened and backed out of reach, she asked quietly, "Do you want me to get rope from their camp?" They could probably still use the cord she'd been tied with. At least until they could find something more permanent.

Jude nodded, and she scurried up the hill, giving Lawrence's body a wide berth. Even so, her wayward gaze caught the dark liquid seeping out from under his lifeless form. *God, have mercy on him.*

She didn't allow herself to ponder that. Once she reached the camp, she grabbed the rope she'd been tied with, along with a small pouch that looked like it might contain bullets and powder—just in case.

When she returned to Jude, he had both of Martin's arms behind his back, wrists gripped in one hand while the other held the blade at the man's neck.

She dropped the rope beside Jude, then scooped up the rifle. "Let me just load this, then I'll watch him while you tie him up."

Jude raised his brows at her, his expression asking if she really knew how to handle the gun.

She gave him a confident nod. She'd never loaded a *rifle*, but she'd spent a lot of time practicing with the derringer she'd bought when she started being given more challenging and dangerous assignments. Also, she'd watched carefully each time Jude loaded his gun after hunting.

The gun was a little different than the derringer and Jude's weapon, but the concept was the same. Once she'd cocked the rifle, she took aim at Martin's head, which was the only place large enough that she was sure she could hit without striking Jude. *Don't let me have to shoot, God. Please.* But if she had to for Jude's protection, she would.

Somehow God had made the impossible happen so far, first giving her the idea of how to free herself, then turning these two blackguards against each other so Jude could make his move. Jude must have been bluffing as he'd laid almost unmoving on the ground. Or...was he truly hurt and now pushing through his pain?

Protect him. Give him strength.

It took Jude less than a minute to bind Martin's wrists tightly behind his back. Then Jude pushed to his feet and turned to her. His gaze ran down the length of her, checking for injuries, no doubt.

She gave him a hopeful smile. She should do the same to him, but she was splitting her focus between Martin and Jude, and her eyes wouldn't leave Jude's face enough to worry about anything else.

He looked dirty and tousled, but oh, so handsome. And *here*. With her.

Somehow, they'd come out of this alive, with both of them standing, and him looking at her as though he had come through fire to find her—and would do it again if he had to.

He closed the distance between them, took the rifle, and held it with one hand, stock braced against his shoulder and his fingers holding the trigger guard, barrel aimed at Martin. Then he wrapped his free hand around her waist, turning her into him so they were chest to chest.

She wrapped her arms around his waist, breathing in the wonderful scent of him. The scent of life and courage and honor. The scent of the man she loved with every part of her. Though emotion welled in her eyes, they weren't tears. Just gratitude.

I'm sorry I've ignored You all these years, God. Thank You for bringing Jude into my life. Thank You for showing Your love through him.

She probably wouldn't have ever understood the fullness of love that was possible without seeing Jude live it out. The thought that God could love her as much as Jude said He could still seemed too wonderful to be true. But she'd seen Him act, here in the midst of this battle, and she no longer doubted that He saw and cared about them. That He listened, even to a wayward woman like her.

I want to be Your daughter. Will You adopt me into Your family?

At her words, the warmth that wrapped around her was

greater even than the comfort of Jude's arms. It filled her insides, soothing the raw places, the hurt, the grief from all she'd lost. Not even the latest betrayal from Winston could penetrate the peace washing through her.

She laid her head on Jude's shoulder and soaked it all in.

CHAPTER 26

Seven days. Seven long weary days since that awful night of the fight with Lawrence and Martin.

Exhaustion had settled deep into Jude's bones, making every movement an effort as he and Angela set up camp after another long day on the trail.

He'd thought Lawrence's death and Martin's capture would be the end of their troubles. That night a week ago had been a turning point, sure. He no longer had to watch their backtrail, searching for signs they'd been followed, that Lawrence and Martin had found them again.

But he was *still* watching. He cast a glance at Martin, tied to the tree where he'd stay all night until they packed up to ride out again in the morning. The man was already looking at Jude, piercing him with that sullen glare that had been his constant expression this past week.

Jude turned away, scanning the camp to see what he should do next. Angela had already built the fire and was stirring something in a pot. The aroma wafting up nearly made his knees buckle.

He stepped closer and inhaled a long whiff. "Boy, that smells good."

She sent him a weary smile. Even with dark circles under her eyes, she was beautiful. "It'll be nice to have a warm meal."

Maybe he shouldn't have pushed them so hard this week. But having Martin in their camp, so close to Angela, felt like too much risk. Like a flame licking up a fuse connected to blasting powder. At any moment, the man could explode. Somehow get free and take revenge on her.

So Jude had pushed them, traveling for several hours after dark and heading out as soon as they could in the mornings.

He crouched beside her. Maybe they should rest a little tomorrow morning. She could sleep in, then they could set out two or three hours later than they had been.

As he opened his mouth to suggest it, a noise sounded from outside the light of the fire. A rustling in the leaves. They'd taken shelter just inside a cluster of trees, a short distance from the river. Was that an animal watching them?

Most night creatures would move *away* from fire, not toward it.

He stood and stepped toward the sound.

"What is it?" Angela spoke quietly, just loudly enough for him to hear.

"I don't know." It might be nothing, but there also might be a person out there, lurking in the shadows. Did Martin and Lawrence have an accomplice who would be looking for them? Had Winston come to ensure his commands were followed?

Jude scooped up his rifle from the scabbard attached to his saddle at the edge of camp. When he straightened, he stared into the darkness, trying to find movement among the shadows.

The rustling sounded again.

His heart pounded. "Who's there?" If it was another traveler, a stranger approaching their campfire, the person would answer.

The caw of a raven drifted through trees.

A raven? At night?

The sound tickled at something in his memory. It was most definitely a raven, not a crow. Some people mixed the two birds, but Jericho had a pet crow who acted as a watchbird on the ranch, alerting if strangers approached. All the Coulters could easily tell the two sounds apart.

Two Stones.

Memory flashed like lightning. That was the call Two Stones often used when they played the signal game as youths. The raven call was the first one he'd taught them.

Jude stared into the woods. Two Stones couldn't possibly be here, though. Nor his brothers. They wouldn't expect him to be riding alongside the river. If they came looking for him at all, they'd stay in Fort Benton, watching for the arrival of steamships.

The raven sounded again, and this time it rang with such familiarity in his mind that he could no longer question. "Two Stones?"

The shadows shifted, though no noises sounded. Then a figure emerged into the ring of firelight, grinning wide.

Jude blinked, his mind still struggling to make sense of this.

Two Stones took a step closer, little more than a stride away. "Don't shoot, brother. I am real, I promise." He nodded toward the gun in Jude's hands.

The voice finally settled the shock in his mind, bringing him back to full awareness. Jude eased the rifle to the ground, his own grin forming.

Two Stones was here. His good friend. Practically a brother. He would help. Now, Angela wouldn't have to take any of the watches, and Jude wouldn't have to worry so much.

He closed the distance between them and grabbed Two Stones for a quick embrace. He wanted to laugh. Wanted to whoop.

Two Stones returned the grip, then held him at arm's length, his brows raised. "I see you've missed us, being gone for so long." His mouth tipped up on one side the way it always did when he teased.

Jude laughed, letting a bit of his relief out. "You have no idea." He turned and gripped his friend's shoulder so he could introduce him to Angela.

She'd risen to her feet, waiting quietly by the fire. Her expression held a tentative smile, like she wasn't certain what was happening.

He stepped forward, bringing Two Stones with him. "Angela, this is Two Stones." Had he told her about their good friend? So much had happened, he couldn't remember for sure.

He must have, for her smile deepened. "Hello. Jude has spoken of you, and I'm honored for the chance to meet you." Her voice took on a more formal tone, a bit of the accent slipping in that he'd heard the first time he awoke on the train to find her sitting next to his bed pallet. She must be nervous.

He pulled his hand from Two Stones's shoulder and moved to stand by her. She would soon feel comfortable with his friend, but he would do everything he could to speed that process. He spoke to Two Stones. "I met Angela on the train back from New York. She's been..." How could he possibly summarize all that had happened? "We've had lots of adventures together. And she's been a godsend through them all." He swallowed. That didn't say even half of how much Angela meant to him.

Two Stones was studying him, his dark eyes probably seeing everything Jude didn't say. The man turned to Angela and offered a friendly smile. "I am happy to meet you, Angela."

Now that introductions were over, he had so many questions. "How did you find us here? And why did you come?"

Instead of answering, Two Stones looked past them,

nodding toward Martin. "If I answer you, will you tell me why you have an enemy in your camp?"

Jude's middle twisted at the accuracy of the word *enemy*. "It's a long story, but I'll tell."

Two Stones nodded, his gaze moving back to him and Angela. "Heidi and I were in Fort Benton, picking up a load of supplies for the people in my village. A ship came to the dock, and I heard two men speaking of a Coulter who had been on board."

His dark eyes homed on Jude. "They said he and his wife had left the ship a week before they reached Fort Benton. They could not understand why these two would choose to travel over land instead of on the big boat."

More questions glimmered in Two Stones's eyes than Jude was ready to answer. Should he tell the truth about all that had happened between him and Angela? Her deception about them being married? Normally, he would keep no secrets from this man. But that felt more like Angela's secret than his own.

Two Stones wasn't requiring answers yet, for he continued speaking. "I too wondered why my brother would leave the big boat that would bring him home sooner. I came to see what trouble he has found." The lines at the edges of his eyes crinkled, the only hint of his teasing.

Jude chuckled, glancing over to meet Angela's gaze. She still looked a little worried. About what though? Surely she didn't think Two Stones was a threat, not simply because he was Salish.

Her eyes didn't hold fear though, only concern. He could ask her later, and see if she foresaw a problem he'd not thought of yet. His mind was too weary to think clearly tonight.

He turned back to Two Stones to offer as short an explanation as he could. "We ran into trouble on the steamer. Two men that Angela knew from New York had been sent to follow me back to the mine. Apparently, their boss has plans to waylay next year's shipment of strawberries." The code word slipped out before he could catch it.

Two Stones's gaze shifted to Martin again. "He is...?"

"One of the two who followed us. We had a tussle a week ago, and he shot the other fellow working with him."

Martin's glare intensified as they all three stared at him, but he didn't speak. He hadn't said much since that fateful night.

Two Stones gave a slow nod, probably still trying to work out the story. Jude could give him more details later.

He turned back to Jude. "What will you do with him?"

"We're pushing to get him to Fort Benton." Jude scrubbed a hand through his hair. "Once there, Angela can wire a family friend in New York City, someone she trusts. We're hoping he can get the right people involved there to stop the man who's put all this together. Then we need to get Martin here back to the city." He let out a sigh. "I'm hoping to find a few guns I can trust to deliver him."

Two Stones considered that. "You wish to return to the ranch, not back across the country. But it would be worse for him to break free."

Jude dipped his chin. "Exactly."

His friend scanned their camp, his gaze lingering an extra heartbeat on the pot of bubbling food. "I am here to help. I will take the night watch. You both should sleep."

Jude allowed his shoulders to sag. *Thank You, Lord.* "That sounds better than I can say."

Angela crouched by the fire. "The stew is ready. Both of you should eat."

Jude looked past Two Stones. "Do you have a horse? I can hobble him with ours while you get settled."

His friend turned and strode back the way he'd come. "I will do it. Then I will be glad for that stew."

As he disappeared into the shadows, Jude turned back to

Angela. She was focused on her work with the food, scooping soup into their bowls. Was she ignoring him on purpose?

He crouched beside her. "Two Stones is a good friend. I trust him as much as I trust my own brothers." He snorted a chuckle. "More really. Especially in this. He's Salish but has spent a lot of time around whites, especially these last few years. His instincts are solid. He'll be a better guard than I am."

Angela finally looked up at him, her expression soft. "I'm glad he's coming. It's good to have a friend."

Something in the way she said that last word made him study her. Did she not have friends back in New York? She'd never spoken of any, except Mr. Stewart, their family friend who had helped her get the job with the Treasury. The one she planned to wire for help when they reached Fort Benton.

Did she have no female friends her own age? Jude wouldn't claim anyone other than Two Stones and his own brothers as friends in that way, but Angela didn't have sisters. No one to share confidences with or rely on in times of trouble.

He rested a hand on her arm, an action he'd not planned, and it seemed to surprise her, from the way her gaze dropped to his fingers before lifting to his face again. "It *is* good to have a friend. I hope you know you have that in me too."

His insides cringed at the notion he'd just voiced. He was her friend, of course. But everything in him—everything save his conscience—craved far more than friendship with her.

The tendons at her throat worked, then she dropped her gaze back to the food. "Thank you." Did her voice crack with those words? As she reached for another bowl, her arm pulled from under his hand.

He stayed there beside her for another few heartbeats. He'd made things worse. Whatever was bothering her, he'd not helped.

So he pushed to his feet. They were both so weary. All would be better after a good night's sleep. "I'm going to gather another load of firewood." Two Stones would likely bring more, but this gave him something to do.

When he returned with an arm full, Two Stones sat by the fire, a bowl in hand as he ate.

Angela was kneeling by her pack but, as he lowered the logs onto their pile, she stood. "I'm going to the river for a few minutes." Her voice sounded more like its usual tone, though he could hear exhaustion in the words.

After she faded into the darkness outside the firelight, he settled beside Two Stones. The man motioned to another bowl full of broth with chunks of meat poking up above the liquid. "She said that's yours."

Jude reached for the dish and scooped a hearty first bite. The savory warmth washed through his mouth, and he enjoyed every minute as he chewed. Angela sure could make a good meat stew, even with what little supplies he'd purchased back at the trading post.

"So you're married?"

Jude nearly choked on his stew at his friend's question. It seemed he still had some explaining to do.

Two Stones took another bite, a twinkle in his eyes telling Jude that he clearly expected an answer.

Jude swallowed his bite. "Not married. Just travel partners." The explanation sounded feeble even to his own ears. But he didn't want to talk about Angela's deception. That had been forgiven. Maybe Two Stones wouldn't press.

"Ah." He gave a nod as though he understood. But after spooning another bite into his mouth, chewing, and swallowing, he added another casual comment. "But you care for her."

Jude said nothing at first, eating his meal, allowing the crackling fire to fill the space between them. Did he dare speak the real reason nothing could last between them? Two Stones would understand. He might even have wisdom to share.

"It's...complicated." He spooned another bite but didn't lift it to his mouth. "I do want to marry her. She's special." His chest tightened with the truth of that. "But she's not a Christian. And I made a commitment to God and myself that I wouldn't marry a woman who doesn't love Him."

Two Stones didn't speak again for a long moment. When he did, his words brought little comfort. "That is a difficult path to walk." He turned to meet Jude's gaze. "As the heavens are higher than the earth, so are God's ways higher than ours, and His thoughts than our thoughts." His gaze softened. "I will pray for you to see His way through this."

Jude swallowed. He'd always loved that verse, but he was afraid to allow the hope that wanted to slip in with the reminder. Still, he nodded. "Thank you."

CHAPTER 27

*A*ngela stood just beyond the perimeter of the camp, her heart pounding. She hadn't intended to eavesdrop, but she'd arrived just in time to hear Jude's words, spoken with a quiet intensity that made her chest ache.

She's not a Christian. And I made a commitment to God and myself that I wouldn't marry a woman who doesn't love Him.

She sank back against a tree, her mind racing. She'd had no idea that was what held him back. Of course Jude's faith was important to him, but she'd not realized her lack of it would keep him from opening to her.

But hadn't he said as much, back on the steamboat, when he first told her he was planning to leave her in Fort Benton? She'd been so panicked about the thought of losing him that she'd not heard his real reason. What a fool she'd been.

She let her eyes drift closed. The men had stopped talking, leaving her alone with her thoughts and her Heavenly Father. *What should I do, Lord? Should I tell him?*

Of course she should tell him. Everything in her felt at peace with that idea—including the quiet place deep inside that she'd begun to sense when she prayed. Not just peace, but *joy*.

They were both so weary, perhaps it should wait until they'd slept. For her part, her emotions were always closer to the edge when she was this exhausted.

But she couldn't stand to wait. Not even one night.

She had to prepare herself for the possibility that, when she told Jude about her new faith, nothing would change between them. He would surely be pleased, but maybe her lack of faith in God was simply an excuse he'd given his friend for not marrying her.

He might simply welcome her as a sister in God's family.

That thought nearly stole the strength from her legs. A daughter of God she very much wanted to be, but *not* Jude's sister.

Still...she needed to tell him. As Two Stones had said, only God knew what would happen here. *Work things out according to Your plan, Lord. Please.*

She stepped into camp, and both men looked at her. Two Stones gave a nod of greeting, then took another bite of stew. Jude's eyes looked wary, not quite meeting her gaze.

Yes, she needed to tell him now. He deserved to know the truth. Then he could do with it what he wanted.

"Jude, I saw something down by the river I want to show you." She motioned into the shadows she'd just stepped from. "Will you come with me?"

He regarded her, his expression unreadable except for his weariness. Perhaps she *should* let him rest first. But he would want to know this. Surely.

At last he pushed to his feet and waved for her to walk first. Her nerves tightened as she and Jude wove through the trees. When they reached open land, the moon cast a soft glow over the river ahead.

The weight on her chest made her breathing harder, but she worked to take in deep, steady inhales. As they neared the river, they both slowed. This was the time. She had to tell him now.

She kept her focus forward, toward the river. "I overheard what you said to Two Stones." She glanced at him. "The last bit anyway. I'm not sure how long you were talking."

His brows lowered, but the shadows concealed his eyes, so she couldn't see his thoughts. He didn't say anything.

All she could do was press on. "I realized I haven't told you what happened to me that night I was kidnapped." She inhaled a steadying breath. "When I was tied to that tree, and Martin and I heard you and Lawrence fighting on the other side of the hill, I was desperate to help you. But I couldn't get free. It felt hopeless." Even now, she could remember that panic. That terror for Jude's life.

She squeezed her eyes to keep herself in the present, then let out a shuddering breath. "The only thing I could do was pray. You'd been telling me that day that God cares about everything that concerns us, so I decided it was worth seeing if He cared about the two of us and the danger you were in."

Jude shifted just enough that she could see the intensity in his eyes. Drilling into her face, as though something she said might be the air he needed to survive. Or maybe he was searching for a word to prove she was lying. Her history would certainly warrant that.

All she could do was be honest and trust God to show Jude the truth. "After Martin disappeared up the hill, I prayed and asked God to show me how to get loose so I could help you. Then the idea came to burn my ropes off. The way it slipped in, so soon after my prayer, I knew"—she pressed a hand to her chest—"something inside me knew it wasn't an idea I'd come up with on my own. Then after I got free and climbed over the hill and crawled to a place where I could see those two had you on the ground, it felt impossible again. I didn't have a gun, and I didn't think you did either." This next part still left her in awe. "I prayed that God would make a way. That He would somehow get us out of that situation alive."

She raised her hands, palm up. "And he did. He made Martin turn against Lawrence, leaving only one man for you to subdue. After it was all over"—she left out the part where she was in Jude's arms—"I told God I was sorry for not believing before. I asked if I could be part of His family, adopted as a daughter." Even now, she could feel the peace from that moment snuggling around her like a hug. She wrapped her arms around herself, holding it in. Relishing the warmth.

"I didn't tell you at first because...it's all so new. I'm still learning so many things. How to talk to God, how to listen. I'm not nearly as good at it as you are, but I can feel Him when I pray."

Would Jude think she was saying this just to take away the barrier between them? That her change wasn't real? She could assure him of the truth of her words, but she couldn't change his opinion. *Only You can, Lord.*

❧

*J*ude studied Angela as the moonlight reflected off her cheekbones. Could this be real? *Lord, don't let it be a lie. Not something she fabricated because she heard me say that's what I wanted.*

He couldn't rush into this. Couldn't grab her up and swing her around the way he wanted to, whooping for joy.

Yet she was waiting for his response. He had to say something. *Is she speaking truth, Lord?* He couldn't tell if this hesitation inside him was the Holy Spirit's prompting, or his own fear of being drawn into another lie.

For now, he could simply respond to the words she'd said. She'd said she asked God to bring her into His family. *That,* above all else, was a reason to celebrate.

He allowed a smile to slip out. "That's wonderful. Truly. It makes me happier than I can say." And with his words, joy seeped into his chest, his body finally reacting to the truth she'd shared.

And it *was* truth. He could see it in every part of her expression. Now that he thought about it, she'd been different this past week. A new peace lingered around her, a smile in her eyes even when she was at her weariest.

Lord, can it really be true? This prayer was different than the ones he'd breathed a moment before. Wonder clouded the thought.

She'd prayed.

She was truly a child of God now. And the fact that she *hadn't* told him rang true with her words. A relationship so new, so wonderful, would be something to hold close until she had more confidence.

She must have seen the shift in his reaction, for a grin spread over her face that illuminated the new joy in her heart.

Maybe giving in to a few reckless impulses wouldn't be out of line. It was right and proper to celebrate news like this. He closed the distance between them, placed his hands at her waist, and hoisted her into the air. And spun a circle.

"Yahoo!" His voice rang across the river, echoing in a way that sounded like the angel chorus celebrating with him. They certainly were.

Angela was laughing as he brought her back to the ground, and the joy lighting her face intensified that same emotion surging inside him. He pulled her close, wrapping her in his arms, relishing the connection between them.

Thank You, Father. Not just that there was no longer a barrier between them, but because He had brought another lost lamb back into the fold.

The sting of emotion rose up to burn his nose. Such a celebration. And he'd been able to play a small part.

Show me my next steps, Lord. I don't want to rush ahead of You. There technically wasn't anything else standing between him and Angela, but he needed to hear God's leading before he asked her what he so badly wanted to ask.

As he listened for any nudges in his spirit, he let himself relish the feel of her. She fit so perfectly in his arms. Holding her made him want to be better. A better example of God's love for her. An example of the way Christ cared for the church.

The rightness of it all resonated in him. *Should I wait, Lord?*

He felt no check in his spirit. No hesitation.

Only an intense, soul-deep thankfulness. More than a feeling, more than emotion, but it rose up so thick he could barely speak.

Angela must have sensed something happening with him, for she lifted her head and drew back enough to see his face. Her brows wrinkled in concern. "What is it?"

He hadn't gathered his wits enough to make a proper declaration, but he could answer this question. He swallowed enough to speak, letting himself sink into her gaze. "It's love."

Her eyes shimmered. Those beautiful, dark eyes that he loved so much. She didn't speak immediately, and when she did, she seemed to have as much trouble getting words out as he was. "Are you sure?"

Another question he could answer easily, without reservation.

"Very sure. I never would have imagined God could work things out the way He did." He tipped a grin. "As Two Stones reminded me a few minutes ago, His ways are much higher than mine. I should know better than to second-guess Him."

Her eyes glimmered with so much emotion. Her beautiful mouth tipped up at the corners. "I love you too."

He blew out a breath, letting go of all the tension he'd carried these past weeks as he'd longed for her, afraid to let himself hope they'd be able to make a life. Then he grinned. "Would it be too much if I spin you around again?"

She laughed. A laugh so beautiful it made him want to swoop in and kiss her.

He raised his brows. "Or maybe you'd be game for a kiss instead." He lowered his forehead to hers, and he could just see her mischievous grin.

When she spoke, her voice held that same teasing lilt. "I don't know. Might be bad for my reputation, kissing a man out here under the stars."

His heart quickened. What better time than now to ask? He lifted his head, meeting her gaze. "Marry me, then." He shook his head to clear it. He could do better than that.

He brought his hands up to cover hers and locked her gaze in his. "Angela Larkin, would you do me the honor of becoming my wife?" He couldn't help teasing a little. "In truth, this time. For the rest of our lives. I'll do my very best, with God's help, to be the husband you need. The husband you deserve." He swallowed more emotion. "I won't always get it right, but with the two of us strengthening each other, leaning on God, I know He'll create something wonderful with us."

Angela's lips parted slightly, and her eyes, bright with tears and moonlight, softened into a tenderness he felt in his very bones.

"I would love to, Jude. With all my heart, yes."

He didn't whoop or spin her in a circle. Instead, he drew her into a hold that felt so intimate, the connection between them went far beyond what words could describe.

Only a Master Creator could have brought them to this point. And for the first time since he'd left his homestead, despite the fact that they still had so many miles to go, he finally felt like he was home.

CHAPTER 28

a warm breeze caressed Angela's face as she rode beside Jude. Two Stones came just after them, with Martin's horse dragging behind.

She scanned the horizon ahead as they rode. Two Stones had said they would see Fort Benton in the distance soon. Anticipation made her want to bounce in the saddle, despite how tired she was.

The plain stretched before them like an unending tapestry. The sky above was a brilliant canvas of blue, dotted with cotton-like clouds drifting lazily by. No wonder Jude loved this land so much. The place had a wild beauty that seeped into her soul, filling her with life and helping her breathe deeper than she ever had before.

"So..." Two Stones's voice drifted forward, drawing their glances back to him. His expression had that bit of mischief she'd seen a few times. "Is there to be a wedding when we reach Fort Benton?"

Heat flushed up her neck, and she turned forward again. Two Stones's chuckle carried on the breeze.

She dared a glance at Jude and met his smiling eyes.

Those eyes. They steadied her every time.

And he was to be her *husband*. The idea thrilled with each remembrance, filling her up with warm pleasure that made it impossible not to smile.

"Well..." Jude kept his focus on her, those smiling eyes reading her thoughts. "I'm hoping we don't wait long for a wedding, but I would like to have my family there, if possible. The ranch would make a pretty spot."

The ranch. Her heart quickened with the word. The fact that Jude trusted her so fully, even after all she'd done. He was taking her not only into his heart, but into his life. Bringing her to the place that mattered to him most. To the people who were not only his roots, but also his future.

No words could express how thankful she was, and emotion stung her eyes. She loved this man so...very...much.

His gaze softened as he watched her. She couldn't tell him everything she was feeling with their audience looking on, but she would do so later.

The last two nights, since Two Stones had been with them, she and Jude had slipped away from camp and sat at the river's edge. Tucked against his side, sheltered in the strength of his arms, she'd shared her heart with him, and he'd shared his with her. They'd talked as long as they dared, telling stories and hopes and thoughts she never would have dreamed she'd be able to tell another person.

But this was Jude.

He never judged her or criticized the way she felt. He listened and encouraged.

She'd never met a man who *encouraged* her the way he did.

It made her want to weep, but not from sadness. The safety she found with Jude made her emotions spring so much more readily. And even that, he didn't judge. When the tears came, he held her. Rubbed her back. Told her it was good to cry.

Then when she lifted teary, red-rimmed eyes to thank him,

he told her she was beautiful. No one had told her that before. Not ever.

These days with Jude felt too wonderful to be real. And the thought of a lifetime with him...

The first time they had a moment alone, she would attempt to tell him again how much he meant to her.

He was waiting for her answer now though, and from the way his brows had started to dip, her delay was worrying him.

She smiled to show him all was well. "My mother once told me that if I ever met a good man who I wished to marry, I shouldn't let worry for her hold me back. I think maybe she meant not to let worry for her stop me from marrying at all, but I also think she would not want us to wait for her to reach us."

She paused. "I would like to invite her to come for a visit though, if that's all right."

Jude nodded before she finished speaking. "Please. Tell her we all want her to come, if she's up for the journey." He tipped his head as his expression turned thoughtful. "She could move here if she'd like. She might enjoy playing with Naomi's little Mary Ellen...and any other children that might wander along." An extra sparkle twinkled in his gaze, bringing that heat once more to her cheeks.

She dipped her chin and turned forward once more. Her gaze found the horizon again, where a few buildings were beginning to take form.

She raised a finger. "Is that it?"

"It is." Jude's voice had a tinge of relief.

The structures grew steadily as they approached, slowly revealing their details—the wooden facades of stores, the wall that marked the early boundaries of the town from several decades ago, even the glint of windows reflecting the afternoon light.

At the edge of town, they reined to a stop.

Jude looked to Two Stones. "You sure you don't mind staying here with him?" He shot a look at Martin.

Two Stones nodded. "It is best."

Jude nudged his horse forward. "We'll send a lawman out to you when they have a place to put Martin." He'd said there was a small jail in town, but it was often full. The sheriff might need to plan other secure accommodations. Surely that didn't mean a hotel, but she'd not asked his exact meaning.

He glanced back at Two Stones. "Once we send the wire, we'll meet you at the hotel?"

Two Stones nodded again. "You can look for Heidi there if I have not come yet."

The thought of meeting this man's wife sent a flutter of nervous anticipation to Angela's middle. She wanted so badly for the woman to like her. She had to make a good impression.

She guided Shadow beside Jude as they started into town. The place was much busier than most of the frontier towns the *Marietta* had stopped at, though everything was dirtier than she'd anticipated. Not like the coal grime of New York City. This was actual dirt covering the once white-washed buildings, probably coming from dust and mud that churned in the unpaved streets.

Jude stopped them at a small structure and dismounted. He glanced around the street as he handed his reins to her. "Can you wait with the horses? If they've a full jail, it might not be a fit place for a woman in there."

Before meeting Jude, she might have been frustrated by a man telling her she couldn't handle whatever she might see or hear in the jail. But Jude's protection came from love, and it only made her love him more.

So she accepted his reins and stayed in her saddle to wait.

The five minutes he was gone gave her a chance to study passersby—men, all of them. Most sported clothing like Two Stones wore, with loose cotton tunics and leather trousers.

Jude emerged from the jail with two men he introduced as Mr. Schindler and Mr. Danvers. After he gave them directions to find Two Stones and Martin, the two rode away and Jude remounted Thunder.

He raised his brows. "Ready to send that telegram?"

Her insides tightened, but she nodded. This was her part of their work, and she had to get this right.

They rode farther down the same street, then turned twice before stopping in front of another white-washed building. This one must have been painted recently, for the white hadn't turned muddy yet.

They dismounted and tied the horses to a rail in front of the building, then Jude pulled her to his side and rested a hand on her back, guiding her to the door.

With his strength bolstering her, she squared her shoulders and entered. This building proved to be a mercantile, with a counter in one corner. Jude led her that way.

An older man met them there, one who looked a little more like a shopkeeper than all those she'd seen on the street. "Mail or telegram?"

"Telegram please."

The fellow took a paper off a stack, then pushed it and a pencil toward them. "Write your message here. Ten cents a word."

Jude positioned the writing utensils in front of her. He leaned close to her ear to murmur, "Say as much as you need to. Don't worry about the cost."

She sent him a look of thanks, then focused on her message. At ten cents a word, she would make it as short as she could, but she needed to ensure Mr. Stewart wouldn't doubt she was the one who'd sent it. He didn't even know she'd left New York, as far as she knew. She'd told her mother she had to leave on a trip for the Treasury but hadn't told her where she was going.

After several rewordings, she finally slid the message across the counter to the clerk. "Thank you."

He read the paper, a frown marring his expression.

Sweat dampened her underarms at what he must be thinking. In truth, she didn't *want* to know his thoughts, she only wanted him to send the message.

Jude must have sensed her unease, for his hand rested on her back again. "How much is the cost?"

The fellow looked up. "Two dollars sixty."

She nearly flinched. She should have taken one more pass to eliminate unnecessary words.

But Jude only laid a coin on the counter. "Please have all replies sent to Angela Larkin at the hotel."

The man nodded and eyed the coin, nearly double the price he'd quoted. Did it cost so much to have a return telegram delivered? This must include an inducement to complete the work well.

"Yes, sir. Thank you, sir."

As they left the building, she inhaled a deep breath, letting the fresh air unravel her nerves.

"Let's see what rooms can be had. I bet you're ready for proper amenities." Jude gave her side a little squeeze.

She met his look with a smile. "I haven't minded sleeping on the ground."

He raised his brows. "Really? We can camp outside of town if you'd be more comfortable there."

For a heartbeat, she couldn't tell if he was teasing or not. Did he really want to camp again tonight? It would save money.

But then a corner of his mouth tipped up, and a twinkle touched his eye.

She breathed a little easier and allowed a teasing tone. "I wouldn't want you to be uncomfortable when there are proper amenities nearby."

He chuckled. "The hotel is next door, so we can leave the

MISTY M. BELLER

horses here for now. I'll take them to the livery once you're
settled."

She could help him with that task, but for now she allowed
him to guide her.

The hotel was a much larger building than those on either
side of it, rising up two stories. It was nothing compared to The
Southern in St. Louis or any of those in New York City, of
course. But this building fit Fort Benton's rustic setting.

As Jude reached for the door handle to let them in, the door
opened before them.

Angela stepped back to allow the person to exit—and was
surprised to see a woman.

"Excuse me." The pretty blonde gave them a shy smile, but
her reaction halted when she caught sight of Jude.

"Heidi?" Jude sounded as surprised as the woman looked.

"Jude." A half-second of jealousy churned in Angela's middle
before her mind recalled that Two Stones's wife was named
Heidi. She should have been expecting to meet her here.

And she was. The angst of sending the telegram was simply
discombobulating her.

Jude drew himself up, pulling Angela closer to his side. "We
were just coming in to look for you. Two Stones is probably
finishing up at the jail, then he'll be here too."

Heidi's expression of pleasure slipped to worry, but Jude
quickly added an explanation. "We had some trouble on the way
back, so Schindler and Danvers are taking possession of the
man for now."

She nodded, then her gaze moved to Angela. "We were
worried about you, especially after Two Stones heard that a Mr.
Coulter and his wife left the *Marietta* a week before coming
here." Her tone held questions, but her expression remained
open and friendly.

Jude chuckled. "We'll tell the rest of the story later. For now though, I'd like you to meet Angela Larkin. Angela, this is Two Stones's wife, Heidi."

Heidi's smile bloomed full as she reached to take Angela's hand in both of hers. "What a pleasure to meet you. I can't wait to hear more about you and all the adventures the two of you had." She cut Jude a look not unlike that of an elder sister at her wits end with a troublesome sibling. "You've managed to bring Jude back in one peace, so you've already earned my respect." Heidi finished with that same smile, so warm and open that Angela wanted to reach out and clutch it.

Instead, she returned the woman's grip and gave a polite nod. "Thank you. We were so glad for your husband's help."

Heidi's gaze lifted from Angela, moving past her. "And there he is." She spared an apologetic look as she stepped around them. "If you'll excuse me a moment."

Angela turned with Jude as Heidi nearly ran across the street to meet Two Stones, who rode toward them. He slipped from his horse in time to meet her partway, scooping her in a hug so tight that her feet lifted off the ground.

The two held each other much longer than a simple embrace, as though they'd been apart for weeks, not days. This was a private moment, and she should turn away. But the tenderness of it...

Jude's arms came around her, pulling her back against his chest. His cheek rested on her hair, cradling her in the warm protection of his love.

She sank into him, sending up another breath of thanks to the Lord who'd brought her to this place of such abundance.

CHAPTER 29

*a*ngela twisted another section of hair, drawing it up to the coif at the back of her head. How wonderful to have both the time and amenities for a real bath and proper morning ablutions. She'd even washed out her blue dress last night, then pressed away the wrinkles this morning. Jude might not even recognize her, so put together like this.

A knock sounded on the door, and she slipped the final hairpin in place. "Coming."

Was that Jude, here to take her to the dining room for their morning meal? Two Stones and Heidi said they had early business to attend to but would meet them in the café at noon.

She opened the door, but instead of Jude, the man from the telegraph office yesterday stood there. He backed a step, seeming nervous. "Miss Larkin?"

"Yes." She smiled at him, then glanced at the paper in his hands.

He held out the missive. "You received a telegram."

She took it. Her fingers wanted to claw it open then and there. Had Mr. Stewart believed her? What would they do if he thought she was making up a wild story?

The man hesitated in the hallway, and she offered another smile. "Thank you."

He nodded and turned away as she closed the door.

She slipped open the telegram with quick fingers and unfolded the sheet, her eyes darting to the rows of neat text.

"HUGH FAULKNER FROM T IN FORT BENTON WITH FAMILY. LOCATE AND DISCUSS SITUATION. CAN TRUST HIM."

She worked to make sense of it. Hugh Faulkner? She'd heard that name... Wasn't he the assistant to Secretary McCullough himself?

Nervous anticipation thrummed through her. She had to show this to Jude. It seemed impossible to believe that a high-ranking Treasury official might be here in Fort Benton. If it was true, though, they had to find him before he left.

She slipped out her door and strode down the hotel corridor to Jude's room. When she knocked on his door, he opened it almost immediately.

His eyes brightened when he saw her, but then he caught sight of the telegram in her hands. His gaze flew back to her face. "He answered?"

She nodded, the nerves in her chest pulling tighter.

Jude looked like he wanted to invite her in, but of course that would be unseemly. He glanced down the hallway, then settled for staying right where they were. "What did he say?"

She handed him the missive to read for himself. He took it, leaning against the door frame as his eyes scanned the page.

Then he looked up at her. "Hugh Faulkner? Do you know him?"

"I think he's Secretary McCullough's assistant. I've never met him, though. How can we find him?"

Jude stepped away from the door frame. "Let's ask the clerk

downstairs. This is the nicest hotel in Benton. They might be staying right here."

Hope bloomed in her chest as she walked with Jude down the hallway to the stairs at the end. Could it possibly be as easy as this?

The clerk, a young man with spectacles and a trimmed beard, looked up from his ledger as they approached. "Hello."

"Morning." A tinge of urgency touched Jude's voice. "We're looking for a Mr. Hugh Faulkner. Would he be staying here, by chance?"

The man's brows rose, and he nodded behind them. "I believe Mr. Faulkner and his family are in the cafe."

She glanced toward the open doorway of the large room, where they'd dined last night. People sat at the tables, the murmur of their conversation drifting into the lobby. Could he be so close?

"Thank you." Jude touched a hand to her back to guide her that direction.

Even before they entered the room, a child's squeal sounded above the conversations. She and Jude stopped just inside the doorway, scanning the sea of mostly men.

"Over there." Jude pointed to a table near the far window. "Is that...?"

She focused on the group. Several children sat with a man and woman. One of the boys stood in his chair to stretch across the table while the man reached for his arm. A smaller girl knelt on her seat, perhaps to make herself tall enough to see over the table. An older girl ate her food quietly, and the youngest—a blond child who couldn't be more than two—sat in the woman's lap.

Angela focused on the woman. Was that...Helen from the steamboat? And her husband, Hugh? The younger couple they'd shared dinner with in the captain's dining room?

She grabbed Jude's arm, darting a look at his face to see if he'd realized the same. "Do you think...?"

He raised his brows, a smile tugging his mouth. "Hugh and Helen. I never caught their surname. Perhaps Faulkner?"

Wonder spread through her chest as she matched Jude's grin. "I can't believe it."

He squeezed her side. "Let's go talk to them."

~

"*I*s it all really over?"

Angela's words matched the sentiment in Jude's chest as he sat at the cafe table with her, Two Stones, and Heidi, sharing the details of their conversation with Mr. Faulkner.

Angela's cheeks nearly glowed as she spoke. "He said they may need my testimony when the trial goes to court, but for now, Mr. Faulkner will take over custody of Martin. He said Secretary McCullough had suspected corruption somewhere in the department, maybe even among the agents."

Two Stones's brow furrowed as he listened to their story. "I am glad this came to light. The evil had to be stopped."

Jude sighed and leaned back in his chair. "I'm glad it's come to light too. And mostly, I'm glad our part is over."

Heidi gave a soft smile. "I'm continually amazed at how God brings things together in ways that only He could manage. Like having Mr. Faulkner here right when you needed him."

"I still can't believe that." Angela straightened in her chair. "He said Secretary McCullough sent him here to make connections with the government officials in Fort Benton and suggested he bring his family along and make a holiday of it." She slid a grin to Jude. "To think, we had dinner with them in the captain's cabin—one of the top Treasury officials—and I had no idea."

Two Stones pushed his plate back on the table. "What now? Will you stay here longer?"

Anticipation slipped through Jude's veins, but he looked to Angela. "We could either leave for the ranch in the morning or stay a few more days. What do you prefer?"

Everything in him wanted to get to the ranch, but he wouldn't rush her if she wanted to sleep on a real bed a little longer. He'd already questioned Two Stones about how everyone at the Coulter ranch was faring, but he'd like to see for himself they were well. And hand off the money.

But more than anything, he wanted to introduce them to Angela. They would love her, he had no doubt. And they'd be more than a little shocked he brought home a woman. Just thinking of that made a grin tug his mouth.

Angela raised her brows at his smile, and he chuckled. "I was just thinking how surprised my brothers will be when you ride into the yard with me."

A flash of uncertainty touched her eyes, though her smile didn't slip.

He reached for her hand. "They'll love you. Wait till you meet them."

She gave a small nod. "We should leave soon. I'm sure you're ready to be home."

Home. That word felt so good. He could almost hear Jericho's voice now, the deep rumble as he gave orders in the morning.

Two Stones sat up straighter, glancing toward the café door that led to the hotel lobby.

Jude paused, sorting through the sounds he was hearing. That really did sound like Jericho's tone, rising above the murmur of other conversations.

The one who answered *had* to be Sean—his high-pitched voice was familiar. What in the red rock hills...?

Jude pushed to his feet and barely remembered to murmur, "Excuse me a minute," as he left the table.

Could his family actually be here? Surely it was another man and boy who just sounded like his brother and nephew.

As he stepped to the open doorway, he paused to take in the group of familiar faces. Jericho was speaking again, his voice quieter this time as he gave directions. Dinah stood at his side, with Lillian and Sean in front of them.

Lillian was the first to spot him, her eyes going wide. "Uncle Jude!"

The rest of them turned, and Sean barreled toward him, crashing into his side as Jude wrapped the boy in his arms. The others crowded around, and he pulled Lillian into a hug on his other side.

"What are you all doing here?" He lifted his gaze to Jericho and Dinah.

Dinah answered first. "We're impatient to hear how your trip has gone. I was also running low on a few supplies for the clinic, so we decided to come see if you'd made it this far yet."

"Jonah's with us too." Jericho spoke up. "He's down at the dock, checking to see if you were on the steamer that arrived this morning."

Jude couldn't shut down his grin. What a relief to see these faces again.

"Wait till you hear Uncle Jonah's news." Lillian turned her blue eyes up to him.

"Yeah, he's getting married." Sean nearly jumped with his excitement.

Lillian frowned at her brother. "That was Uncle Jonah's news to tell."

As the two squabbled, Jude worked to decipher what they were talking about. Jonah? If he was getting married, the only woman it might be was...

He looked at Jericho and Dinah to see if he was following the right trail.

Jericho gave a nod. "He and Naomi. They're waiting till you get home."

Something in his middle tensed. Was he just being petty, wanting to be the only one with that particular kind of news? A look at Dinah's face showed she was excited about the prospect of her sister making a match with their brother. He would need to work through this unease before he voiced it.

For now, he said, "That's something."

A presence behind him brought him back to his own surprise, and he stepped to the side to allow Angela, Two Stones, and Heidi to join the group.

As his family greeted Two Stones and Heidi, Jude pulled Angela a little closer to him. It didn't take long before silence settled and they all looked from him to Angela.

He grinned. "It's been an eventful trip, to say the least. We'll tell you all about it, but first I'd like to introduce you all to Miss Angela Larkin. Angela, this is my oldest brother Jericho and his wife Dinah." Then he motioned to the younger pair. "My niece Lillian and my nephew Sean."

Angela dipped a slight curtsy. "I'm honored to meet all of you."

"As are we." Dinah stepped forward to take Angela's hand, her eyes twinkling with warmth. "We were impatient to hear news of Jude, so we came to town early. What an unexpected pleasure to meet you here too." She glanced from Jude to Angela. "Did you two meet on the journey?"

Jude held in a chuckle. His sister-in-law was working to ferret out the details already. "We did. We'll share the entire story." He motioned toward the café. "Have you eaten?"

Before they could answer, the door to the street opened, the light catching Jude's gaze. Jonah's outline filled the frame as he stepped into the lobby, and another man entered behind him.

Jonah spotted them right off and came to greet Jude. "There you are." He clasped Jude's hand.

Jude used the grip to pull him close. "I hear congratulations are in order."

Jonah chuckled as he pulled back. "I'm a happy man."

Then he motioned toward the fellow who'd entered with him. "When I was looking for you at the dock, I met him coming off the steamship. He's looking for someone we know."

The man stepped forward to join the conversation. His gaze seemed focused on Dinah for some reason, though he slid a glance around at the rest of them.

For Dinah's part, her expression had lost its smile. In fact, she'd gone pale, her hand gripping Jericho's with white knuckles. What in the world...?

"Hello, I'm Eric LaGrange." The man glanced around the group, but his gaze landed on Dinah again, staring at her with an intense focus.

Jude's hackles rose, and Jericho stepped closer to his wife, slipping an arm around her back.

LaGrange seemed to realize his error, for he shifted his focus to Jericho and Jude with a small smile. "I've come looking for Naomi Wyatt." He nodded toward Dinah. "I'm a friend of the Wyatt family, from back in Marcyville."

That knot in Jude's belly clenched tighter. He found himself slipping his arm around Angela, pulling her a little closer to his side. Something didn't feel right about this man and his presence here.

Dinah still looked tense, but she nodded. "Hello, Eric. I didn't expect to see you so far from Virginia."

He gave her a tight half-smile. "Naomi sent me a letter. I came as soon as I received it." He pulled a folded paper from his pocket.

Jude glanced at the missive, then focused on it as realization slipped in. That was the letter Naomi had asked him to mail in Fort Benton on his way east with the sapphires.

"Well." Dinah's voice had a forced brightness. "I suppose she'll be happy you've come." Her eyes flashed with something that didn't look like pleasure, especially when she darted a look at Jonah. "Naomi is still back at the ranch, and it's a couple of weeks' travel to reach it. We just came from there, but now that we've found Jude"—she motioned toward him—"I imagine we'll set out soon. You can see if the hotel has an extra room for the night, then travel with us if you'd like."

The uneasiness in Jude's middle pulled even tighter. She was inviting the man to their ranch? He glanced at Jericho, whose brows had gathered in concern. Surely Dinah knew what she was doing. This man must not be a scoundrel, or she wouldn't invite him to travel with them.

LaGrange nodded. "Thank you." He turned toward the clerk's desk on the other side of the room.

When he was out of hearing range, Dinah blew out a breath. "Shall we take a table in the café? I can explain who he is"—she honed a look at Jude—"then I can't wait to hear everything about your journey." Her expression brightened with that last bit.

As they all turned back into the dining room, he kept his arm around Angela, nestling her close to his side. She sent him a quick smile, her dark eyes meeting his for a moment that lingered. He let himself sink into her gaze, let his heart find the balance that came with her nearness.

This new fellow's presence was likely to cause a stir, and Jude's discomfort with the thought of Jonah wedding Naomi needed to be dealt with. But for now, he would settle into the peace of having Angela at his side. This woman was far more than he'd ever imagined.

Thank You that Your ways are so much better than my own.

CHAPTER ONE

Unrest gripped Eric Carpenter's chest as he rode near the back of the group traveling up the steep path that led toward the Coulter ranch. Though the bright afternoon sun illuminated the snow-capped peaks to the west, a lurking danger seemed to circle overhead like a vulture searching for its next meal.

This place reminded him of another treacherous slope. That jagged ledge had been far away from this incline, yet he prayed this trek would not end in tragedy again. Though they'd only been boys, daring to play in the spot they'd been warned against, his best friend's life had changed forever that day.

He couldn't let the same thing happen to his daughter.

His *daughter*.

The word still sounded so foreign. How could he have had a child—been a father—for nearly a year and not known? Shouldn't he have *felt* something? Somehow been different? Maybe sensed a gaping hole in his heart?

He *was* missing a part of his heart, but that piece had been gone for more than the ten months his daughter had been alive. A year and seven months, as a matter of fact. Since the last time he'd seen Naomi.

What he thought would only be a few weeks away to handle business while his father recovered from a surgical procedure had turned to four long months. Four months during which Naomi never responded to a single letter. And when he finally managed a short trip back to Marcyville to see her, she'd been gone.

He'd never learned where she and her sister had gone, no matter how hard he tried to find out, not until the letter arrived from her two and a half months ago...telling him he had a daughter.

Now he'd come to find what he had lost. The autumn air nipped at his exposed skin as he breathed it in. Cold weather would arrive sooner than he wished. How bitter the winters must be in these heights. His mount trudged up, picking its way around the boulders scattered up the sharp mountainside.

"Eric, are you all right?" Dinah slowed her horse to ride beside him, her expression concerned. "You look pale."

He forced a smile. "Just lost in thought." He couldn't afford to show weakness now, not when so much was at stake. He'd once thought Dinah a friend, back when he and Naomi were courting. The two were twins, but you wouldn't guess it to look at them. They possessed completely different personalities and tastes, yet they'd often known what the other was thinking.

Did Dinah's kindness to him now mean her sister would feel the same when he saw her again?

Maybe not. Dinah also seemed to be fully entrenched in this place, having married Jericho Coulter and now living on the Coulter ranch with the rest of these people. She was likely responsible for Naomi's engagement to Jericho's brother, Jonah.

He wouldn't be unkind to Dinah, but he certainly didn't think of her as a friend anymore.

As the trail narrowed around the side of a cliff, the group spread out single-file. He would have preferred to remain at the very back, but Jonah, Naomi's intended, slipped in behind him. He'd noticed one of the three Coulter brothers always stayed near the lead, with another at the tail of the group. Maybe it was protectiveness, but it felt like an effort to control them all.

The group was large enough that Eric had been able to stay at the fringe during the two weeks they'd been traveling.

Between Dinah and Jericho, the other brothers, Jonah and Jude, plus Jonah's intended, Angela, who seemed to be a newcomer here, and the niece and nephew, Lillian and Sean, it was easy enough to keep to himself.

"Almost there." Jericho's voice sounded from the front.

Eric's gut tightened. They'd built a house this close to such a cliff? His daughter was being raised in conditions far more dangerous than he would have thought. How could Naomi allow this?

Anger spurred through him. It wasn't as if she didn't have another choice. If she'd answered any one of his letters, he'd have dropped everything and come to her. They could have married immediately. He would have done whatever she needed.

Instead, she'd waited until six months passed to even tell him his daughter existed. Was it because of her impending marriage to Coulter that she finally sent word to him at all?

Maybe Eric should thank the man. He barely kept in a snort. He couldn't bring himself to do that anytime soon.

"We're here!" The young girl's voice must belong to Lillian, the Coulter's niece who looked to be about twelve. "There's Naomi." The riders in front were spreading as they left entered a clearing.

Eric's insides squeezed tighter. He would see Naomi in less than a minute.

Would she look the same? What would she think about how he looked? What would she say to him? Her letter had been to the point, giving details but not what she thought about the news she shared.

They entered the yard and the horses in front of him parted. Several buildings came into view, but a commotion at the corral drew his attention.

A young woman with the same willowy figure he remembered struggled to close a gate. The horse on the other side pushed, determined to charge out of the corral.

And no wonder.

Eric's gut twisted. Another horse occupied the corral, kicking out furiously with both hind legs. Kicking the other horse into the gate that Naomi fought to close. He had to get to her. Now.

"Let them out!" Jericho kicked his horse forward at the same time Eric dug in his heels, pushing his tired gelding into a lope.

He needed to go faster, but his creature was incapable of more after two weeks on the trail. Eric's heart galloped. If only he had Gypsy here. Naomi needed help. This time he had to be there for her.

At last, he reached the corral where two of the Coulter brothers had already leapt from their horses. Naomi must have heard the command to open the gate, for it swung loose and a horse ran free on the other side of the yard.

Then another form caught his gaze. Something or someone in brown cloth, lay on the dirt in front of the gate.

A dress? A person? Jericho sped to the place and dropped onto his knees.

Eric's lungs locked as he leaped from his horse and sprinted toward them.

Dinah screamed. "Naomi!"

Fear strangled Eric as Dinah knelt at her sister's side. Had the horse trampled Naomi? She lay there so still. What should he do?

Dear Lord, help her.

He started to press through the crowd gathering around her, but they were already shifting to let Dinah kneel at her sister's side.

Dinah been a doctor back in Marcyville, so maybe she'd know how to help better than he.

Eric stood and moved to Naomi's feet, though he had to stand behind Jude and Angela.

Then, Naomi lifted to her elbows. "I'm all right." Her face held a pallor, her voice sounded far from steady, but she was alert.

Thank you, God.

Eric's heart hammered as he took her in. So familiar, yet different. Her frame was thinner than he remembered, and she'd added a few fine lines at her eyes.

But those eyes. They were still just as wide and deep brown. Like the James River on the summer night he'd asked her to marry him. He could still remember how her smile lit them from within and held him so transfixed he had no desire to look away.

Dinah spoke to Naomi, spouting a rapid-fire series of medical questions that sent Naomi rolling those eyes in a way that was so familiar it hurt. Eric's fingers itched to reach out. To touch her face. To hold her tenderly, the way he once had.

He started to edge around to her other side, but Jonah beat him to it. The man crouched beside Naomi. He placed his hand on her shoulder, and it took everything in Eric not to step forward and jerk Jonah away.

Naomi hadn't even seen him yet, as focused as she was on her sister and Jonah. Her intended.

Clenching his fists, he forced himself to look the other direction. He scanned the ranch yard. The buildings sat on a hill, with the house at the upper part of the clearing, the barn and corrals down the slope. Constructed of logs, the homestead was nothing near as large as he would have expected for a family this size.

The door of the house opened, and he waited to see who would emerge. From what he understood, aside from Naomi and the baby, three other Coulter brothers ran the ranch while the rest had gone to Fort Benton. Also an elderly Indian man and woman, the parents of Two Stones, a fellow Eric had briefly met when he arrived in Fort Benton were staying here as well. Two Stones and his wife had planned to stay in Fort Benton a few more days to finish business, but they'd return eventually.

All these people on this ranch...strangers knew his daughter far better than he did. He inhaled a breath to keep his anger at bay.

He glanced back at Naomi. They weren't strangers to her, but it still didn't settle right in his chest.

Movement caught his eye again by the door. Likely the native woman.

But it wasn't a white-haired grandmother. The tiny figure who appeared in the doorway couldn't be more than a year old, and even from this distance he could make out the fringe of reddish curls that matched his own as a child.

This had to be his daughter.

His body froze as he took in every part of her. Not that he could make out many details. The child wore a dress that fell to her knees, with pants underneath, probably because of the cold winds here. On her face, her pudgy cheeks were the only detail clear enough to see.

But the entire vision was...beautiful. An uncanny warmth spread through his chest. And a love so powerful, his heart could explode. Who knew a man could feel such intense emotions?

The tiny girl turned around knelt in the doorway, then slid a leg down to the stoop. Her next foot reached down to the ground.

With a jolt, Eric realized she was leaving the house. Who was supposed to be watching her?

No adult appeared in the cabin behind her. His pulse thrashed. She could get hurt.

He strode up the hill. Meanwhile, she'd already found her

balance on the slope and was toddling down toward him. Running, that was. Down another steep grade.

His breathing stalled as he pushed into a run himself. Any moment she could trip and tumble forward, rolling downward. Memory flashed of the last time he'd watched someone slide down a mountain.

Nathan had never walked again. There weren't loose rocks here, but she could still be injured.

She was just a baby.

At last, he reached the child, stopping her forward motion with a hand on each shoulder. "Whoa there. Not so fast."

He dropped to his knees in front of her, letting himself study her cherub face. She regarded him with wary eyes. Wide eyes. Brown just like Naomi's.

A knot clogged his throat as he stared at his daughter.

His baby girl.

She started to back away from him, pulling from his hold. Was she afraid of him?

He had to say something. Quick. He couldn't let her be frightened.

He managed to force out a word. "Hello." His voice came out rough and scratchy, so he cleared it.

She stopped backing, but still eyed him with suspicion.

He smiled. "Are you Mary Ellen?"

The distrust in those big brown eyes melted into curiosity. "Me-me." She patted her chest with chubby fingers.

Her voice was music to his ears, the sweetest symphony he could hope to hear. Emotions tumbled inside him. This tiny being before him, with curls like autumn leaves and eyes like endless pools, was his child. His flesh and blood.

He extended a hand to her, palm up, an offer as much as an invitation. "I'm your papa. I've come a very long way to meet you."

Mary Ellen gazed at his hand, then back up to his face. She

didn't speak again, but no hint of wariness remained in her gaze. At least she wasn't afraid of him. That seemed a good first step.

She shifted her attention past him and her eyes lit. "Ma-ma."

He turned to look down the slope, toward the group still gathered in front of the corral. Naomi was on her feet now, brushing herself off with the help of her sister.

They all looked up at him. Did they realize the child had come outside on her own?

He rose to his feet but kept himself positioned where he could make sure Mary Ellen didn't scamper down the slope again. Whatever Naomi had been doing with the horses had clearly taken her away from caring for their daughter. Such errors in judgment could be disastrous for a child.

Despite their stares, he stood to his full height. Now that he'd finally been united with his daughter, he would make sure she was cared for. This wild land was much too dangerous, especially for a child so young.

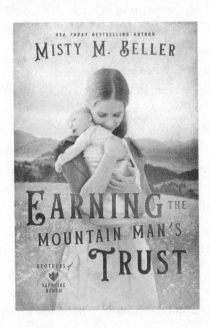

Get EARNING THE MOUNTAIN MAN'S TRUST, the next book in the Brothers of Sapphire Ranch series, at your favorite retailer!

Did you enjoy Jude and Angela's story? I hope so!
Would you take a quick minute to leave a review where you purchased the book?
It doesn't have to be long. Just a sentence or two telling what you liked about the story!

To receive a free book and get updates when new Misty M. Beller books release, go to <u>https://mistymbeller.com/freebook</u>

ABOUT THE AUTHOR

Misty M. Beller is a *USA Today* best-selling author of romantic mountain stories, set on the 1800s frontier and woven with the truth of God's love.

Raised on a farm and surrounded by family, Misty developed her love for horses, history, and adventure. These days, her husband and children provide fresh adventure every day, keeping her both grounded and crazy.

Misty's passion is to create inspiring Christian fiction infused with the grandeur of the mountains, writing historical romance that displays God's abundant love through the twists and turns in the lives of her characters.

Sharing her stories with readers is a dream come true for Misty. She writes from her country home in South Carolina and escapes to the mountains any chance she gets.

Connect with Misty at <u>www.MistyMBeller.com</u>

53041405R00152